# NAKED ISIS

William Bond

PublishAmerica
Baltimore

© 2005 by William Bond.
All rights reserved. No part of this book may be reproduced, stored in a retrieval system or transmitted in any form or by any means without the prior written permission of the publishers, except by a reviewer who may quote brief passages in a review to be printed in a newspaper, magazine or journal.

First printing

At the specific preference of the author, PublishAmerica allowed this work to remain exactly as the author intended, verbatim, without editorial input.

ISBN: 1-4137-9695-8
PUBLISHED BY PUBLISHAMERICA, LLLP
www.publishamerica.com
Baltimore

Printed in the United States of America

# CHAPTER ONE

I was bored by Freemasonry. It had been exciting when I was first invited into the Brotherhood, with its strange rituals, but now it felt all too commonplace. As far as I could see, most of the members of my lodge treated it like a gentleman's club. I was now only going to the meetings because I had been told to do this and tried my best to conceal my boredom. Then salvation came when at the end of one meeting a grey-haired man approached me. I'd seen him before and vaguely knew that he was a very high-degree Mason.

"Hello Arthur," said the man, smiling, "I hear that you've been asking too many questions."

"Is there anything wrong with that?" I snapped.

"Not if they are sensible questions," he replied calmly, "and you don't cause any trouble."

He held out his hand.

"My name is James Ashe," he told me, as we shook hands. "Would it be possible to go somewhere where we can speak in private?"

"Well, yes, all right," I stammered uncertainly. I now recognised the name and knew for certain he was an important member of the Brotherhood. He led the way out of the building and I followed.

"Do you mind if we go for a walk?" he asked, when we were outside the Freemason's hall.

"Er, no," I said, by now confused and a bit frightened about what was happening.

We walked up the road for a short way in silence and only when we were completely on our own did he begin to talk.

"I hear you have a interest in finding out the truth about Freemasonry."

"Yes," I said forcefully, "I find it very strange to belong to an organisation that doesn't know its true origins and the real reason it was first created."

"Doesn't the explanation given, satisfy you?" he asked.

"No," I said firmly. "It might if there was only one. The problem is that there are so many theories about Freemasonry, even among the members. Some claim it was originally just a working Mason's guild, others claim it is a secret society that goes back to before the time of the Pharaohs or King Solomon. Other people claim it was started by the Knights Templar. It seems to me that people just latch onto any explanation they happen to like. Personally I think they are all wrong."

James smiled.

"Why do you think that?" he asked.

I gave a deep sigh.

"I thought I would find out the truth when I became a Mason, but it's not the case. All I get are speculations and theories. I feel we are treated like mushrooms; fed bullshit and kept in the dark. I think all these different explanations are red herrings to lead people away from the true reason, why and how Freemasonry was founded."

He patted me on the back.

"I can understand your frustration," he said, "so what do you think would be the true reason for the origins of Freemasonry?"

"I really don't know," I said. "The explanation I liked best was the one which claims that Freemasonry is a coded word for the preservation of ancient knowledge. To carve writings and symbols into stone is the best way of saving information, because paper or wood can burn or rot away. We can see this in the ancient Egyptian civilisation. Archaeologists and scholars know so much about this culture because the people used stone for their temples and pyramids and carved writings and images on the walls. We know far less about the ancient Sumerians and Mesopotamians because they built in mud brick, which erodes. So the work of the mason, more than anyone else, does preserve ancient knowledge. I've also thought about why the word free is used at the beginning of the name Freemason. At times in the past when knowledge was censored by the State and Church, it suggests that the masons had knowledge that was free from this."

"What do you think this uncensored knowledge might be?"

"Again, I can only speculate," I said. "When the Christian Church took over societies, they destroyed all ancient knowledge and burnt down libraries, the most famous one being the great library of Alexandria. The Moslems did the same later on. So I would guess that perhaps scholars at the time preserved what scrolls they could in secret societies. The problem with that explanation is that you would have to believe the secret society existed for over a thousand years. I just can't accept one could last for that length of time without being betrayed at some time to organisations like the Inquisition."

"I see you have put some thought into this," he said. "Do you believe there's any way secret information might have survived for so long?"

"At a guess this knowledge would have to survive in wealthy families," I said, "since they would have the means and education to hide and rewrite scrolls that are rotting away. There's some justification for believing this; in the time of Renaissances in the 8th, 9th and 12th centuries, when the Church briefly relaxed its repression, suddenly a great deal of ancient knowledge came to light. Like the works of Plato and Socrates. For that to happen, people must have been hiding away it somewhere. Then there's the problem with the beginnings of Protestantism. I cannot believe that Martin Luther created a breakaway Church on his own. I wonder if he was given the support of some secret society that protected him and his supporters from being murdered or executed - in much the same way as Freemasonry gave help and support to American leaders during the American Revolution."

"You are thinking seriously about this," he commented gravely.

He was quiet for a few seconds, then frowned.

"Arthur," he said very quietly, as if he was frightened of being overheard, "What would you say if I told you I belong to an extremely ancient and secret order, that created organisations like Freemasonry and the Rosicrucians. We're looking for young people to keep its traditions going and you seem to be a likely candidate."

"If I didn't know you were a prominent member of our brotherhood," I said, "and a very well respected member of the community, I would say you were playing a joke on me."

"This is no joke," he said firmly, "I am very serious about this."

"I'd like to know more about this organisation first," I said cautiously.

"I'm afraid I cannot tell you anything. It works through a long series of initiations, tests and instruction. These might take many years. You'll be tested on the intellectual, emotional and spiritual levels. If at any time you fail one of the tests or you feel that what we are teaching is not for you, then the initiations will stop and we'll go our separate ways."

I paused to consider his words.

"Can I think about this?" I said.

"If you're uncertain, it's better for you to say no," said James. "I'm afraid you have to make up your mind right now."

"Why does it have to be now?"

"If you have to go away and think about it," he explained, "then you have doubts, and these may resurface at a later date. You might also be tempted to discuss it with others, which is forbidden. As far as I'm concerned, this conversation never happened, and if you don't respect our need for secrecy then there's no point in continuing."

I sighed.

"All right, Yes, yes, yes," I said quickly. "I am very interested; it's just this cloak and dagger stuff I find off-putting. I don't see why you have to have secret societies nowadays. We don't have to worry about the Inquisition anymore. Aren't we supposed to live in a free society where everyone is at liberty to express whatever religious or political beliefs they like?"

He laughed.

"So we are told," he said, "but there's still knowledge and beliefs that are considered to be highly dangerous. As you say, people are treated like mushrooms. We are in the possession of secrets that, if revealed, might threaten the stability and power of every ruling elite in the world. People in the past have been murdered because of these secrets and it goes on even today."

"Oh," I said, "this sounds a bit dangerous."

"No, it isn't dangerous," he reassured me, "If you don't attempt to rock the boat and cause trouble."

"So what exactly is this knowledge that gets people killed?"

"You ask too many questions," he said solemnly. "Now please take this very seriously; you are not to speak about this to anyone. If you do, then I will deny everything and we will wash our hands of you. I'll get in touch with you later on and arrange for your first initiation."

"Can I ask just one more question?"

"Very well," he assented.

"Why me?" I asked, "I don't have great academic qualifications or anything else special about me. In fact I've been told that I will never amount to anything."

He smiled.

"Your humility does you credit," he teased, "We are looking for special people, but not in the sense of what makes a person successful in the material world."

"I'm not deep into spiritual stuff either, if that's what you're looking for."

"I assure you," he said, "we have looked into your background and you are exactly the type of person we need."

"In what way?"

"We live in a world of sheep and goats," he said. "Most people are sheep and they accept what's told to them without question. They don't want to know about anything beyond what is considered normal. Then there are the goats; they do question what has been told them and are willing to step outside comfortable normality. It would be impossible for us to initiate anyone who wasn't willing to question traditional beliefs and fashionable thinking."

"So you're looking for mavericks? I concluded. "I don't see myself as a maverick or a rebel. All right, I admit I have a mind of my own but I keep my ideas to myself. I'm not interested in making waves and causing trouble."

"I'm glad to hear it," he said. "We're not looking for people who want to change the world dramatically. For us, that would be dangerous. I admit we are in the business of evolving society, but we do it behind the scenes, and we do it bit by bit. We've found that violent change and chaos can be harmful to our cause."

"So in what way are you attempting to change the world?"

"I'm afraid I can't discuss that with you at this stage," he said flatly.

"But what would happen," I went on relentlessly, "if I found out I entirely disagreed with your ideals?"

"Then our assessment of you would have been completely wrong. Don't worry though. You'll go through tests to discover your deep-seated values. We will also feed you knowledge and teachings that are not secret but relate to our deeper beliefs. If, during the initiations, you find that you disagree with what we are doing, it will show up. If you decide our way is not for you, that will be fine, because we won't have revealed anything more than a member of the general public can find out."

"I see," I said, though I didn't see at all.

"So, are you happy?" he asked, "You haven't suddenly changed your mind?"

"Oh no," I said quickly, "I'm still very interested."

We said good-bye and went our separate ways. He returned to the Freemasonry hall to pick up his car, while I kept on walking to a public car park. Driving my car home, my mind was racing. I felt both excited and frightened at the same time, but most of all I had a burning curiosity.

I kept looking in the rear-view mirror to make sure I wasn't being followed and when I was satisfied I wasn't I stopped at a pay-phone box and went inside it. I then phoned a number that I had remembered for more that a year now. I had been told only to use a pay-phone and not to use a mobile phone or the phone in my house as they can be bugged.

"Whom do you want?" asked a female voice on the phone.

"Angel Lyons," I replied, I knew this wasn't her real name, it was the code name I had told to use in contacting her.

"Who is calling?"

"Timothy Cotterell," I said with growing excitement. This was my code name.

"What is it?" asked the voice.

"They have taken the bait," I said quickly, "I have been asking the questions you have suggested and now I have been invited to join a secret society."

"What secret society is this?" the voice asked.

"I don't know, but I was approached by James Ash," I replied.

"That's good," came the voice, "It may take a few years before they fully initiate you, if you pass all their tests. Don't contact me unless you have something important to pass on. Understood?"

"Yes," I said, "could you give me some idea what these tests will involve so I can prepare for them."

"We told you before," said the voice impatiently, "We don't want you to know too much, so you will behave in a natural way. They might get suspicious if it seems you know what is coming. We would prefer you failed the tests than reveal that we are targeting them. That is your main priority. Not to reveal you are a spy. Understood?"

"Yes, understood," I said with a sigh.

"Don't worry," said the voice more softer this time, "You fit the profile of the type of people they want, nicely. You should do well. Good luck."

I heard a click on the other end.

I now felt frightened and very much alone. I had been warned that they only wanted the minimal contact between me and the government agency that had recruited me. I remember being greatly surprised at being approached at university to be a spy and took a lot of persuasion it wasn't a elaborate joke. Even when I was convinced, I couldn't see what use I could be to them. I had received virtually only a weekend course on being a spy, they said I didn't need to know much, because they wanted me to behave like a ordinary member of the public.

I began to wonder, how it was I fit their profile so well. It seems both organizations checked my background and claimed that I was somehow right for them. I wondered what they had found out about me and worried that perhaps there had been a mistake. As far as I could see, there was nothing in my life to check. I didn't belong to any political party or religion. I didn't even express any political leanings, because in my opinion there was little to choose between political parties. I did have a mild interest in religion and spiritual matters but again, I thought all religions seemed to be saying the same thing. I had dabbled in New-Age spirituality but only because an ex-girlfriend had been deeply interested in that sort of thing.

The only reason I had become a Freemason was because my father was a Mason and I was invited in as his son. As far as I knew, my father hadn't been involved in any activities besides Freemasonry. In fact he didn't seem to be interested in anything outside of his job and family. I remembered his views were distinctly conservative. Up to the day he died, he was telling us that life had been better when he was a child and everything was changing for the worse. I couldn't see him wanting to belong to any organisation those aim was to change society, unless it was to drag it back to the 19th century. So I doubted if this secret society had anything to do with him.

I felt very flattered and excited that this mysterious organisation wanted to choose me, but I also felt uneasy about their motives. Yes, I was a person who questioned everything, but I couldn't believe that was the only reason. Time would tell.

## CHAPTER TWO

A few days later James phoned me, telling me to come to his house that evening. I thought this was very short notice; although I wasn't in a serious relationship it would have been awkward if I'd already made arrangements. I arrived at the appointed time and was invited in. I had never been to his place before but was not surprised to find it was a large and luxurious house. His living room looked more like a library, with crammed bookshelves covering most of the walls. He picked up a box from a small table and then unclipped a rod from the side of the box that was attached to it by a wire.

"I want you to stand with your arms wide open and your legs apart," he said.

"What is that?!" I exclaimed looking at the box.

"It detects bugs or any other electronic devices," he said, "now do as I tell you."

"All right," I said reluctantly.

He switched it on and scanned my body, and even got me to lift both my legs one at time to scan my shoes.

"I'm sorry to be so melodramatic," he said, "But we cannot afford to risk a bug or a tracking device being taken to the place of your first initiation. I'm sure you wouldn't do this, but a electronic device could be planted on you without your knowledge. I will have to do this every time you come here."

I now realised the wisdom of my controllers in not putting any bugs on me. If they did, I would have been discovered at my first meeting.

He offered me a drink and we chatted for a while about subjects that had no relevance to the real reason for my visit. Suddenly, he got to his feet and picked up what looked like a black cloth bag from the table.

"I'm going to take you to your first initiation," he informed me, "but I'm afraid I have to blindfold you."

Gently, he placed the bag over my head and I found I could see nothing. I realised it was a hood, with a small opening near my mouth so I could breathe. The bottom of the hood had drawstrings, which he tied loosely around my neck so I couldn't remove it easily. Then he led me though the house to his garage, where I found myself getting into his car. All this was accompanied by apologies and reassurances that I would be quite safe, though I did wonder how he would explain the situation if we were stopped by the police for any reason.

I have no idea how long the journey took; I lost track of time having a hood over my head. I had a feeling he took me to the place in a very roundabout route because we always seem to be swerving around so many corners, to the degree I began to feel nauseous. I wondered if the secret service that had recruited me was now following his car, it seems the obvious thing to do. Yet they also said the empathise was not to reveal they were targeting the group James belonged to. So perhaps they may not risk following the car, in case they were spotted by James. I was a real beginner at this spying game, they had gave me only the briefest training so I didn't know how they operated. I now began to feel frighten again; what would happen to me if the group I was trying to infiltrate found out I was a spy? Would they go as far to murder me? I wasn't a hero, I was just a normal person who happened to get caught up in all this. If they did catch me out and tried to torture me, I was sure I would quickly confess all. I had been told they were a very dangerous group, so were they terrorists? I had been assured they wasn't, but then they might of told me this to allay my fears. I was still thinking these endless possibilities when presently I felt we were going up a drive and into a garage. We entered a house through a side door to the garage and I was led into a room. Only when James had closed the door did he remove the hood. Looking around curiously, I saw a small room, completely bare except for two chairs. The window was covered by thick curtains which didn't allow me to look out. We sat down and he allowed my eyes to become used to the artificial light after being in darkness for such a long time.

"I'm afraid I will have to ask you to remove all your clothing."

I was somewhat surprised.

"What kind of initiation is this?" I asked, baffled.

"You won't be hurt," he said, "but you have to do this as part of the initiation. We need to see your reaction."

"What, my reaction to taking off my clothing?"

"No. Now just do as I ask."

I hesitated for a minute, and then slowly undressed. I hesitated when I stripped down to my underpants but James gave me a node to indicate he wanted those off as well. I now felt very vulnerable. Here I was, completely nude, in a strange house, waiting to be part of some unknown ritual.

"Now go out of the door into the passage."

"What do I do then?"

He smiled enigmatically.

"Whatever you want."

"Is this part of the initiation?" I asked.

"It is a test," he admitted.

I trembled as I opened the door and let myself through. At the far end of the passage I saw an elegantly but strangely dressed woman, seated on a highly elaborate chair. The neckline of her dress was cut so low her two large firm breasts were exposed. Thinking someone had made a mistake, I tried to dive back into the room before she saw me, but the door was locked. It was embarrassing, being stark naked in the presence of a well-dressed woman. When I realised she had a veil over her face, the situation seemed even more bizarre. She stared at me as if I was somehow doing something wrong. I was completely at a loss as to what to do.

"How dare you stand in my presence," she suddenly shouted. "Kneel!"

I gaped at her for a moment; the situation was so strange that I became confused. Then I found myself obeying her and knelt on the floor, feeling a complete idiot.

"Nose to the floor," she ordered in a gentler voice.

I complied. In my stunned imagination I wondered if this was a trick. Soon people would spill out of one of the rooms to laugh at me. I also didn't know if I would pass the test my obeying or disobeying her. I decided it was more likely I would pass by obedience.

"Now crawl towards me," she said interrupting my chain of thoughts.

I lifted my head and began to crawl forward.

"Keep your nose to the floor," she repeated sternly.

It was difficult. I found I had to rest on my forearms and knees. I felt so foolish that I had to suppress a fit of giggling. As I moved closer to the woman, I realised her chair was on a small platform, making it appear more like a throne. Her bare feet peeked out from her long elegant dress, and embroidered slippers were neatly placed in front of the platform. When my face reached the platform I became keenly aware of her staring down from what seemed to me a great height.

"Look at me," she commanded.

I looked up and my eyes focused on her bare breasts, I also noticed the fact that she had a stylised apron over the front of her dress.

"You may have the honour and privilege of kissing my slippers," she intoned suddenly.

Quickly, I kissed the toe of each slipper, then waited to see what else she might want me to do.

"You may have the privilege of more than one kiss on my slippers," she said archly, "you may lick them as well."

I noticed they were open slippers with a fairly high heel so I began to kiss and lick the heel end. It was clear she had been wearing the slippers for most of the day because I could discern the distinct smell of feet. Soon I was engrossed and began to lick the sole area of both slippers. When I paused for a moment, she remained silent, so I continued – for how long I don't know. Somehow I had become lost in the sensual smell and taste of this woman's shoes.

"That is enough," she said abruptly. "You are dismissed. Go back to your room!"

To obey her I began to turn around, but she immediately stopped me.

"You do not turn your back on me," she said, and I froze at the lash of anger in her voice.

For a few seconds I waited for my heart to calm, then tried crawling backwards.

"Keep your nose to the floor," she reminded me.

Very slowly I managed to retreat backwards down the passageway. It took a long time. When I came to the door by which I'd entered the corridor, it opened. I dived through it in relief. It was James who had rescued me and was now closing the door again. I broke out into uncontrollable giggling.

"Why are you laughing?" asked James.

I shook my head.

"I don't really know. I suppose because I found the situation so bizarre. I know some of the Freemasons' rituals are a bit weird, but this one is really off the wall. It just seems to have had a strange effect on me."

"All right," he said, "sit down and stay here until I come back. And do not try to look out the curtains when I am gone, as they have a burglar alarm on them."

"Do I put my clothes back on?" I asked, realising I was now feeling slightly chilly.

"No; don't do anything unless you are told to," he answered and left the room.

I quickly began to get frighten again after he left, and the fact I was nude made my vulnerability even more acute. It was more than a half an hour before he returned.

"We will have to wait here," he said.

We sat silently for about ten minutes until we heard a knock on the door of an adjoining room.

"That's your signal," said James, getting to his feet. "As I open the door I want you to crawl through the doorway on your hands and knees. Keep your eyes on the ground and don't look up unless instructed to do so."

I crept slowly forward as he opened the door. This time I found myself in a far larger room. At the far end I saw three veiled women on three seats above a platform. Again dressed in a similar fashion to the woman in the corridor. These women were clearly older as their bare breasts were not as firm and their dresses seem to be cut to hold their breasts up. This bizarre scene increased my fear and I found myself shaking as I crawl towards them. Fortunately, it wasn't so far to crawl this time.

"It is customary to show homage by kissing our feet," one of the women said as I approached them.

I kissed the feet of each woman, noticing that they all wore exquisite slippers.

"Very well," I heard a female voice, "sit on that cushion."

There was one just in front of the platform so I slid onto it with head bowed.

"We wish to learn about your emotional and spiritual selves," said a voice above me.

"Oh," I replied, my voice barely above a whisper.

"Look at us," said the same voice.

I looked up at the three veiled women; from my sitting position on the floor below the platform they seemed to be surveying me from a very great height. From my slightly greater height now, I saw that also wore aprons with symbols on them. I could just make out from my position, one had a symbol of a bird of prey, the other a bull and the third, a snake.

"We have learned from James," said the woman in the centre of the group, "that you do not express yourself emotionally. We understand that. Many men find it hard to reveal their feelings, but this is what we want to know about you. Tell us how you feel about women."

"Well, I am very attracted to women," I said, and paused. "I never really thought about it until now."

"So, is it the only feeling you have about women?" said the woman on the right hand side, " that you want to fuck them?"

The directness and calmness of the question took me by surprise.

"No," I said hurriedly, not knowing what to say, " I do like their company as well."

"Tell us about your relationships," said the woman at the centre.

"I only had two girlfriends at university," I said. "The first one was called Jane. We got on very well together but she was into Buddhism and New Age stuff. I was happy with this until she tried to convert me to the same beliefs she had. That caused trouble between us. My second girlfriend, Mary, was a very ambitious career woman. I didn't see much of her because she was always studying. Looking back now I think she got involved with me because I was so easygoing. I suppose she had me on a bit of a string. When she had some spare time she would call me up and we would either go out together or have sex, but it was always when it was convenient to her. When she got a job in America she just went off and left me."

"How did you feel about her doing this?" asked the woman on the left.

"Very upset," I said, "even though she warned me it would happen."

"Has she been in touch with you since then?" the same voice enquired.

"Well, yes," I admitted. "She sometimes phones me or sends a email. She also comes back to visit her parents and might pay me a visit for a few hours."

"Do you have hopes that you will get together?"

"Not now," I said. "The last time she phoned I was a bit angry with her, and she hasn't phoned or emailed me since."

"Why were you angry?"

"At the time, I didn't know," I said, "but thinking about it since, I've realised I couldn't handle not knowing whether she really wanted me or not. My friends were telling me she had me on a piece of string and was just using me. When she phoned or emailed me I would have hopes of starting to see her again. Then I'd have the disappointment of not hearing from her for a long time. I cared about her a lot but I just couldn't handle the emotional ups and downs she kept putting me through."

The three women looked at each other.

"We would like you to contact her again and apologise for your rude behaviour," said the woman in the middle. "Express to her how you feel, and how much you love her."

"If I do that," I objected, "I'll give her license to walk all over me and use me how she likes, and that's exactly what she will do."

"Do you love her?"

"Yes," I admitted. "I still love her."

"If you truly love her," she said emphatically, "you will accept her no matter how she behaves towards you."

I was outraged.

"This is my life," I said with anger creeping into my voice. "She's told me it would help her career if she married a wealthy man she could control. She's also told me I'll always be a loser and only useful for a bit on the side. So she hasn't exactly encouraged me to stay loyal to her. It's very clear her career comes first, well before anything else, so I don't really think there's any room in her life for me!"

The women totally ignored my anger. It disappeared into a black hole somewhere in the room.

"Do you want to learn how to love?" asked the woman in the centre.

"Of course," I said, though I wasn't entirely sure what it meant.

"Mary provides you with the perfect way to do this. She was testing your devotion all the time."

"Well it's a test I failed," I said defensively.

"You haven't failed," she replied, "you have done well. Ignore what your friends tell you. For a man at your stage of development, you have shown great loyalty and understanding, so far, as well as love. We realise Mary has pushed you to your current limit, but because it became too difficult for you doesn't mean the situation is irretrievable."

"But what if she genuinely doesn't want me?" I asked plaintively.

"If that is the case, from what you tell us about her, I would say she will let you know. I doubt if she'd keep you hanging around if she didn't want you at all."

"You're asking me to suffer again emotionally," I said miserably. "I really couldn't cope if I contacted her again and she rejected me. Or we started to communicate again and she decided to marry someone else. She's someone who can really get to me. Do you know, I have even thought of suicide because of her."

The women exchanged glances again and I detected what looked like a concealed smirk from one them.

"The fact that she does get to you, as you put it," one said, "makes her the perfect spiritual teacher for you. In the time the relationship existed, you probably learnt more about love than many men learn in a whole lifetime. It was difficult because there was no help or support. You were following your emotions and instincts, yet your friends were insisting that you were a fool. Yet on the spiritual level it is mostly the fools that make the greatest progress. No one was congratulating you on your loyalty and understanding. It's no wonder that in the end you gave up. Learning to love, whether it is love for yourself or love for others, needs to be encouraged, more than anything else in the world. If you are willing to try again, we will give you all the support and help you need."

"How will you do that?"

"You may question James but not us. It is not your right."

"Sorry," I said, now feeling very frightened once more. There was no doubting these women's innate authority, despite the soft voices.

"Another way you to learn to love is learn how to care and support others. What do you think about helping out in a shelter for homeless people?"

That completely threw me, I have always been uncomfortable with seeing beggars on the streets and do my best not to look at them and hurry past.

"I don't really know," I said with trepidation, "I have never considered ever doing something like that."

"Do you think you would be better off looking after children, or old people or the disabled?" said another voice.

"I just don't know," I said, "I have never thought about doing any of these things either."

"So in your life you have never have had to care for another human being."

"No."

"Then it is about time you started. Many young men of your age are now living with a partner and fortunately young women today make their men get involved in caring for their own children. That doesn't seem to be option for you at present. So we need to find another way you can learn how to care for others. Are you willing to help at a homeless shelter?"

"I will give it a go," I said uncertainly.

"You may go," the central woman said, dismissing me.

I bowed my head and found myself thanking them and crawled backwards to the door, which magically opened when I came close to it, allowing me to reverse through the gap.

James closed the door after me, then picked up the hood.

"We can't hang around," he said urgently, "we have to be getting away now."

"I have to get dressed first," I objected.

"We haven't the time," he said. "This room needs to be clear for another initiate; we can't keep the Goddesses waiting while you get dressed."

Hastily, I picked up my clothes, he put the hood over my head, and I was led back to his car. On the return journey I found it impossible to stop myself from laughing nervously at frequent intervals. Shock and disbelief chased each other round my head. I struggled to dress myself, hampered by both the seatbelt and the hood over my head, added to my hysteria. In the end I gave up and finished dressing only after we had reached his place.

"How are you feeling now?" he asked, after we had got back to his sitting room.

"I still feel a bit strange. I didn't think a ritual like that would have such a powerful effect on me."

He nodded.

"Now you have calmed down," he said, "take a seat and tell me why you think it was so potent."

Once seated, I considered his question for some time, but no instant insights arrived.

"I really can't say," I confessed. "It might be to do with the fact that I wasn't expecting anything remotely like what actually happened."

I leaned forward in my chair.

"All right then," I said. "What was that stuff all about? If it was a test did I pass it?"

"We'd rather you work that out for yourself," James answered.

"Oh," I said, leaning back again, "I just wouldn't know where to start."

"You have a very questioning mind. It's why we became interested in you. Can you think of any reason why we used a ritual like this and why it has a strong emotional effect on you?"

"No I can't," I said, and my voice betrayed my distress.

James said nothing, making me feel very uncomfortable. I had the feeling he wanted me to make a confession of some kind.

"Do you want to stop this?" he asked, breaking the silence. "After all, this ritual is only a taste of what is to come. If you don't think you can cope, then don't continue."

"No, I want to go on," I said quickly, and I was surprised at the eagerness in my voice. "I just want a better understanding."

"All right. I will help you," he said. "Have you read anything by Carl Jung?"

"I've heard of the name," I admitted. "Isn't he some sort of psychologist?"

James nodded.

"That's right," he said. "He is the only one I have encountered who gives an accurate insight into the psychology of rituals. Your first assignment will be to study Jung and work out from his ideas why we used the particular initiation you just went through and why it has affected you so deeply. I have some of his books here."

He left his seat and walked over to one of the many bookshelves. After sorting through them, he took down four large books, which he placed on the table in front of me.

"Another thing," he said, "have you any comments about the dresses the Goddesses you worshipped."

"I don't understand why they had bare breasts," I said, "but I did notice they all wore aprons, with symbols on them, like Freemasons wear. Does this mean they are Freemasons?"

"That is for you to work out for yourself," he said, "but is will give you a big clue. Do you know anything about the Minoan civilization of Ancient Crete?"

"No I don't," I admitted.

"Then I want you to research it, and that may give you a few answers."

"Another question you refer to the women as Goddesses, is this group all about Goddess worship?"

"Yes, does that worry you?"

"Well, no," I said, "It just raises a question that puzzled me for some time. Is the Statue of Liberty which was built by French Freemasons, also a Goddess?

"What makes you think that?"

"Well, some time ago we had a prominent Freemason gave a talk in our lodge about the Statue of Liberty. He told us that originally the French wanted to build a giant statue of the Goddess Isis next to the Suez Canal. This fell through because Egypt is a Moslem country, and it would upset too many people. So they decided to build it in New York Harbour instead. Then when I asked if the Statue of Liberty is really the Goddess Isis, and why would Freemasons want to build a extremely large statue of a Goddess in America, I didn't get a satisfactory reply."

James gave a quiet chuckle.

"He probably wasn't used to people asking such direct questions," he said.

"Well, I'm asking you the same questions," I said, "Is the Statue of Liberty the Goddess Isis and why would Freemasons want to build a giant statue of a Goddess in such a prominent position?"

"The important point is that she is a Goddess, the name doesn't matter, as all Goddesses are one Goddess. If you want to give her a name, she is a Sun Goddess."

"Why a sun Goddess," I asked in puzzled tone, "I thought Goddesses were moon Goddesses."

"No, in pre-Christian times there were both sun and moon gods and Goddesses. It is to do with symbolism. The sun is the greater light so a sun deity would be more important than moon deity. This means that if a male sun god paired with a moon goddess would symbolise that the sun god was dominant partner. This was why the Statue of Liberty was made into a Sun Goddess to show she wasn't taking second place to anyone. We symbolised this by having the sun rays in her head dress, and if you still don't get the point, we had her holding up a blazing torch."

"Isn't it a bit audacious and provocative to have a giant pagan statue in a Christian country? How did the Freemasons get away with this?"

"Simply by not calling her a Goddess, we have been getting away with using Goddess symbols in our symbolism for years by simply not spelling it out. People assume that Freemasonry symbols are incomprehensible and don't bother to try and understand them. This means we can use very obvious Goddess symbols, without people pointing the finger and saying we are a secret Goddess organization."

"Oh," I said, and fell quiet for a moment this got my mind racing to other Freemasonry symbols that had puzzled me.

"There is a mystery made about the letter G you find in the compass and square symbol. Some Masons claim it means geometry but I never been satisfied with that explanation. I did think it might stand for God, but when I suggested that, I was told I was wrong. So what does it mean?"

"What do you think it means?"

I shook my head.

"Your not suggesting that it means Goddess."

"Correct."

"Oh." I said again, "And what about the letter M you also find in the same place?"

"I'll rather you answer that yourself." He said quietly.

I thought this over for a minute, then it became obvious.

"It must mean mother," I said.

He nodded in agreement.

"The two words together mean Mother Goddess." He said.

I was quiet for a moment thinking things over.

"All right," I said, "what is the real meaning of the compass and square symbol."

"Again, I would rather you worked that out for yourself." He replied.

He went to a desk and opened a draw and pulled out a large folder, he looked through them for a minute and then handed it to me."

"What can you understand from this picture?" he asked.

I looked at the picture, it had a image of two angels and in between it had the compass and square symbol. At the bottom it has the words, faith, hope and charity. I pondered for a few minutes.

"The angels I suppose are Goddesses," I said, trying to say something intelligent.

"Yes," said James slightly impatiently, "I pointed that out before."

I got the feeling that he expected me to see instantly what the picture was saying, but I was still puzzled.

"Faith, hope and charity are names of the triple Goddesses," he said trying to help me, "The Triple Goddess is very Ancient Symbol, known originally as the Maid, Mother and Crone. They were also later known as The Three Grey Ones, The Three Harpies, The Three Fates, The Three Graces and The Three Maries. In the Egyptian Isisian religion they become Isis, Osiris and Horus. While in Christianity they are father, son and holy spirit.

"Yes but there is only two Goddesses in this picture," I objected.

"So what is that telling you."

I looked that the picture again.

"Where is the third Goddess," he said patiently.

"Are you saying that the compass and square symbol is a Goddess?"

"A Goddess symbol," he corrected me.

I stared at the picture again.

"How is that a Goddess symbol? I asked.

"I would prefer you worked that out for yourself. Alright, I will give you something a bit easier."

I now felt very much out of my depth. I was able to ask some intelligent questions about Freemasonry symbolism, because I had been told the meaning of some, by the government organization that recruited me. They had told me the meaning of the Statue of Liberty, but they never gave me any clues to the meaning of the square and compass symbol. He looked through the folder again and pulled out another picture which I had seen often, a Freemasonry first degree tracing board.

"There are many symbols in this picture which ones do you want?" I asked

"Anything you like."

I looked for a minute and picked out the most prominent symbol.

"Well the ladder in the middle of the drawing has three women on it, so I assume they would be the triple goddess and I now notice that the ladder has a key hanging from it. So would this drawing be saying that understand the meaning of the triple goddess is the key, to climbing to the top of the Freemasonry organization?"

"That would be one explanation. Another would be that the goddess is the key to spiritual enlightenment."

"Why a goddess and not a god?"

"The answer to that is all around you. The major religions of the last few thousand years have all worship gods and all have totally failed to create a loving, caring and peaceful world for their followers."

"Buddhism doesn't worship a god," I objected.

"Yes and it is noticeable they have a better track record than either Christianity or Islam for not starting religious wars. Unfortunately the finer points of Buddha theology is lost on it's ordinary followers and they worship Buddha as a god even though he claimed he wasn't one."

"So why would worshipping a goddess be better than worshipping a god?"

"I think I am now in danger of overloading you with information. It is time you went home."

"Well, can't you just answer this one question?" I asked in exasperation. He had presented me with a puzzle but was now refusing to answer it.

"It doesn't have a quick and easy answer, we could end up discussing it for the rest of the night. I would prefer you to think about it and try and answer it yourself."

"I suppose I'd better get going." I said, in agreement, realizing I know felt very tired. I picked up the books, "Thank you for a very interesting evening."

"Just one thing," he said and handed me a card.

"This is the address and phone number of a homeless shelter, we would like to contact them and volunteer your services. They are short staffed so need all the help they can get."

"Is this another test?"

"Only in the sense of finding out what sort of person you are, so we can best know what is need for your spiritual development. One other thing, do you practise meditation?"

"I did for awhile when I was with a girlfriend who was into Buddhism and the New-Age."

"I would like you to start again practising at least once a day."

"What sort of meditation? There are many forms of meditations."

"Any form of meditation that makes the mind quiet, you may try different types to find out which suit you the best."

He smiled and escorted me to the door.

"I'll give you time to study those books, and do your research " he told me, opening the door to let me out, "then I'll contact you again."

I nodded, we said good-bye to each other and I was soon driving away in my car. When I parked my car I suddenly felt I was being watched. I tried to tell myself it was imagination and hurried up to my flat.

That evening I set about composing a message to Mary. I felt slightly resentful that the leaders of this organization were now interfering with my private life and wish now I didn't mention Mary. But I also realized that deep inside I wanted to try and contact Mary again and they had given the push I needed to do this. It seemed better to use email rather than the telephone since I could spend time thinking about what I wanted to say. After a while I realised that an abject apology plus a declaration of my continuing love was necessary to heal the breach. I expressed it as unequivocally as I could manage, then sent it off.

For the next few days I found myself doing what I normally did after writing to Mary; logging onto my email every few hours to see if she had replied. A week later she phoned me. As usual, I spent the whole time telling her how much I missed her and how much I loved her. Then she finally rang off, not telling me when she would contact me again, I realised that I was dancing on her string yet again.

## CHAPTER THREE

It was nearly a month before James phoned me again, to invite me to his house. I brought three of the books he lent with me. He let me in, scanned me with his device, indicated a seat, then offered me a drink.

"How did you get on with the homeless shelter?" he asked

"I only went once," I admitted.

"What happened?"

I took a deep breath.

"When I walked through the door the smell was terrible. Most of them don't wash and go to bed drunk, and piss and shit on the beds they sleep on. I also couldn't relate to any of them, I just didn't know what to say. It was very depressing experience and I had nightmares about it when I went to bed that night. I really don't want to go back there."

James sighed.

"I can understand how difficult is can be, if you never done anything like this before." He said. "How would you feel about helping out in a old people's home, instead."

"That would be just as bad," I said, "My sister done that for awhile and she told me what it was like. She said she had to help old people on the toilet and then wipe their bottoms afterwards. There is no way I could do something like that."

"What about looking after children or the disabled?"

"Do I really have to do something like this?"

"No. If you are unhappy about trying this, you can go to a dominatrix instead."

I thought for a moment is had made a joke and gave a polite laugh but then I realised from the expression on his face, he wasn't joking.

"Are you serious about this?" I asked.

"Very serious, dear boy."

I frowned trying to make sense of it.

"Is this all about learning humility? If I am not willing to humble myself in caring for homeless people, then I have to do it, through going to a dominatrix. Is this, what this is, all about?"

"If you say you have to humble yourself to care for homeless people, then the assumption is, you regard yourself as superior to them." He pointed out.

"I suppose I must do," I admitted, I felt very uncomfortable with this suggestion but also realised that deep down I did feel that way.

"Humility is very important aspect of all spiritual paths," said James interruption my thoughts. "Yet more important than this, is the need to learn to love. For instance Jesus teaches us we all need to learn to love our neighbours yet the Christian Church makes no attempt to teach people how to love in practise. They may of encourage women to be humble and loving, in the past. By once restricting them to do only the most menial low paid work and take on the greatest burden of caring for children, old people and the disabled. But men were not encouraged in any way to learn to love and care for others. As you can see with your upbringing, you were never given the opportunity to learn how to care for no-one."

I thought this over before replying.

"I don't understand how going to a dominatrix will help me learn how to love." I said, finally.

James was quiet for a minute, his face showed he was thinking what he was going to say next.

"In your generation you are used to women getting the same pleasure out of sex as men," he said slowing, "It wasn't always like this. In the 19th century it was believed that women didn't enjoy sex and was even capable of having a orgasm. In many Moslem countries today they still practice genital mutation where they cut off the clitoris of women, in attempt to make sure they don't enjoy sex. So why was female sexuality so restricted? In strict patriarchal countries their custom, taboos and laws are focused so that women are only allowed to express their emotional life in loving their husbands and children. While men are encouraged to only love themselves. This is expressed in the sexual act where men are free to enjoy sex however he likes and women to only be concern in giving him sexual pleasure."

He paused.

"I don't understand what all that is to do with going to a dominatrix?" I said with a puzzled voice.

"I haven't finished yet," he said patiently, "The patriarchal system, was very good at teaching women unconditional love for others and for men in learning to love themselves. Now we don't condemn this, because these are very important spiritual lessons. But there comes a time when women need to learn how to love themselves and men to learn how to love others. And this time is now. If you look at the behaviour of the dominatrix and client relationship it reverses in many ways, the behaviour of the normal 19th century marriage."

"Yes, but I have already done this," I protested, "I have always been attracted to bossy girls and they have been the dominant partner when we have had sex."

"If you weren't like this, we wouldn't be interest in you," commented James, "but this is only the beginning of your spiritual journey in returning to the Goddess, not the end. You still have a lot to learn on the emotional and spiritual level."

"So you are saying; I can learn important spiritual lessons by going to a dominatrix. I really find that hard to believe."

"It is true that no patriarchal religion or sect would suggest this. But we are not a patriarchal religion. In pagan times patriarchal priests would condemn the priestesses of Goddess temples as temple prostitutes, because these priestess would have sex with the men who worshipped at these temples. What they don't tell you is that these men worshipped the priestesses as living goddesses. And the priestesses taught these men how to best serve and pleasure women without any thought of their own pleasure. This is why patriarchal religions have very anti-sexual doctrines, because they were very frighten of female sexuality power."

"It sounds like I am joining some kinky sex club," I protested.

James shook his head.

"I can understand your assumptions," he said, "but if you think about it, many religious rituals even today have a sadomasochistic element. We are very aware of this, while most religions completely deny that it's happening. If you look at the central drama within the Christian mystery, it's about Jesus allowing one of his disciples to betray him and deliver him into the hands of his enemies. He makes no attempt to defend himself. He is whipped, humiliated and finally nailed on a cross to die. Yet everyone is frightened to suggest that this might be the act of a masochist."

I laughed uneasily.

"I can't imagine any Christian accepting that theory." I said. "Surely they would say it is an act of supreme sacrifice."

"Yes of course it's a sacrifice, but why?" asked James. "Many Christians claim that Jesus surrendered his life to his own father, God, to atone for the sins of mankind. There's no avoiding the implication that this god is a punitive and judgmental deity. To me that seems the act of a real masochist - to sacrifice yourself for someone else's sins, not your own, in order to earn the forgiveness of a vindictive and cruel god. If, like us, you refuse to believe in an unloving God, then there's an important question; why did Jesus voluntarily allow himself to suffer extreme pain and humiliation?"

"It could be," I said, "that it's to demonstrate his kingdom is not of this world. He wasn't interested in material wealth and power, and the torture and death of his body was irrelevant. Spirit continues whatever is done to the flesh."

"That's a much more sensible explanation," he said, "but it still seems an extreme way to illustrate this truth. After all, Buddha said much the same thing, but his way of validating it was to live the life of an itinerant beggar and holy man. Isn't that a more sensible and reasonable way to get your message over to your followers?"

I frowned, not willing to accept his implication.

"So are you saying Jesus was a pervert of some kind?" I asked angrily.

James shook his head.

"No, I'm not saying that," he said. "The Christian Bible has been changed, censored and downright fabricated over the last two millennia. Scholars today can prove this incontrovertibly. This means that the story of Jesus in the Bible is an incomplete story to say the least. Without some key elements which have been omitted or censored, it makes very little sense."

"So what are these missing keys?" I asked.

"I can't tell you until you've finished your initiations," he said, "but hopefully you might be able to guess some of them already."

I stared at him in bewilderment.

"Are you saying I will be doing the same thing as Jesus by visiting a Dominatrix? I asked, "Is this what this is about? Are you saying Jesus was so depraved he went to prostitutes who whipped him?" I was incensed by this idea.

James laughed.

"You're just trying to be provocative," he said. "Don't forget that, traditionally, Christians claim Mary Magdalene was a reformed prostitute."

"Are you serious about this?" I asked, "Are you now saying Jesus and Mary Magdalene were a pair of perverts."

"Why do you use the word pervert?" he asked calmly. "Isn't it just a way of passing judgement on someone whose behaviour you don't approve of?"

"Yes," I said, "though I wouldn't try to stop anyone who has strong masochistic desires expressing them. That's not the point. I'm not that way inclined myself and I'm shocked by your suggestion that Jesus was a masochist. You haven't yet denied this is what you believe either." I looked at him sharply, folded my arms and waited for an explanation.

He regarded me thoughtfully.

"I may have introduced you to these ideas too quickly," he said. "You see, we've all been taught that masochism is completely different from sacrifice. Sacrifice is a noble act but masochism is somehow sick - a mental illness. Yet the behaviour is exactly the same."

"All right then," I said. "If a man pays a Dominatrix in order to be whipped or tortured, what cause or person is he sacrificing himself to?"

"To the Dominatrix," he replied.

"Yes, but they are just playing a game," I said insistently. "He has a sexual fantasy about being whipped by a woman in black leather and he asks the Dominatrix to act it out. I don't see how he is sacrificing himself to her."

James smiled yet again.

"I agree they are playing a game, but it might more accurately be described as a drama of sacrifice which they are acting out," he said. "If you go to Church every Sunday, the priest acts out the drama of the last supper, before Jesus voluntary allowed himself to be crucified."

"So you see no difference between a man going to a Dominatrix to get his rocks off and Jesus being crucified," I said disgustedly. "I can't think of any Christian who would find that acceptable."

"We're not trying to appeal to staunch believers in the Christian doctrines," he said. "We want people who are open-minded about new ideas. The fact is that Jesus, historically, forms part of a long line of sacrificial gods such as Osiris, Dionysus, Pan, Odin, Bader and Mithras. All of these gods acted out a sacrificial drama in which they were killed to save humankind. These were the gods of mystery religions, and they have been around a very long time. If you are not prepared to look past the beliefs presented to the general public, to find the roots of these perennial myths, then we have misjudged you."

"You're not trying to say sadomasochism is the root of all religions?" I asked.

"No," he said patiently." The injunction of all mystery religions is; KNOW THYSELF. Many of the ancient pagan religions were very aware of the need to understand the sexual drives and sadomasochistic desires in people. As Sigmund Freud stated, only a hundred years ago, the suppression of sexual desires can lead to stress and mental illness. The same is true of so-called sadomasochistic needs. Modern psychiatry is only rediscovering what the ancients knew about human behaviour thousands of years ago."

"Are you pagans then?" I asked.

"Not in the sense that we have specific doctrines imposed on our members," he said, "but we do have ancient knowledge that has been preserved for thousands of years. To those who pass all our initiation tests we give this wisdom freely."

"Why do you restrict this information to a chosen few?" I asked. "Why don't you simply present it to all people?"

"We'd love to do that," he said feelingly, "and we have leaked it out bit by bit over many centuries. The problem is that the ruling elites of the world perceive our knowledge as unacceptable and dangerous. We're part of a secret war that's gone on for thousands of years. At present there is a truce; we will be left alone providing we don't attempt to give away what we know to the general public. Individuals who have tried to do this in the past have been murdered, and not just by those in power. If you think this is exaggeration, consider what happened to someone who has nothing to do with our organisation - Salman Rushdie - when he published 'Satanic Verses'. A Fatwah was declared and he had to go into hiding to avoid being murdered. All because he expressed controversial views on a religious topic. Look at your own reaction to my comments about Jesus - and you're not even a Christian!"

I shivered.

"It sounds a bit dangerous to join your religion, " I said.

He shook his head.

"Not if you follow the rules," he said. "The people who have been killed are those who attempted to use the secret knowledge to change the world too quickly. Over the last four hundred years we've been successful in imparting it bit by bit. While we exist we can continue to do this, but there have been some too impatient for change. They are the ones who are murdered. I'm afraid we cannot shield those who step out of line, because we need to protect the organisation as a whole."

"So who are they; the ones who go round persecuting your members?" I asked.

He stood up.

"I think that's enough for now," he said. "Shall I arrange for your next test?"

"But what will happen," I said anxiously, "if I don't have any masochistic desires? What if I don't want to be whipped or tortured by anyone, even if it's a glamorous woman."

"You won't be forced to do anything against your will. Not at any stage. You also don't have to go to a dominatrix to be whipped and tortured there are other things you can do. Now, do you want me to continue with this test?"

"What would happen if I refused to see this woman?" I asked.

"Nothing," he said, "but it would be a indication to us that you are not suitable for our organisation. You also have a choice you don't have to go down this path, we can help you find ways to learn how to actively care for others."

My thoughts went back to the homeless shelter, and I suddenly realised that compared with going back there, visiting a dominatrix didn't seem so bad.

"I don't know myself if I am, suitable for you organisation" I said. "Is a pagan religion with violent sexual rituals and orgies?"

He grinned.

"I can understand your concern," he said. "No. We care deeply about the knowledge and mystery of life. The foundation of most mystery religions is, as I said - 'know thyself'. If you don't undertake the quest to discover who you are, the knowledge we could give you would be of little benefit. It might even be harmful to you. These initiations and tests are a journey of self-exploration. If you decide in advance that certain areas are forbidden, you limit what you can discover. Unless you are willing to delve unreservedly into your deepest desires and emotions, then we are wasting each other's time."

"So what would happen if I go to this woman and find out I'm not a masochist?" I asked, unwilling to let the subject go.

"It won't matter," he said. "What is important is your willingness to explore yourself."

I gave what I thought was a nonchalant shrug.

"No problem then," I said. "I'm interested in finding out everything I can about myself."

"Good," James replied. He picked up his phone, dialled a number and began arranging an appointment for me.

"Will next Tuesday at 7 o'clock be all right for you," he asked, calling over to me.

"Fine."

Having completed the arrangement he replaced the phone.

"I've arranged a four hour session," he informed me as he walked back to his seat.

"Isn't that a bit long?"

"It might be," he admitted, "but we want you to take your time. The woman is not a member of our organisation, nor does she need to be. As far as she is concerned, she's simply providing a service. The reason we use her is that she is very good with beginners. She will be gentle and give you time to explore how you feel. I think you'll be safe with her."

I gave a short laugh.

"I still think it's very strange that you use a Dominatrix as part of your initiation test."

"So you keep saying," James replied wearily, "but it only feels odd because, like nearly everyone else in our culture, you have been taught that sex has nothing to do with religion, that it's somehow the enemy of spirituality. As you learn more, you will understand sexual energy much better and realise its tremendous potential for transformation."

"Oh," I said, completely lost again. "Sex is just sex isn't it?"

"Perhaps it would be a good idea to study the Tantra." He said.

"Oh," I said, "Isn't that just about sexual positions or something like that."

"No, it is a very ancient religion," he said, "though now it is only a Hindu sect. Some of its ideas have been taken over by the New-Age movement. I wouldn't read about the New-Age interpretations for the present, they could lead you astray."

"So does the Tantra use priestesses that act like Dominatries?

"Not now,"

"So does your group do this?"

"That is a secret but I can tell you that in the past, we had to teach our initiates everything ourselves. This was because the authorities had such a strong grip on all written knowledge that candidates could only learn from heavily censored scholarship. Now, through our efforts, censorship has become more difficult. So we can teach you a lot in the early stages of initiation without revealing too many of our secrets. Now did you find anything about the Ancient Minoans." He said changing the subject.

"Well, I discovered that Minoan women wore dresses very similar to the women of my first initiation." I said.

"What did you glean from this?"

"Not a lot. I found it interesting that the Minoan priestesses seem to wear aprons similar to Freemasons. Which seems to suggest that perhaps Freemasonry was started by the Ancient Minoans.."

"That would be one explanation, but it is not suggesting that Freemasonry was started by just the Minoans but by all the ancient civilizations that lived at that time. It would be helpful to you do find out more about the first Neolithic civilizations."

He went to his shelves and took down an armful of books, which he placed on the table in front of me.

"These are from an ordinary book shop ," he said, "but they do give an insight into the ancient mystery religions. Christianity itself started off as one, until it was taken over by people who only knew about its outer mysteries. These books are by scholars who have some awareness of how Christianity began. There are also books on

Gnosticism and ones about pagan mystery religions. They won't give you any illuminating facts about the inner mysteries of these religions; that knowledge has largely been lost or destroyed. Mostly they discuss the rituals and beliefs taught to the ordinary devotees rather than the inner elite, but they'll give you a start. Now did you try and work out the meaning of the compass and square symbol?"

"I have been told that it is a hexagram, but that doesn't make sense as it is used by the Jewish faith as the Star of David. Surely Judaism wouldn't be using a Goddess symbol."

"The hexagram symbol is far older than Judaism," said James, "did you find out anything else."

I shook my head.

"Very well keep looking," he said, "It may become clear in your research."

He looked at the books I had brought back

"Have you finished reading these?"

I nodded.

"Did they help you understand your feelings about the first initiation?"

"I think so," I said uncertainly. "Jung writes about Archetypes. They seem to be powerful instinctive feelings we all have, like say the Hero Archetype, which leads men to act out the role of a hero. The ritual I went through must have been designed to activate a powerful Archetype within me."

James indicated agreement.

"So which one did it trigger?"

"It could be the Great Mother, " I mused, "though I personally didn't think the first woman who made me worship her acted like a mother. But I suppose the other three women did."

James smiled at me.

"I'd agree with you that the Great Mother Archetype is the closest guess you can make after reading Jung," he said. "What Jung didn't mention is the Goddess Archetype; that's the one that applies to a woman who sees herself as a Goddess."

"So did the women really believe they were Goddesses?" I was incredulous, and it must have shown on my face.

"Correct," he said. "But it required them to play the role and you to accept it, for it to work. Some men would have been repulsed or frightened and refuse to go through with the ritual."

"Well, I have to admit I was a bit scared myself," I admitted, "but not enough to run away."

"This kind of ritual can affect men in many different ways," he said. "Your reaction was interesting; you giggled. Do you know why?"

"I think it was just to cover up my fear. I felt I'd been thrown in at the deep end and I was in a situation that was really bizarre. Feelings came up which I didn't really understand."

"Sorry about not warning you first," he apologised, "but we have some treacherous and dangerous people trying to join our organisation. So we need ways to discover the psychology of the people we instruct. It's one of the reasons why we need a long initiation program."

"I still don't understand why you're so frightened of spies in the 21st century," I said. "I can appreciate it was necessary in the past, but what secrets can you have that are so powerful you have to subject candidates to masses of tests?"

"If I told you, they wouldn't be secrets," he explained. "I can assure you this isn't just a tradition. We have very good reason, even in the modern world, to hide what we know."

"All right," I said, sighing, "but I must admit I'm really curious to know what they are."

"All in good time," James said consolingly, "if you pass all our tests."

He took a sip of his drink and looked at me intently, as if trying to work me out.

"Are you ready for another one – a test that is?"

"Yes, of course," I said emphatically.

"I will arrange it then," he said, and stood up. I realised it was now time to leave.

I picked up the books, was shown to the door and began my drive home. Though I was now feeling somewhat confused about the possible role of a Dominatrix as part of my training, I had to admit my curiosity. I also remembered what he said about Jesus and began to realise why they were considered by the authorities as a dangerous secret society. He claimed they worshipped a Goddess but the thought crossed my mind they perhaps might be Satanists. I shivered at this thought, I didn't want to be mixed up with people like this. Yet James came across to me as a sensible and decent person in spite of his outrageous beliefs. That thought helped comforted me, but not too much, I didn't know James that well and he could have another side to him that was very different.

I also was worried about what he said about the treacherous people who have betrayed them. I realised now, I was probably going to be one of these people. If James was a kind and decent person what was I doing in betraying him? He claimed that people in his organization had been murdered. Surely the government organization I worked for, wouldn't do something like that. The 007 types with a licence to kill, were just a fantasy. Then I remembered that I read that Ian Fleming, the creator of James Bond, served as a secret service agent in the second world war. So was there a element of fact in his stories? I found the thought so disturbing, I done my best to dismiss it from my mind.

# CHAPTER FOUR.

It was Tuesday. My car was parked outside an ordinary house in a middle-class suburb. There was no denying I felt nervous as I walked slowly to the front door and rang the bell. What would she look like? How would she behave? Come to that, how would I behave?

The door opened in less than a minute. A well-dressed middle-aged woman let me in. It was not what I expected; she looked far too ordinary. After a brief greeting she led the way up the stairs and showed me into a spacious bedroom. It was the most bizarre room I had ever seen. The walls had been painted black, the ceiling was red and a crimson carpet spread out over the floor. A line of built-in cupboards covered one wall, each with a full length mirror on its door. The effect was to make the room appear even larger than it was. In the centre of the room was a double bed. Near the door were two chairs and a small table. In one corner I noticed what looked like medieval stocks.

"Is this your first time?" the woman asked gently, observing my shocked expression.

"Well, yes," I admitted.

Her smile was kind.

"When your friend James phones me," she said, "he always sends me men who have never experienced this before. I don't know why he is so busy finding customers for me because he never been one of my clients. Do you even know what you want to do?"

"I'm not sure," I replied, though the truth was that I had no idea at all.

"Fine, dear," she said. "Would you like a cup of tea? We can discuss it then."

"All right," I said, relieved. I wasn't in a hurry as I wasn't paying for her time.

"You can save a bit of time as I make the tea," she said, going out the door, "if you take your clothes off now. Would you like me to dress up in black leather or PVC?

"Neither," I said. "I'm not into clothes like that."

"That's no problem," she replied and left the room. Left alone, I wandered around the bedroom, taking a closer look at the sexual paraphernalia she had on display. In one corner was a frame, whose purpose I could only guess at. In the opposite corner were the pair of medieval-style stocks I had noticed earlier. Next to them was a large table covered by whips, canes, chains and strap-on dildos of all kinds. I began to feel nervous and contemplated leaving there and then. In the end I decided not to; the Dominatrix seemed a nice person and James had said I would be safe with her.

I had just gotten undressed when she re-entered the room with a tray. She was completely nude and I suddenly realised she was old enough to be my mother. In spite of her age she still retained a slim figure and I got the feeling she probably done regular exercise. She placed the tray on the small table and we sat down.

"Do you have milk and sugar?" she asked, pouring the tea.

"Milk and half a spoon of sugar, please," I said, stifling the sudden urge to laugh at the incongruousness of the situation.

"Did you look around my room?" she asked, as she passed me my cup. I nodded.

"Is there anything you want to try?"

"I don't know," I said, "Some of the things you have in this room make me really nervous."

She patted my hand.

"Don't worry dear," she said. "I don't force anyone or push them past their limits. You don't have to use the whipping frame or stocks if you don't want to."

"Well what else could you do?" I asked.

"You can have an over-the-knee spanking, body worship or I can pee into your mouth," she suggested.

"What's body worship?" I asked.

"Just kissing and licking my body," she said. "Some men like to kiss my feet or my pussy or my ass."

"I think I'll try those," I said, suddenly emboldened.

"The spanking, the body worship and drinking my pee?"

"Not drinking your pee," I said firmly. It sounded unhygienic to me.

"Finish your tea first," she ordered and the urge to laugh returned, though I was careful to keep a straight face as I sipped the remainder of my drink. As she chatted about the weather, I began to realise that she was a very ordinary person except for the fact that she made her living as a Dominatrix. I could have had the same conversation about the constant rain in any other middle-class home. The only difference was that we were both naked and surrounded by instruments of sexual torture.

After drinking her tea the woman rose to her feet.

"Would you like to start now?" she asked.

Suddenly I felt nervous again.

"Do you want to try an over-the-knee spanking?" she continued.

"Yea, all right," I said, attempting to sound casual.

She pulled her chair away from the table, sat down and patted her lap.

"Come on," she invited.

I felt both embarrassed and awkward as I stretched face down over her lap. My feet and hands rested uncomfortably on the floor.

"Are you comfy?" she asked.

"Yes," I lied, unwilling to change my position.

She began slapping my bottom. There was no holding back; she was spanking me as hard as she could, surprising me with her strength. It hurt right away and just got worse. I couldn't see for the life of me why any man would pay to be spanked, caned or whipped by a woman. I endured it for a few minutes - my pride wouldn't allow me to end it too quickly - then I asked her to stop, got back to my feet and clutched my stinging bottom.

"Oh, I can see you enjoyed it," she said brightly, looking at my lower regions.

I glanced down in surprise to find I was sporting an erection. How had that happened when I was only conscious of pain?

"What would you like to do now?" the woman asked, breaking into my confusion.

"Um, the body worship, I suppose."

"Do you want to start by kissing my feet?"

"Yes," I assented, though I really had no preferences as yet.

"Very well," she agreed. "Take a cushion off the bed to save your knees."

I knelt before her and she lifted one of her feet, making it easier for me to kiss. I was soon licking her feet enthusiastically, but to my surprise and disappointment, it had no effect on me. I tried everything; licking the soles of her feet, sucking between her toes. Somehow it was different from my first experience and didn't produce the same emotions. Suddenly I had a desperate craving to recapture the same feeling.

"Can I kiss you between your legs," I asked.

"Of course you can, dear."

She stood up and faced me with her legs apart. I reached forward and kissed her vagina.

"Perhaps I had better lie on the bed, if you want to do that," she suggested.

She placed two large pillows at the end of the bed and lay on her back, elevated by the pillows. Her legs were wide apart.

"Are you comfortable like that?"

"Yes," she said. "I've been practising Yoga every day for the last twenty years so I have a very flexible body. Just put your cushion at the foot of the bed and you can kneel on it."

I did as she suggested and found I could comfortably kiss her vagina. I was soon hard at work, licking her clitoris and running my tongue around her labia. At first it was quite exciting, but as time went on and I felt no response from her, the pleasure died. I brought my head up to tell her I was finished, then noticed a flushed expression on her face; I realised it was affecting her after all. Greatly encouraged, I continued, even though my tongue was becoming tired. After a while I was rewarded by a gentle sigh from her, and a movement from her hips. Though my tongue now felt very fatigued, I was determined to keep on until she reached orgasm. I reapplied myself to her vagina with enthusiasm. The hip movement escalated into a violent rocking motion that I found hard to follow with my head; one of the pillows under her hips fell off the bed and I had to bend my head down lower. Finally she did orgasm. For a moment she gripped my head between her thighs and reached down with her hands to pull my head closer to her. Briefly I felt a real sense of accomplishment.

"Thank you, that was nice," she said, kicking the last pillow off the bed. "I very rarely orgasm with a client."

"It was my pleasure," I said, with a fervour that surprised me.

I lay down beside her. She lit a cigarette and we were soon chatting easily together. As I'd been booked for four hours we had the chance to indulge in a long conversation. Time passed very quickly. I was halfway through a story of my student days when she abruptly interrupted me to ask,

"We have a hour and a half left. Is there anything else you want to do?"

I looked over to the stocks and whipping frame and decided I wasn't ready to try any of these.

"I don't know," I said. "I think I'm satisfied with what we've already done."

She looked at me thoughtfully.

"I don't normally have sex with my clients," she said, "unless they're regular customers, but you did bring me to orgasm beautifully. I think with you I'll make an exception. Would you like to have sex with me?"

"Please," I said, at which point she reached over and began to play with my penis, then when I was erect she put a condom over it.

At first we used the normal man-on-top position. Then she rolled us both over, sat on me and began pumping up and down on my penis while I ran my hands over her hips and breasts. Finally, after what seemed a long time she had another orgasm. This time she cried out.

She slumped down on the bed next to me.

"You're a long stayer," she said, "Why haven't you ejaculated yet?"

"The girlfriend I had at university trained me to be like that, " I explained. "She insisted that I didn't come until she'd had an orgasm. She taught me to use the squeeze method to make sure I didn't ejaculate. I've been the same ever since."

"So how did you bring yourself off?" she asked.

"Sometimes we came together," I answered, "but if not, then she told me to play with myself,"

"And you didn't mind that?"

"Sometimes," I admitted, "but I realised I was just being selfish. I think I learned a lot from her."

"Are you still with her?"

"No," I said wistfully. "She wanted to pursue her career and went to live in America. She seems to have the attitude that staying in a long term relationship might get in the way of her ambitions."

"I'm sorry to hear that," she said, with what sounded like real regret. "Is there a chance you'll get together again?"

"I don't really know," I said. "We did keep in contact, but even that has fizzled out a bit."

"I just hope it will work out for you two," she said, at the same time reaching over to grab my penis. "Perhaps I can bring you off."

She manipulated my penis until I finally came, then reached for some tissues to clean the sperm from my stomach and chest. From her facial expression I realised that she actually enjoyed doing this. She'd probably got the same satisfaction from my orgasm as I got from hers.

We took our time getting dressed before she showed me out of the house. She kissed me as she showed me out the door, and even thanked me for a lovely time. I now realised that James was right; she was very good with beginners. I had enjoyed the session far more than expected. But I did wonder about the whips and canes I saw, not to mention the equipment hidden in the mirrored cupboards. I couldn't imagine such a nice person whipping men, but she certainly hadn't held back when she spanked my bottom. I wondered if she did the same with a thick cane in her hand.

# CHAPTER FIVE

It was several days before I visited James again. As we sat in our usual places in his living room, he began to question me with his normal directness.

"How did you get on with the books I gave you?"

"They were an eye opener," I confessed. "I didn't realise that modern Biblical scholars are doubtful about the authenticity of the Bible and unsure whether Jesus was an actual person."

"How do you feel about it?" he asked.

"I was never a committed Christian," I said, "so it doesn't mean a lot to me. I can see it would really upset those who believe the Bible is the word of God, though."

James sighed,

"Yes it can," he said. "Since the 19th century, scholars have shown that the Bible has been tampered with and extensively rewritten. Not many of the general public are aware of this; not only would the knowledge undermine the Christian Church, but it would also upset too many people, so the Church tries to ignore it. However, I didn't want you to read these books to knock Christians; they're free to believe what they want. What I wanted you to understand is the long history of censorship and distortion of the truth that has been going on in all the major religions. I'm afraid most religions have been hijacked by people only interested in political power. They twist or suppress the truth to suit themselves, and from our point of view give religion a bad name. It's not surprising that so many people today are atheists. All they can see when they look at most religions are people with illogical and contradictory beliefs who are being used by a power-hungry and corrupt priesthood. We wanted you to read the books I gave you in order to realise that the accepted wisdom disseminated by most Western religions may not be true. Some of the time it can even be a shameless lie. Now how did you get on with your research into Neolithic Age?"

"Well I found it difficult," I said, "There is not a lot of stuff on it in my local library or bookshop, and what I discovered was a bit on the heavy side."

"Perhaps I can help you."

He rose to his feet and walked across the room to his bookshelves. Soon another pile of books was in front of me.

"I haven't finished reading the last lot," I protested.

"You're not required to read them all," he reassured me. "Sort through them and choose those you like the look of. Like the previous ones, these are just ordinary books you can buy anywhere. They're about the excavations of the oldest cities discovered by archaeologists in the last fifty years or so. Hopefully they will give you some insight into the true nature of human beings as we see it, without revealing any of the hidden secrets we have."

"This is worse than being at university," I objected. "I never had to do so much studying in my life. And I'm still not sure what all this stuff about religions and the past has to do with being whipped by a Dominatrix."

"If you keep on studying and practising what we tell you," James said, "You'll eventually understand. Now, did you study the Tantra?"

"I found one book on it in my local library," I admitted, "I have to say I have been doing something similar in my relationship with Mary. Tantra teaches men not to ejaculate during sex and this is what Mary taught me to do. The only difference is that she allowed me to masturbate afterwards but in Tantra the man is even not allowed to do this."

"How do you feel about this?"

"Well I can only say these men must get very sexually frustrated. It must be even worse than monks who remain celibate, in Christian and Buddhism orders."

"Have you thought, why these men would do this?"

"Well, they claim they save spiritual energy by not ejaculating."

"Do you think that is true."

I shrugged.

"I have no idea."

"Do you think a more sensible explanation would be that Tantra sex it give women a big advantage during sexual intercourse?"

"Well, I suppose it would."

"Think about it. Read about the Tantra more and well as Taoism which is also similar."

He stood up.

"The Goddesses want to see you again, to decide if you've progressed."

I found myself once more with the hood over my face, driving to an unknown destination. At the end of the journey, there was the same room as before. I was told to remove my clothing and we waited for a knock on the door.

"Right," James said when it came, "Just do as you did last time."

I crawled into the room, where I saw the same three veiled women as before, dressed in the same way as before. I continued my slow progress towards them and kissed their feet.

"Sit up on that cushion, but keep your head bowed," ordered a female voice above me and I quickly obeyed.

"Have you contacted your girlfriend Mary?"

"Yes," I said. "She phoned me a week after I e-mailed her and we talked for a while."

"Have you resumed your relationship?"

"I think so," I replied. "She rang off not saying if she would phone or see me again, so I can't be sure."

"Very well," she said. "Now, how did you get on with Liz, the Dominatrix James sent you to?"

"She seems a very nice person. We got on pretty well. But she didn't have the same effect on me as the women here."

"In what way?"

I struggled to explain.

"Well, when I kissed the slippers of the first woman here," I said slowly, "it felt very powerful. When I did the same at Liz's house it just didn't have the same emotional impact."

"Describe the feeling you get when you kiss our feet."

"I'm not sure what it is," I said, "I suppose it's a feeling of devotion - I think."

"And why didn't you get this reaction with Liz?"

"I don't know," I said. "She's just different from you."

"Think about it," came a different voice, "Remember what you've already discussed this with James."

I concentrated for a minute before venturing an opinion.

"Is it about Archetypes? You are able to evoke the Goddess Archetype but Liz couldn't. I felt your control from the very beginning, but Liz gave her power away. She thinks being a Dominatrix is only about catering for men's funny little fantasies, so she asked me what I wanted to do. In effect she put me in charge. Is that why, when I attempted to worship her, it didn't work?"

"You learn quickly," said the voice, "you're quite right. Now, did you try out her sex-toys?"

I shook my head.

"No. I'm not really interested in having pain inflicted on me. She did spank me for a while and that was as far as it went."

"So what did you do in those four hours?"

"I tried what she called body worship," I replied. "I ended up going down on her and bringing her to orgasm - then we had straight sex. We also talked a lot. I enjoyed doing that, while lying naked on a bed."

"Are you sure she didn't fake the orgasm?" It was the voice of the third woman this time, coming from the left.

"I don't think so," I said, feeling slightly angry, "I must have spent an hour licking her. I had to work really hard at it. And the way she came -well if she faked it, then she's a damn good actress!"

"The fact that you were willing to spend an hour on oral sex," said the original voice, "does give us an insight to your character."

"I've been used to doing that with Mary."

"Give us more details," said the voice from the left, "We want to know more about your sex life and feelings."

"Well," I said, "Mary sometimes wanted what she called quickies. She would call me on my mobile phone and tell me to come around straight away. When I arrived she would be in her dressing gown. She'd lie back on the bed and tell me to give her cunnilingus. After I had given her an orgasm or two, she'd say she was busy with her studies and order me to leave."

"How did you feel about that?" asked an amused voice from the centre.

"Admittedly I did get pretty annoyed after a while," I said. "I felt she was just using me. We nearly had a row over it. I said a few words about being exploited. She said I didn't have to do it if I didn't want to and threatened to end the relationship. It was then I realised how much she meant to me. Once I began to see that I enjoyed giving her pleasure, I stopped complaining."

"Good!" said the voice from above. "We can see you are learning."

"Now clearly," said another voice, "you prefer to avoid pain, so we won't force you down that path. However, you do seem to like giving pleasure to women so we will build on that. Have you ever massaged your girlfriends?"

"Sort of ."

"Have you ever been on a massage course?"

"No."

"It would probably be best if you were properly trained," one of the women said. "Tell James and he will help you to enrol on a massage course. We'd also like you to have few more sessions with Liz. Try out all her services and find out how you feel about them. While you're doing that, you can make a start on helping Liz learn to feel like a Goddess. It's one of the ways you can serve her. Just because you don't get the same feeling from her as you do from us doesn't mean you have to give up. The next time you give her oral sex, put as much devotion in it as you can."

There was a pause while some silent consultation between the women was concluded. Then one addressed me,

"We accept that you may not enjoy pain, but we want you to explore it further for the moment. Our insight tells us it's important. Try out some of Liz's toys and report back to us."

"Right," I sighed.

"You are dismissed."

I had begun to crawl backwards away from them, my nose touching the rough floor, when an icy voice stopped me in my tracks.

"We realise that you are still a rough uncarved block," the voice said witheringly, "but you need to learn better manners. Last time you thanked us with feeling. Why haven't you done so this time?"

"Sorry," I said hesitantly, "I didn't realise it was expected of me." Even to myself the excuse sounded lame.

"Are you not grateful for our instructions?" she asked.

"Of course,"

"Then it is polite to express this gratitude," she said in a steely tone.

"Thank you very much for all you have taught me," I mumbled; my only desire was to escape the room and these terrifying women.

"You can do better than that," another voice commented.

"Thank you very much for all the wise wisdom you have given me," I said, with as much feeling I could muster.

"Clearly, wisdom is something you have yet to learn," said the voice from the middle with a sigh, "Very well. You may go."

I backed into the next room and found James waiting for me. I did wonder if I would be rebutted for my failure to stick with being a volunteer at the homeless shelter, but the subject never mentioned. James hustled me out of the house even faster than on the previous occasion.

"Why do I have to be undressed when I see these Ladies?" I asked him in the car.

He chuckled.

"All sorts of reasons. Did you know a woman can gain an insight into how a man is feeling by looking at his penis?"

"Oh," I said, wondering if I'd had an erection when I was in the presence of the Goddesses.

Back at James' house I dressed, picked up the books he'd selected for me and left. I was still trembling slightly as a result of the women's reproaches, and wondered how I would cope if they really became angry with me. I even contemplated giving up on my initiation, but dismissed the thought quickly. It would be the act of a coward and I didn't want to see myself that way. For now I would continue.

It was a week before I could arrange another session with Liz. This time I had to pay her myself. Once I became aware of how expensive her time was, I only booked two hours. When she met me at the door, I felt reassured, like we were old friends, so after we undressed, I nervously suggested I try out the stocks. She took me over to the table with the sex-toys, asking me to pick which instrument of punishment I preferred. I chose an innocuous-looking strap, hoping that it wouldn't hurt too much. Some of the objects on the table frightened me; I could imagine them doing real damage to my tender skin.

Liz led me over to the stocks. My head and hands were placed in the padded half-round notches, then the other half of the stocks was fitted over my head and hands and held in place with a catch. Without warning, a wave of fear washed over me, leaving me shaking with feelings of intense vulnerability. Liz appeared not to notice.

"Are you ready?" she asked.

I looked up. In the mirror I could see her standing behind me, strap in hand. Then she brought it down hard on my bare bottom. Before I had time to recover she gave me another hard blow. I could see in her glistening eyes that she was enjoying herself. It was a side of Liz I hadn't seen on my previous visit; though she was clearly a nice person in some ways, it seemed she truly enjoyed spanking or whipping men. After four blows I couldn't take any more.

"Please! No more," I said, but she still gave me one last whack.

"I haven't given you many," she complained, and I clearly detected the disappointment in her voice.

"I'm a coward," I admitted. "Please. I've had enough."

"All right, dear," she agreed reluctantly and released me.

I spent the rest of the time giving her oral sex. Remembering to follow the instructions of the Goddesses, I tried to invest as much feeling into it as I could. I also tried to imagine Liz as a Goddess and wondered if this was having any effect on her. I'm happy to say I was able to bring her to orgasm again and gained a real sense of satisfaction from it.

As I drove away I reflected on the irony of the situation. I had paid her money, given her oral sex and in return all she had done was inflict a painful strapping on me. Logically, it didn't make any sense at all. Yet at the emotional level it seemed to have its own logic. I was now glad I'd only stayed for two hours. I knew that a longer session would have led Liz to 'pay me back' by giving me ordinary sex. For some reason I didn't want this. What I now desired was to give without expecting anything in return.

I was soon taking weekend courses on how to massage and had a weekly arrangement with Liz. Since I needed someone on whom to practise my massage skills, I asked Liz. I found myself paying her for the privilege of both massaging her and giving her oral sex. Though I was perfectly happy to do this, I remembered only too well that I was supposed to try out all Liz's equipment. I definitely did not want to use the whipping rack, but wondered if I could cope with the strap-on toys.

The next time I visited Liz I discussed this with her. She appeared happy to go at the pace I could cope with and suggested I pick the smallest piece on her table. I was then locked into the stocks. All of her strap-ons had double dildos. In the mirror I saw her push one of them inside herself before strapping it around her waist. Then she rubbed cream on the remaining one.

"Are you ready?" she asked.

"Yes," I agreed, tensing up for the expected pain.

She laughed.

"Relax," she said, "It won't hurt."

I saw her position herself behind me in the mirror. As my legs were longer than hers she made me bend my knees slightly. Then when she felt satisfied she had the right height she pushed the dildo inside me. I was incredibly relieved that it only felt slightly uncomfortable. Compared to being beaten by a strap it was nothing.

She set to work buggering me, Watching her in the mirror as she thrust inside me, I realised I was clearly in a role-reversal situation. I reflected that if I had been a really 'macho' man I would now be feeling violated or shamed. But I wasn't disturbed in any way.

"You are so much more relaxed," Liz commented, "are you enjoying yourself, dear?"

"I think so, but it's pretty weird," I said.

"That's only because it's your first time," she said gently. "Some of my clients really like this; one young man who comes to me seems to be addicted."

There was no adequate response that occurred to me, so I remained silent, keeping my focus on the pleasurable feelings from her rhythmic movements.

"Perhaps I'd better stop now," she said at some point, leaving me with a faint sense of disappointment, "as it's your first time."

She pulled out of me, then released me from the stocks. I gave her the usual massage and oral sex. Because I was endeavouring to feel as much devotion as I could towards Liz, I noticed that my emotions were becoming stronger every visit. Liz commented that her orgasms were more intense than at first, leaving me wondering if my attentiveness was having an effect on her. I drove away from her house knowing that although I had been buggered I felt fine because it had been a woman doing it. How would I have felt if it had been a man? Everything in me screamed that it would have seemed a total violation, but there was much, much more to this response than the fact I was a heterosexual male. James was right. The Goddesses were right. There was so much I had to learn about myself; as yet I had only scratched the surface.

It was over a month before James phoned me to arrange another meeting. This time I was aware that I was excited at the prospect of seeing him again; there was a lot I wanted to tell him.

"So how are you getting on?" he asked me, as we eased ourselves into comfortable chairs in his living room.

"The massage course is good," I said, "but I need girls to practise on. At the moment I've only got Liz."

"Sometimes if you get friendly with a few of the students on your course you can arrange an exchange massage," he suggested.

"I did ask one of the girls there," I said, "but she was a bit wary of me. I think they all assume it will lead to sex. There is a middle-aged man who offered, but he's homosexual and I'm positive he wants sex. It's not easy to find an exchange partner."

"I may be able to help you," he said. "I know a woman who adores massage. She's in her sixties - I don't know if that will worry you. She lives in the country so it would be about an hour's drive to visit her."

"I don't think it will be a problem," I said, "Liz is old enough to be my mother and that doesn't worry me. In fact I don't even think about it now."

"Good," he said. "I'll arrange it with her later on. I would also advise you to buy a massage table and take it with you. Now - how have you been getting on with your studying?"

"Well," I said slowly, "I thought that the Egyptian and Sumerian civilisations were the oldest ones, but civilisation seems to go back thousands of years earlier than they do. I've been reading about Catalhoyuk and Asiklihoyuk in Turkey and the theories of Marija Gimbutas in some of the books you gave me."

"How would you sum up what you've read so far?"

"From what I have looked at," I said, "it seems that archaeologists have theorised for a long time that the first civilisations were started by war lords who built cities and fortifications against invasion by other war lords. This theory was contradicted in the 1960's with the discovery of Catalhoyuk, the oldest city ever excavated, and other Neolithic settlements throughout Eastern and Southern Europe.

Archaeologists couldn't find any evidence of fortifications, weapons of war or any form of violence in the earliest settlements. This is what Marija Gimbutas revealed in her books. She was condemned and ridiculed for a long time for daring to write about this. Then more recently scholars have found the oldest city in South America, called Caral, in Peru. Again, archaeologists couldn't find any evidence of warfare and violence in this city. The people who lived there weren't like the bloodthirsty Aztecs later on. Not surprisingly, this has undermined the warfare theory a lot. Archaeologists are now accepting that the people in the first civilisations might have lived in a peaceful world, where widespread aggression was unknown. So it seems they're beginning to accept that Marija Gimbutas might be right."

"A very good summary," he complimented me. "Did you also read about what they found in the Indus Valley Civilisation in Pakistan?"

"No," I said, "I haven't read all the books you gave me."

He grinned at me.

"Sorry, I didn't mean to push you. I can see you've been studying hard." He thought for a moment. "From what you read did you form any theory about why the first civilisations were basically so peaceful? And why did we move to an age of brutality and warfare that is still going on today?"

"The only person who seems to have a theory on this is Marija Gimbutas," I said. "She points out that all these Neolithic civilisations worshipped a Mother Goddess and lived in a matrifocal society where the sexes were equal. Then about 5,000 years ago, patriarchal tribes swept in from the north and conquered them. Since then we've had nothing but domination through fear and violence. Mostly by men."

"And what do you think of this theory?" he asked.

"I really don't know," I said, "I can't imagine a civilisation where people were able to live in peace for thousands of years. I have no idea whether it has anything to do with worshipping a Mother Goddess either. Perhaps the priests or priestesses of this religion had such a powerful hold over the people that they never thought of using violence."

James frowned. I could see there was something he didn't agree with.

"You're half right in that it has to do with the religion of the Great

Mother," he said.

Getting to his feet, he walked over to one of the bookshelves and returned with three slim books.

"Have you ever read the Tao Te Ching?"

"No," I said, " but I have heard of it. I came across references to it studying Taoism. Isn't it a sort of a Bible for this ancient Chinese religion?"

"You could say that," he said. "Many people find it hard to understand, so I've given you three translations. You may find one translation explains certain verses better than others. Unfortunately, many of its teachings are in coded form, to overcome the threat of censorship that existed when it was written. The key to unlock these coded references is to remember that it contains the teachings of an ancient Goddess religion. The writing describes an ancient feminine philosophy, rather than the masculine one we've had for the last five thousand years. If you keep this in mind, the book will make sense to you. If you have problems, then you could also research the Golden Age that's written about in Greek, Roman, Egyptian and Hindu mythology. The story of the Garden of Eden was also a Golden-Age myth, so you can read that as well." He concluded, "The Tao Te Ching is really the Golden Age myth of the Chinese."

"I was taught that Golden Age stories were only utopian myths," I said, "so why do I need to find out about them?"

"Well, of course you were," James replied, "but through your research of the Neolithic age you will find that they are based on truth."

"How can you be sure that the Golden Age written about in Greek myth," I asked, "refers to the Neolithic age?"

"You'll find that out when you investigate the legends in more detail," he said. "I'm aware this is all very new to you, because we are brought up to believe that the further we go back in time the more primitive societies were. The fact is, there's a lot of evidence that contradicts such an assumption. For instance, linguists who study ancient languages have a real problem. We would assume that the further we went back in time the simpler language would become. What linguists have found is the opposite; the further they went back, the more complex language became. The English language was more complicated 200 years ago that it is today, ancient Greek and Latin are more complex than modern Greek and Italian. While the ancient Indo-European languages were even more complex than Latin and Ancient Greek. There's also a problem with the Cro-Magnon people who were our ancestors in the Stone-Age. From the fossils discovered, it seems that on average their brains were larger than modern people's." He paused. " The point I am making is that Golden-Age myths claim we have degenerated since the last Golden Age and there is now evidence to support this."

"So why would language become more complex the further you go back in time?" I queried. This was all news to me, not to mention the fact that it seemed highly unlikely.

"It has to do with the very different natures of men and women," James explained. "Scientific studies comparing the sexes always show that in general, women are better communicators than men. The average infant girl starts speaking before the average infant boy. Linguistic studies also reveal that the average woman has a larger vocabulary than the average man. All of this suggests that language would be far richer in a society ruled by women, while the reverse would be true in a society dominated by men. One of the conclusions you can draw from language studies of the past is that society was female-centred. Now, our world is dominated by men and language has become increasingly simple because of this."

"Are you saying that the people of the Neolithic Age lived in a matriarchy?"

"Yes."

"Can you prove it?"

"Not officially, but there's a lot of circumstantial evidence. I've already covered the indirect proof from language studies. Then there's the fact that we can't find indications of systematic violence or weaponry in Neolithic sites. Every civilisation since then has had to arm itself against conquest. We believe this is the result of men's unchecked aggression. It's unlikely that testosterone-driven men could create a world of peace, so the most likely scenario is that it was women who governed communities during the Neolithic Age."

Seeing my interest in his theories, James continued enthusiastically.

"There's a mystery about the type of housing built in both Catalhoyuk and Asiklihoyuk. Unlike any form of accommodation in later civilisations, the houses of these two communities were built so close together that they had very few streets. The only way residents could get to their own homes was to walk over the roofs of other people. It seems to me that people must have been amazingly tolerant and responsible if they could live in such conditions without arguments between neighbours. To me, this again points to communities operating by the feminine values of co-operation and sharing rather than the masculine ones of separation and conflict."

"So what about Marija Gimbutas's theory that the sexes were equal in those days?"

"She was probably being politically correct," he said. "Apart from that, she might have been one of the many women who have problems with the concept of women dominating men. When people use the word matriarchy, they often assume that it's just the flip side of patriarchy; women controlling men in much the same way men have subjugated women in the past. The problem with this idea is that women and men are very different in lots of ways. It's hard to say anything for sure after so many years of patriarchal conditioning, but it's unlikely that women would use a rigidly hierarchical system. They don't have the alpha-male drive to be top-dog for a start. They're far more likely to emphasise teamwork to achieve goals than use fear of punishment. Being less belligerent and competitive than men, they're more likely to create an equal society. There's one big problem though. For men and women to live together in harmony, women would have to find a way to curb the negative side of men's behaviour."

"How did women do that?" I asked curiously. It seemed a completely impossible task to me. My estimation was that most of the world's problems arose from the egocentricity and aggression of selfish men.

"Testosterone in men drives them to be aggressive and competitive," he said, "but testosterone is also an important factor in men's sex drive. I haven't got time to go into it, but studies show that there are fundamental similarities between anger and sexual arousal. Castrate any man and both his aggression and sex drive are greatly reduced. So if you can change the focus of a man's sex drive, you can also change the direction of this kind of behaviour."

"How do you do that?" I asked, still baffled. "You're not suggesting that women in Neolithic times had to castrate men?"

"That's far too crude," he said. "Women on the whole are much more subtle than that. The way it's done is similar to the teachings you are getting in your initiation."

He rose.

"Now it is time for you to go for another test"

He put the hood over my head and we went on our usual mystery tour. On the journey, I wondered what this test would be like.

When we reached our destination, I took my hood off and found myself in a very ordinary room; it looked as if it was someone's living room. James produced a mask that reminded me of Batman's mask without the bat-ears.

"Put this on," he instructed. "We have to keep your identities secret from each other."

I held it to my face and he tied it at the back, making it difficult for me to remove without help.

"I will have to leave you now," James explained. "Your teacher will come into the room when she is ready. Do the usual thing of kneeling before her and kissing her feet."

After he left the room, I waited for about ten minutes before the door opened and a veiled woman entered the room. Quickly, I knelt, allowed her to sit down then kissed her feet. She laughed nervously as I did this.

"I'm sorry," she said in a girlish voice, "I haven't quite got used to men kneeling before me and kissing my feet. I've been told how important it is, though. They tell me you have to train men the same way as you would a dog."

She laughed again.

"Take off one of my shoes," she ordered.

I obeyed.

She put one leg over the other and extended it towards me.

"All right Rover," she giggled, "lick my foot."

I licked it all over. She seemed to be perfectly happy, until suddenly she told me to stop and put her shoe back on. There was none of the composure of the other veiled women James had taken me to. This was clearly an immature teenager.

"That was nice Rover," she sniggered, bending down to pat my head. "But the fun's over and we have to be serious. When I was given the assignment to become your teacher they gave me a dossier on your background. It says you were at university for three years but you didn't get a degree. Why is that?"

"Perhaps I wasn't good enough."

"The file says you didn't bother to study," she said. "Why?"

"I didn't know what I wanted to do," I explained I felt uncomfortable in being questioned by a girl probably ten years younger than myself. "I tried a number of subjects but couldn't find any I was really interested in. The only reason I was at university was to please my parents. They were willing to pay my fees."

"According to James." she went on, "you've studied hard when he's given you a task. Does that mean you're interested in our work?"

"I suppose I must be," I conceded.

"Well I think you are a hanged man," she announced and then looked down at me. "Do you know what that is?"

"No."

"It's a Tarot card," she explained. "The Hanged Man is the man who is no longer interested in power, wealth or status, but he doesn't know what to do with his life if he doesn't pursue these conventional goals. In a way, he's in limbo while he's searching for a meaning to his life outside of material possessions and a high place in the pecking order. You're a Freemason. I thought you would have learned about the Tarot at your lodge."

"Not in the lodge I go to," I said.

"And hasn't James told you about the Tarot?"

"Not so far."

"People use it for fortune telling," she continued, "but that wasn't its original purpose. It was created to give a pictorial history of the Great Cycle. It shows the eternal loop of matriarchal and patriarchal cycles. You should ask James about this."

"I will," I said, feeling more uncomfortable.

"The Hanged man is paired to the Strength card," she went on. "You must have seen it. It shows a woman holding open the jaws of a lion. Hanged men are always attracted to strong women, I bet all your girlfriends were like that."

"I've only ever had two real girlfriends in my life," I pointed out, "but yes; I suppose they are pretty strong women."

"Did you contact your girlfriend in America?" she asked, swerving to another topic.

"Yes," I answered warily. I wasn't too sure I wanted to discuss my private life with a teenage girl.

"Oh good!" she exclaimed, "and how did it go?"

"Well, I sent an email to her, and she phoned me back a few days later."

"So are you together again?" She seemed excited, for reasons I could only guess at.

"I think so," I replied, hoping she was going to leave it at that.

"Oh, I know you find it hard to be hooked on someone who only seems to care for herself," she said, "but this has been the lot of women for centuries. Women find themselves strongly emotionally attached to their children or husbands. They give them unlimited love no matter how badly they behave, and put up with terrible mistreatment. You don't have to look far, either in the past or the present, to discover women who've been beaten and abused yet still love their husbands unconditionally. In the same way, if not more so, they love their children."

She warmed to her theme. "Of course there's lots of women today resisting their maternal instincts because they know motherhood knocks it on the head for having a life of your own. That's why many women today go into a depression once they have children; doctors call it post-natal depression, but it's not just hormones – it's the realisation that you are irrevocably trapped for the next twenty years or so. You men don't know about this do you?"

"I suppose not," I agreed reluctantly.

"You see," she said, reverting to her earlier subject, "by getting hooked on Mary, you're learning about unconditional love. So even though it's difficult, it's a very important spiritual lesson."

"Right," I said, wondering why suffering was necessary to my progress. Wasn't love supposed to be about mutual support and caring?

"You have the perfect relationship with your girlfriend in America," she continued. "Your emotional attachment to her is teaching you to love someone whatever they do, while she is learning how to love herself by putting her career before anything else, including your feelings."

I nodded, though I was still not sure what she was talking about.

She looked at her watch.

"It's about time I left," she said, and leaned forward. "This is only a introduction, so we can get to know each other and I can decide whether I want to teach you. For now I have to teach you manners. When I go you will kiss my feet and thank me."

I did my best.

I remained in the room for nearly a half hour, listening to the faint sounds of talking in other parts of the house. I wondered if the women were discussing me. Then James returned.

"All right," he said, "time to go."

He put the hood over my head and shepherded me back to his car.

"I don't want to seem ungrateful," I began as we drove away, "Why am I assigned to a teenage girl who's probably had very little experience of life."

"She is like you a beginner and she has to start somewhere in learning how to teach men."

"I see," I said and fell quiet for a few minutes. My sense of self-importance had taken a dive. Somehow I'd seen myself as the favoured pupil of the Goddesses, in spite of my ignorance, and I was having trouble readjusting my expectations. It was hard to accept that I was just an ordinary novice, with many lessons ahead of me before I could be of any use to James' organisation.

"She said I was a hanged man, like in the Tarot. She also said the Tarot is a pictorial history of our world. Is that right?"

"Yes," he said, "though I have to admit I am not a expert on the Tarot. It also shows the spiritual journey of both men and women."

"I thought the cards were just for reading people's future."

"That's what they're mostly used for," he agreed, "but it wasn't the original reason why the Tarot was created. Like a lot of other things, it was just a means of giving out coded information."

I spent the rest of the journey in silence. I didn't like talking with the hood over my face.

At home that night, I pondered on how much I had to learn. James was encouraging me to study the peaceful civilisations of the Neolithic age, yet at the same time sending me to a Dominatrix. I still wasn't sure how these two activities were connected, except that both appeared to involve some form of Goddess worship. Then there was the female teacher they had given me. I felt comfortable being taught by James, Liz and the three wise Goddesses. They were all older and more experienced than I was. But I wasn't so happy about having a girl as my teacher, someone who was clearly younger than me. I wondered if this was another test for me, and if so, whether I would pass it.

# CHAPTER FIVE
**(note: this is the second chapter five)**

The following Saturday, I found myself driving into the country with my newly-bought massage table. I reflected that my initiation was becoming more and more expensive. Fortunately, James was lending me some of the books I needed, but I still had to pay Liz, the fees for the massage course and now, the cost of the table. I knew James was a rich man; perhaps my expenses seemed like chicken-feed to him. I wondered if he knew that I was still at the bottom of the ladder in my career, in a job that didn't pay very well.

I was also puzzled as to where all this was taking me. James had more or less told me that he belonged to a secret Goddess religion. Presumably I was going to a Dominatrix to learn how to worship a Goddess or perhaps priestesses. Yet the nature of this religion was unclear. He had repeatedly hinted that his beliefs were peaceful and non-violent. So why was I visiting a woman who would gladly beat me with a whip and enjoy doing it? Even the Dominatrix seemed a paradox. Liz was one of the nicest people I had ever met, yet she was also a sadist, even though it was unlikely she would ever hurt anyone without their consent.

I also wondered about the motivation of the men she whipped. From my own limited experience I knew she didn't hold back. What sort of agony was she inflicting on those who asked her to use one of the more vicious pieces of equipment and what on earth were they getting from it? My imagination failed me.

Did it mean that in the ancient Goddess civilisations men were frequently whipped by women? Was this how men were kept in order? The idea seemed nonsensical; there had to be a more sensible explanation. I scoured the pages of the Tao Te Ching looking for answers, but I found it incomprehensible.

I was still mulling over these questions when I came to the small hamlet that was my destination. I had to drive through it twice before I found the house I was looking for. It turned out to be a small cottage with a thatched roof. Having parked my car, I walked up to the front door and banged on a large old-fashioned door-knocker. Seconds later, an extremely plump grey-haired woman answered the door. She was nothing like I'd expected and I was caught off balance.

"Is your name Arthur?" she asked, cocking her head slightly to one side.

"Yes," I said, suddenly feeling very nervous.

"My name is Anne," she said. "Come in."

I passed through her living room as she led the way to the back kitchen.

"Would you like a cup of tea, or coffee?"

"Tea will do, please," I said. "I have a massage table in the car. Shall I get it?"

"Please do," she replied.

I hurried out. When I returned, we settled down cosily to drink tea together, just as I had done with Liz. I wondered if Anne was a member of the secret society that James belonged to, but it seemed unwise to ask. I contented myself with looking round the room, which was ordinary enough, and admiring the small garden which I could see through the open kitchen door. It was at least half an hour before Anne stood up and said briskly,

"I think it's time I had my massage."

I followed her upstairs, carrying my new massage table and we went into a small bedroom containing a single bed. The room was extremely warm and I felt the heat instantly. There was just enough room for me to set up my massage table and I began to sweat at even this small amount of exertion. Anne noticed my discomfort almost immediately.

"Is it a bit too hot for you?" she asked. "I'm afraid I feel the cold at my time of life, so I like the room to be really warm when I have a massage."

"That's quite all right," I said, wondering how I was going to survive the tropical atmosphere. Again, Anne picked up on my thoughts.

"You can take your clothes off," she suggested. "I don't want you to get hot and sweaty."

Without a word, she unzipped her dress and let it fall to the floor. Underneath it she was naked. Her body was completely shapeless; large breasts, stomach and thighs merged into one rotund form. As I undressed, I thought about the carvings of similarly shaped Goddesses found in many Palaeolithic and Neolithic excavations, like the famous Venus figurines of Willendorf, Laussel. Malta and Catalhoyuk. Perhaps in those days, very fat Goddesses represented prosperity and abundance. I knew that even today, large women are considered beautiful in some Arab countries. Clearly, female beauty is a cultural decision, whatever the preference of individual males might be.

By now I was down to my underpants.

"You don't have to be shy with me," Anne commented. I took the hint and removed them, feeling the same vulnerability as I did with the Goddesses. What was it about exposing my genitals that scared me so much? There was no-one else here and the window overlooked nothing but a copse of trees,

"I have my own oil," Anne said, pointing out its location on her dressing table.

Then I helped her onto the massage table. She positioned herself on her stomach with her face resting in a hole at the top of the table. Because I had never massaged a large woman like her before, I felt unsure what to do.

"You don't have to be gentle with me," she said, reading my thoughts once more. "I prefer a hard massage."

I pressed as hard as I could as I moved down her back and bottom towards her legs. It was gruelling work, requiring all my concentration, so I was taken by surprise when she opened her legs in a dramatic gesture. The invitation couldn't have been clearer, yet I hesitated. The previous weekend at the massage course, the instructor had given us all a lecture about being careful around people's genitals and women's breasts when massaging. Gently, I lightly stroked her inner thighs, brushed her vagina with my hands and withdrew. She said nothing so I repeated the motions.

"I don't want any massage oil in my vagina," she suddenly said, "there's a tube of cream next to the massage bottle. Use a little bit of that."

I followed her instructions. Massaging her vagina and clitoris with my finger, with my other hand I kneaded her back and bottom I continued doing this until she reached an orgasm. She cried out loudly and her whole body shook like jelly. After a while she turned on her side.

"I think I'd like a break," she informed me. "Could you make another cup of tea and bring some of the cake from the tin near the tea pot. You can go down as you are; no one is likely to call."

When I came back with the tea and cake, Anne was lying on the single bed. I poured out the tea and passed her the cake, then we talked for over an hour. I still wondered if she was a member of the secret society, but there was no way to find out directly. I tried to steer the conversation onto ancient mythology and religion but I got nowhere. She was mostly concerned with talking about herself and seemed to have no interests beyond the commonplace. Either she was determined not to reveal anything or she was what she seemed, an ordinary person. Finally she decided to continue the massage. This time she lay on her back and told me to begin with her face and upper body. As I moved downwards, she opened her legs again.

"I've been told you're pretty good at cunnilingus," she began.

So I was now about to worship a corpulent Goddess like those of the Stone Age. Was this another part of my initiation? I crawled between Anne's legs and began to lick her; I could taste the cream I had used on her vagina. As I'd learned with Liz, I concentrated on her clitoris, but the result was completely different. Her whole body jerked in small spasms.

"Do it the same way you used your finger," she instructed. "Move your tongue over the whole area."

I realised I wasn't the expert I thought I was; not all women were the same, especially in the area of oral sex. I continued to suck away, but apart from the occasional sigh, there was no response. Was she lying there enjoying herself and in no hurry to orgasm? I tried practising all the feelings of devotion I could summon. As I did this, I began to sense a stronger sensation of worship within myself. There was no way of telling whether it was because I was improving or because Ann was more in tune with the Goddess archetype than Liz.

My tongue began to tire and I became grateful that the muscles were now stronger because of the exercises with Liz. Then the back of my neck began to ache. Eventually, to my relief, Anne's hips began to rock backwards and forwards until she came. Again, her whole body shook and she cried out. I continued to caress her until she told me to stop, then she held out her arms.

"Give me a cuddle."

I climbed on top of her and was enveloped by soft flesh. Her hands moved over my back and bottom and I hardened up immediately. But there was to be no penetration. She kissed me briefly before I was dismissed.

"That was very nice," she said. "I think I will now get dressed."

He attitude now changed and I sensed she now wanted to be alone, so I suggested I leave and within ten minutes I was back on the road, thinking over the experience. James had told me Ann was much older than me, but hadn't mentioned that she was vastly overweight. Why was that? What if I'd refused to go down on her? It wouldn't have been very pleasant for Anne. The only conclusion I could reach was that James had enough confidence in me to risk that possibility.

A few days later I visited James again.

"Anne was impressed with you," he enthused. "She thought you were very good at massage, even though you're still a beginner."

"Oh good," I said, feeling slightly embarrassed by the compliment.

"She wondered if you could come for the whole weekend next time," he said. "She has some decorating to do. Can you do that?"

I think so," I said. "I haven't made any other plans."

"Oh good," he echoed with a smile.

"Um, do I still see Liz?" I asked.

"That is up to you, dear boy."

He could see I felt troubled by his answer, and waved his hand for me to continue.

"Look, I know the relationship between me and Liz is really a business one," I began, "in that I pay for her time. The problem is it now feels personal. I don't feel comfortable about suddenly not seeing her."

James smiled warmly.

"Your concern for Liz does you credit," he said, "but you have to remember that she has many more clients than you. Because of her nature she becomes friendly with all of her customers – it's why nearly all of them are regulars. I'm sure Liz will have regrets about your departure, but it's a normal part of her business. It happens all the time."

"It's partly because I can't afford to pay her fees every week," I said with some trepidation. "I know my job has good prospects but I don't get paid very much at present."

"I understand," he said. "There's no reason why you can't see her once a month or so if you still want to visit her."

"I suppose I could do that."

"Now, how about the studying?" he asked, changing the subject completely.

"To be truthful," I said, "I didn't think that the Tao Te Ching was that much different from the New Testament or Buddhism."

"Have you studied Buddhism then?" he asked.

"No," I replied. "It's just that I once had a girlfriend who became a Buddhist and she tried to convert me. So I learnt a bit from her."

"So in what way do they seem the same?"

"I suppose in teaching humility and non-violence," I said. "Jesus taught people to 'turn the other cheek'; Buddhism and the Tao Te Ching seem to say the same."

"Did you get anything else from the Tao Te Ching?"

"I did see a few Goddess references," I said, "in that the Tao is also called the mysterious female or the mother. It also mentioned a sort of Golden-Age, long ago, when life was far better, so I started looking at similar ideas from other cultures. According to Greek legend, in the Golden Age people lived in peace and prosperity. It was an age of innocence and happiness. Truth and right prevailed but weren't enforced by laws, judges or threats of punishment. The forests hadn't been cut down and there were no weapons of war. The rivers flowed with milk and wine - in fact it was all too good to be true. Then there was the Silver age when things were not so good and the Brazen age when more or less everything had degenerated. Finally, we arrive at the Iron Age of warfare and brutality. Hindu scriptures more or less say the same thing; they claim we live in a repeating cycle of the Golden Age followed by Silver, Copper and Iron."

"Do you see the connection between the Greek, Hindu and Chinese legends of an ancient Golden Age and what has been found in Neolithic sites?"

"Yes I do," I said emphatically. "There were no weapons of war or fortifications in Neolithic communities and that's also what's recorded in ancient Greek legend. I did also learn something from an Internet site. I wrote it down."

I felt in my pocket, brought out a piece of paper and read my scribbled notes,

"The next god in line is Harpocrates (or Hoor-Paar-Kraat in the Egyptian form, Harpocrates being the Greek), Horus' twin brother. He is also Hawk-Headed. But as Horus is the Active, Harpocrates is the Passive. Horus is the God of the Violent Transition, Harpocrates is the God of the Golden Age."

I stumbled over some of the pronunciations but still managed to read it out.

"So the suggestion from this," I summed up, "is that while the passive Harpocrates ruled we had a world of peace and when the active Horus ruled we had a world of violence. That supports the Tao Te Ching, about men learning to be passive and humble in order for us to have a Golden-age."

"Very good," James applauded. "So what do you think you have learnt so far?"

"Well I seem to be learning a completely different history," I said, "than the one I was taught at school."

"Have you considered that the official history, that is fed to the general public, is not correct."

"Well how am I to know if your version of history is more truthful, than what I was taught at school."

"By using your questioning mind. To give an example, you know about the Venus of Willendorf which is probably the oldest carving ever discovered. Can to tell me what is strange about this carving?"

"Well no." I said after a minutes thought.

The carving is over 20,000 years old when according to official history, human beings lived in hunter-gathers communities. Yet she is carved as a very obese woman. Now hunter-gathers live a active lives where they are always moving from location to location to follow game or to find seasonal plants. Also a hunter-gathers diet didn't have a lot of fats and sugars in it. So it would be very unlikely for a obese women to live like this."

"Perhaps she was carried." I ventured.

"Which would bring up a number of questions. For humans to

carry her would be very difficult, they would need some sort of sedan-chair. So this would suggest she was very important to the tribe, suggesting she was a queen or high-priestess. Or perhaps animals like horses and cattle were domesticated far earlier than we believed. So she could of rode about on one of them. Or perhaps she didn't need to move about because people began farming far earlier than we thought. Her obesity raises many questions like this, that conventional history has so satisfactory answer to."

"All right, if that is right what is the true story?"

"I can't tell you yet at your stage of initiation. I just told you this, to give you something to think about."

This made me feel very frustrated. He gives me a puzzle and then refused to give me the answer.

"Now what else have you learnt?" he asked, interrupting my thoughts.

"I've learnt massage and been practicing cunnilingus," I said. "I have discovered there was a Golden-Age in the past when people worshipped the Great Mother - that's now confirmed by modern archaeological finds. So does this mean that becoming skilled at giving pleasure to women is also about worshipping the ancient Great Mother?"

"Of course," he replied, "although that's just one aspect. Now, have you any questions?"

"Yes," I said. I was keen to have some of the puzzles clarified for me. "If there was a non-violent age in the past, why do we now live in such a world of war and conflict? How on earth do you stop people from being aggressive? I know Jesus, Buddha and Lao Tzu taught pacifism and humility but it hasn't done much good, has it? Violence and war have continued over the last two thousand years despite Buddhism and Christianity becoming major religions."

I took a deep breath before continuing. I was bursting with the need to have someone join the dots for me.

" You seem to be teaching me humility in a very unusual way, sending me to a Dominatrix, or getting me to practise massage and cunnilingus on women. I mean, is that your solution to the world's problems? Make all men see a Dominatrix?"

James laughed at my tone of indignation.

"Not quite," he said. "Look. What's become clear from the

experiences of the last two thousand years is that you can't teach men to become gentler by imposing moral codes, threatening them with hellfire or putting them in prison. These are all masculine solutions. The secret ingredient to solving these problems is love, which is not an intellectual concept but an emotion. If everyone felt love for others as well as themselves, all conflict and violence would disappear."

I couldn't believe his naiveté.

"Sure. But Jesus taught love, didn't he? People still hate each other."

"I agree," he said, "but the Christians taught love as a command or instruction, like 'Thou shalt love God,' or 'Love thy neighbour as thyself.' Nowhere do they explain how you learn to love God or your neighbour. Love is an emotion. You cannot intellectually decide to love your neighbour, especially if you don't like him."

"So what's your answer?" I challenged him.

"To get away from the masculine emphasis on laws, rules and the intellect," he said, "and in touch with the power of the emotions. For most women, learning to love is not a problem, because they have a maternal instinct. If you go on a passenger aircraft, you'll find that the safety instructions say. 'If the oxygen mask comes down during an emergency, a mother must put her mask on first before she puts one on her child.' This is because the airlines know that a mother will instinctively place the welfare of her child before her own." James regarded me gravely as if I was to listen carefully to his next point,

"Loving others is not an issue for most women, because their maternal instinct teaches them how to do it and they can easily extend that love beyond the family. It's far more difficult for men. Their paternal feelings are generally weaker and they're not provided with an alternative way to learn how to love people. It's assumed they will be selfish and uncaring, so they oblige. Unless they encouraged to get in touch with their maternal feeling, which are not as strong as a woman's. Or get in touch with the Goddess archetype and learn to worship women."

"So you're saying men can only learn to love by going to a Dominatrix?" I asked. He sighed deeply.

"No, of course I'm not," he replied. "Men can learn to love in an enormous variety of ways. They can become deeply involved in caring for their own children, for a start, which is becoming more commonplace for young men today. Sometimes it can be dangerous to encourage men to do this, before they are emotionally ready, because all sorts of power and sex issues are unresolved. Some men end up sexually or emotionally abusing their children. But in most cases, it works perfectly. Depends on the man." He continued,

"Because the major religions have been dominated by men for the last two thousand years or so, any teachings on love have been largely ignored. You only have to look at the number of religious wars we've had to see what kind of people have been in charge of the church hierarchies. Men who wanted power, wealth and control. They might have paid lip-service to ideas about humility and forgiveness, but they certainly didn't practise them."

"So you're saying that going to a Dominatrix is just the easiest or best way for a man to learn to love?"

"You seem to be obsessed by the Dominatrix," he said patiently. "No. It's one of the ways we teach men to change their attitudes to women and the feminine. They have to learn respect for women and be willing to learn from them, but not via intellectual routes. They have to feel differently before they can think differently. But it's certainly not the best or only way for men learn to love. Some have learned it on a battlefield when they've sacrificed themselves for their comrades. Some find it in serving a political cause or fighting for those weaker than themselves. Homosexual men who play the passive role can also learn about loving service in their relationships with other men. There's an enormous variety of ways by which a man can learn to love others. However, as most men are heterosexual and have strong sexual drives, one of the most accessible routes to change is through an emotional attachment to powerful women."

"So are you suggesting," I said, "that during the Neolithic age women walked around in black leather and whipped men to keep them in line?"

James laughed at my repetitive attempts to provoke him.

"I'm sure many men have sexual fantasies about that," he said, "but I certainly don't believe women have to whip men to control them. It all goes back to the Goddess Archetype. Both men and women worshipped the Great Mother as the Creatrix, but men also worshipped women as Goddesses, because they represented Her on Earth. It was through their devotion and service to women as Goddesses that men learnt how to love."

I stared at him.

"So that is what you're teaching me," I stated flatly. "How to worship a woman like a Goddess,"

"Yes," he said, adding mockingly, "if that's all right with you."

"I think so," I said, ignoring his sarcasm, "but surely not all men will want to do this. You can't force them."

"We have no intention of coercing anyone," he said, "but remember that powerful sex drive I mentioned earlier. It can be satisfied in all sorts of different ways. Men can go down the road leading to the abuse and degradation of women, as we see in a lot of pornography, or they can go the opposite way. Gratification from serving and pleasuring a woman. For the last few thousand years, we've generally had societies which encourage men to look down on women and treat them as sub-human. Naturally, sexual feelings have followed in the same direction. If our culture changes and men are encouraged see women as Goddesses, then there's the opportunity for men to redirect their sexual energy. They can move in the direction of wanting to serve and worship women instead of abusing them."

"Is it what you did in your initiation? Did they send you to a Dominatrix, if they existed then, to learn about submission?"

He shook his head.

"No. My lessons in humility were different. I came from a rich and privileged family. I'd been brought up to see myself as superior to the poor, and because I knew nothing about them, I went along with it. The organisation sent me to do the housework of a widow who was recovering from illness. She had no money to pay for help and no family left to assist her. It was a revelation to me. I'd never lifted a finger before, because we had servants, so I was pretty useless at first. I learned quickly, because I could see how needy the woman was. When she was better, they sent me to work in a home for disabled children and a soup kitchen for the homeless."

"Well I wish they sent me to something a bit easier first, like looking after a widow." I complained. "Going to a shelter for the homeless was a like throwing me off at the deep end."

"That option is still open to you," explained James, "We can try and find you a place as a volunteer carer if you want, instead of going to a Dominatrix. It is entirely up to you which route you wish to take."

I realize he had called my bluff. Yes I was still nervous about going to professional dominas but given the choice I still preferred this, than becoming a carer.

"Um, I think, I have to think about this," I stuttered.

Mollified, I returned to safe questions about the past.

"Can I ask you about equality?" I asked James. "Marija Gimbutas claimed that people in the Neolithic age lived in equality, not the matriarchy you say existed."

"Although she could be correct, I have to say that feminist ideology can be dangerous for women," said James. "It was silly ideas about equality that destroyed the last Golden-Age. Some women began to believe men were harmless and felt it unfair that they were subject to women. So they began to encourage men to see them as ordinary mortals. They even changed the religion of the Great Mother, giving her a son who in time became her lover or brother. In this sense, feminists are correct - there was a period in pre-history when men and women lived together in relative equality. Unfortunately it didn't last long. A few generations down the line, many men no longer worshipped women and felt completely free to behave in aggressive and competitive ways. Not only with other men, but with women as well. As you can imagine, this resulted in some highly anti-social behaviour. When women attempted to restrain these men, they responded with violence.

"Without the mystique of being Goddesses, women found themselves completely defenceless against the aggressive actions of men. Naturally, they realised their mistake and tried to remedy the situation. They went back to teaching their sons to respect the wisdom and power of women. Other women learnt to fight fire with fire and became Amazons, assisted by those men who still remained loyal. There was a valiant attempt over a long period of time, to bring men back into the fold, but in the end it failed. Worse was to come. Many women learnt to worship and serve men as if they were gods, succumbing to male propaganda. It was this more than anything else that made it impossible to put chaos and violence back into Pandora's box. Until now."

I stared at James thoughtfully, trying to digest everything he was saying.

"What about now," I said. "Women are moving towards equality but I don't see any men worshipping women as Goddesses."

He smiled,

"Men today are making exactly the same mistake that women did at the end of the last Golden-Age," he said. "They assume that women are harmless and if you give them a slice of the cake they'll stop pestering you. The patriarchs of the past knew differently. They were aware that the sexual drive in man was his weakness when it came to women and could easily lead to his downfall. That's why you have so many religions like Christianity, Islam and even Buddhism attempting to underplay the importance of sex and creating sexual taboos. It becomes dirty, unspiritual or a necessary evil, suitable only for procreation. Knowledge of the last Golden-Age has been lost or destroyed, so it is hard to convince men of the authority women possessed. Today, women are regaining their strength and power. People are becoming sexually liberated. This allows the Goddess Archetype to be released once again in the psyches of both men and women.

"Does this mean equality between the sexes is impossible?" I said bemusedly.

"I'm afraid it is at the moment, while men have a drive to be competitive. If you look over the last two thousand years or so of history, you find that men have completely failed to create an equal society. The French revolution, the American Revolution and all the Communist Revolutions were unsuccessful in this. All the idealism didn't work in practice because men are too interested in scrambling for personal advantage. Even when they live in a relatively equal society, they still compete with each other for power, wealth and status and create hierarchies of importance. If you try to make women equal with men in such a society, all you get is the rise of aggressive women who are just as happy to trample on your face as patriarchal men. Overall this does not have the effect of adding to the sum of human happiness!"

He continued, attempting to clarify his point,

"This is one of the reasons why so many marriages fail today, because people try to live out an ideal of equality. The competitive nature of men has created a world of winners and losers. We live in a world where the few have enormous wealth and power, while billions of people live in poverty. There's just the same dynamic in the relationship between a man and a woman. A man can only see himself as a winner or a loser, whatever his surface behaviour. There has to be someone he feels superior to, even if it's only a woman, his wife. Equality is not an option for the masculine mind at the moment. Either men will win the current battle and we will remain a patriarchal society, or men will lose, creating a matriarchal one."

"Let me get this straight," I insisted. "You're saying that equality is impossible just because men are competitive?"

James was quiet for a moment.

"Women have a role in this as well," he said. "Women are generally more co-operative than men, so for many of them an equal community of caring and sharing people would be the ideal. But women today have largely lost touch with any aspect of the sacred feminine other than nurturing. During the patriarchal age they learned to be masochists. There was no other way to survive in a world where you were seen as property, valuable only for the services you could provide men. Women swallowed their pain and anger until it disappeared from view, and loved their male oppressors. However, the abuse and degradation of women by men has created an imbalance. To correct this means that men have to repay a karmic debt to women and help restore their self-esteem. The gentlest and most helpful way is to serve and worship them as Goddesses."

"And before you ask," James went on, "It's not the only way. Some men feel a need to be punished for their supposed crimes against women. They feel that a good whipping expiates their guilt, and they're willing to pay good money for their atonement."

He got to his feet.

"I've told you too much," he said. "Think about what I have said and we'll discuss it further when I next see you. Now it's time to see your teacher again."

We went through the routine with the hood and the drive to the unknown destination. I got the same Batman mask.

"Just wait here," James told me as usual.

I'd been examining the wallpaper for about fifteen minutes before my teacher came through the door. I knelt on the floor and kissed her feet.

"How is Rover?" she asked, patting my head.

"Very well."

"Has your girlfriend in America contacted you?"

"No, I'm afraid not," I said regretfully. It was a sore point.

"Never mind," she consoled me, giving my head another pat, then briskly changed tack.

"So what are you learning?"

I started to tell her about the ancient civilisations I'd been studying, but she stopped me.

"I'm not interested in all that book stuff, " she said dismissively. "James can teach you that. I want to know about your emotional and spiritual development."

I didn't have a clue what to say. It was hard for me to work out what I felt about anything, let alone explain it to a stranger.

"You know what I mean. Are you learning to love more deeply?"

"I think so," I said uncertainly.

"How?" she demanded.

"I suppose by doing things for women and serving them."

"Give me a bit more detail!"

"Um, well," I said hesitantly. "When I give oral sex I try to put as much devotion as I can into it."

"Very good. And does that make a difference?"

"I think so," I replied. "It does bring up some strange feelings."

"I hear you gave cunnilingus to a woman in her 60's," she said. "How did you feel about that?"

"I suppose I would never have dreamed of going down on a woman of that age," I mused, "before I became a initiate, but I found I had no problems. I think it was because I liked her."

"I know young men who might have refused," she commented knowingly. "It's good that you can see past the body and relate to the real person inside.."

"Really," I said. "Well it wasn't difficult for me. I'm not influenced by cultural stereotypes of what a beautiful women should look like."

"I'm glad to hear it," she said firmly. "You wouldn't have got very far in your initiation if you were." A pause. "Is there anything you do have a problem with? I might be able to help you."

"Only that I don't like pain," I said. "The whips that Liz had, frightened the life out of me."

"Sounds perfectly normal to me," she giggled. "Most people avoid pain. Is that all?"

"All I can think of."

"So what did you do with this Liz?" she asked curiously.

"Well, just massage and oral sex."

"And nothing else?" she probed.

"I did try her stocks," I confessed, "and she used a strap-on dildo with me. She caned me a few times as well."

"And how did that make you feel?"

"I didn't have any problems with the dildo inside me," I said. "I didn't like or dislike it, But I hated being caned."

"Sure you didn't try anything else?" she pressed.

"No," I said, shaking my head.

"Some men will pay a Dominatrix to pee in their mouth," she divulged. "Or allow them to kiss their ass. Did you try that as well?"

"Oh, no," I said, horrified.

"What's the big deal with that?"

"Well it's a bit unhygienic isn't it?"

"So you wouldn't want to do that to any woman?

"No, of course not," I said indignantly.

"Oh goody," she sniggered. "I think you've just made my day."

She stood, pulled up her dress and pushed her panties down her thighs. After resuming her seat, she lifted her legs.

"Take my knickers right off," she ordered.

I obeyed, wondering what she was up to.

"Pee is also called golden nectar," she informed me. "Do you know why?"

"No," I said, fearing what was going to come next.

"It's because it comes from the body of a Goddess. Am I not a Goddess?"

"Well, yes," I admitted.

"You don't seem too sure."

"Oh, I am sure," I said quickly. "Yes, you are a Goddess."

"So to drink golden nectar from the sacred body of a Goddess," she said provocatively, "would be a great honour and privilege. Don't you agree!"

"Yes, it would be a great honour and privilege," I was forced to admit.

"Are you sure?" she said mockingly.

"Very sure," I replied in a whisper. My mouth was dry with fear and I found it hard to speak properly.

"All right then," she said, with such a big smirk on her face that I could see it in spite of the veil. "I am going to grant you the great honour of drinking my golden nectar. What do you say to that!"

She had me completely checkmated. There was no way I could get out of it.

"Thank you for the great honour and privilege," I squeaked in a strangled voice. I knew I had to push my fears to the back of my mind and get through the experience with as much dignity as possible. My laughing teacher sat on the edge of her seat and opened her legs wide.

"Here Rover! Open your mouth and put it here," she instructed, pointing at her vagina. "And I don't want you to waste a drop of it. Got that?"

"Yes," I said hoarsely, wondering anxiously what urine tasted like.

She gave a sigh of pleasure and I felt the stream enter my mouth. The taste wasn't as bad as I feared. The stream continued for what seemed an age then finally stopped. Remembering what she had said, I kept my mouth in place as she forced out the last of it in small spurts.

"All right Rover," she said in a satisfied tone. "Clean up any drops left."

I used my tongue to lap up any liquid around her vagina. I could taste the urine quite strongly in my mouth, but somehow it felt refreshing.

"Now that was impressive!" she exclaimed. "I had far more in my bladder than I thought, yet you drank the lot without having to take a breath."

"I swim to keep myself fit," I explained. "I can keep my head under water for over two minutes. I can easily drink a pint of beer in one gulp, so it wasn't a problem for me."

"Well good boy Rover," she said patting my head. "You have some surprising talents. But you haven't thanked me yet," she complained archly.

"I'm sorry," I said quickly. "Thank you very much for the great honour of drinking your golden nectar."

"I want you to put a bit more emotion into it," she said, trying to keep a straight face. "After all, you are extremely privileged that I am so kind and generous as to allow you to drink the golden nectar of a Goddess!"

"Oh Goddess," I said, with all the emotion I could muster, "thank you so much for the honour and privilege of drinking your golden nectar."

"Oh well, that will have to do," she sighed. "though I don't think you either understand or appreciate the gift you've just received."

She regarded her panties, now in her hand.

"Are you one of those men who has a panty fetish?"

"Oh, no," I said.

"Well it's about time you were!" she said forcefully, again struggling to keep a straight face. "Put them to your face and start sniffing!"

I was soon enveloped in womanly smells. It was astonishing to me how much I enjoyed the aroma of her underwear.

"You're getting very spoilt," she pouted. "You are greatly privileged in sniffing the panties of a goddess."

I couldn't stop myself from giving a giggle at this remark and she immediately rose to her feet.

"I can see how completely undeserving you are," she asserted with great dignity, "but I have decided to forgive you. You can borrow my knickers as a present from me, but I want them back clean and ironed."

She sailed through the door in regal fashion. Five minutes later, James came in looking deeply concerned.

"Are you all right?"

"I think so," I said. "I just got another attack of the giggles."

"I had better take you home," he decided. We drove back to his house in silence. I was deep in thought, trying to sort out the emotional effect my young teacher was having on me.

"James," I asked suddenly.

"Yes?"

"Is it possible for us to refuse an order?"

"There are no rules that I know of," he said, "but in general the idea is that you obey the women because you want to please and serve them."

"And what happens if there's a time I don't?"

"Nothing. It might be an isolated event – just something you have a problem with. If it recurs in different situations then it's a sign that maybe you're not right for our organisation. There's no shame in that, but obviously they don't want any man joining us who is not fully committed to serving and worshipping the Sisterhood."

"In other words, if I don't obey on a regular basis, I'm out."

"There are probably situations where that wouldn't be the case," he said. "If two Goddesses gave you contrary orders for example, you would be forced to disobey one of them. Or if you were ordered to do something that the Sisterhood as a whole thought was unreasonable. Personally, I don't know of a case of that happening."

I remained quiet for the rest of the journey.

Back in his living room, James gave me a large drink of brandy to calm me,. I took a few sips and put it down. My stomach was now full with urine and I didn't feel like drinking.

"I think I had better get home," I said, standing up to go.

"I haven't given you any homework yet," James complained. "Do you know the story of the Holy Grail from the Arthurian myths?"

"I read a bit about King Arthur when I was a kid," I replied. "And I've seen Walt Disney's 'The Sword and the Stone' as well as 'Indiana Jones and the Holy Grail'." I paused to dredge my memories. "Oh, and 'Monty Python and the Holy Grail'."

He smiled amusedly.

"You won't learn a lot from those films," he said, "so I'd like you to study the Holy Grail stories. Many of them are very Christianised, though, so you'll have to keep in mind that the story of the Holy Grail is far older than Christianity. Like the Tao Te Ching, most stories of the Holy Grail have coded symbols and messages within them. Try to see if you can break the code and understand their original meaning."

I gave a slight groaned, I didn't feel like trying to solve ancient mysteries.

"I think you have gone as far as you can with Liz," he continued, "We have another Dominatrix we use, she has a degree in psychology and is very interested in the mental and emotional state of her clients. I would like you to book a session with her."

He then reached into his pocket and gave me a card and then he showed me to the door.

When I got back to my flat, I found the knickers in my pocket. I couldn't resist sniffing them again. I also had very mix feelings about drinking my teacher's urine. One part of me was revolved by the whole experience while at the same time I also found it exciting. It seems I was slowly being taught how to become a pervert. When I was ready for bed, I lay down and draped the knickers over my face. It was a shock to realise I was getting hooked on those womanly smells.

# CHAPTER SIX

Next weekend found me driving to Ann's house. On the journey, I reviewed what had happened to me since I began my initiation. Some of the events brought a smile to my face, until it occurred to me that I didn't know what the group might demand next. That sobered me up. Social convention and accepted wisdom didn't seem to mean anything to them, so there was no way of guessing the next move. I just hoped they wouldn't tell me to do something way beyond what I thought was acceptable.

But I had already been forced to revise some of my boundaries, with surprising results in some cases. Clearly the initiation process was affecting me both intellectually and emotionally. Certainly, my relationships with women were changing, as was the way I viewed history and my beliefs about religion and human behaviour.

When I reached Ann's house, I found it was swathed in dust sheets. After a quick cup of tea, I was put to work painting a ceiling, then after lunch I gave her a massage. It followed exactly the same pattern as the previous week. That evening we had dinner together, giving me an opportunity to find out what her relationship with James might be. It turned out she was his cousin. Apparently, they were both from wealthy families and had known one another since early childhood. The flow of information stopped there. As far as I could discern, Ann regarded her cousin as a perfectly normal individual, who led an exemplary life. There was no hint that he might be involved with secret societies or weird esoteric cults.

So how come he could provide her with male masseurs? Didn't that strike her as a little odd? I'd already discovered that James had been sending young men to her for fifteen years, following the death of her husband. Their attention to her had been a wonderful revelation, after a marriage where her sexual needs were not only ignored but not even permitted to exist. My feelings towards her, already warm, developed further as she described her first experience of cunnilingus with one of the 'boys'. His actions had shocked as much as delighted her. James' reassurances that she was not a depraved and unnatural woman, but an important mentor for his pupils set the seal on her acceptance and she had never looked back.

I was reflecting on the new picture of James that was forming, when Ann turned the tables on me and my nosy questions.

"Why do you come to massage me?" she asked.

"Well, um, it's just that I'm doing a massage course and I need someone to practise on," I explained.

"That's what James says," she said. "Every time I get a new boy it's the same story. But you don't want to be a professional masseur do you?"

"No," I confessed, now becoming a little worried. I didn't want to lie to Ann, but I also didn't want to reveal anything confidential to her.

"All the young men who come here say the same thing," she said, laughing. "But don't worry. I'm not going to kill the goose that lays the golden egg. I don't know what goes on between you and James - and I know I shouldn't pry, but you have to forgive me for getting curious at times."

I slept in the spare bedroom overnight. The next morning was spent tidying the garden. After lunch she took me up to her bedroom, which she had previously warmed to a hothouse temperature.

"James said I can do whatever I like with you," she said bluntly.

"Well you can, more or less," I admitted.

"Great!" she said. "Would you mind taking off your clothes?"

I undressed in front of her watchful eyes, wondering what she had in mind. When I was completely naked she reached out and began to run her hands over my body. I felt them move briefly over my chest before she stepped forward to stroke my buttocks.

"You have a beautiful firm body," she sighed, reaching round to grab my penis, which was hardening as a result of her caresses. While one hand played with my penis her other hand moved over my bottom. Soon I was completely erect and swaying sensuously to the rhythm of her strokes. She whispered gently as she manoeuvred herself onto the bed,

"Get on top of me." I entered her, half expecting that my whole body would disappear inside her vagina, but it was simply warm and embracing. So comfortable and comforting that I was almost disappointed when she eventually shuddered into orgasm. We lay quietly for a while, cuddling, before she heaved me off the bed and gave me my new instructions.

"Go and make us a cup of tea, dear."

As I made the tea, a thought struck me. Maybe Ann thinks I'm some sort of trainee gigolo and James is in charge of the school. It was an amusing idea, considering James' position as a respectable member of society, but not too far from the truth. I took in her tea. After she had drunk it, she turned to me,

"You didn't come." It was a flat statement and clearly the prelude to some form of action.

"No," I agreed, wondering what came next.

"Lie on the bed," she ordered.

She sat beside me and began to caress my chest. With her other hand she gripped my penis and leaned over it with her mouth open. Soon she was sucking and rubbing me into an explosive orgasm.

"God, that was hard work," she stated, and I could see beads of sweat on her forehead. "but I haven't lost my touch. Do you know, I had to do that to my husband nearly every day. I got very good at it, so it wouldn't take long. It's nice to share it with someone who isn't a selfish pig. Now go and clean yourself up in the bathroom,"

I left the room. When I came back I found her stretched out on the bed, languidly stroking herself.

"Playing with you has made me feel sexy," she said. "I'd like to use your cunnilingus skills again."

When I finally drove off, it was late in the afternoon and I was bone-weary. Ann had certainly worked me hard. I was surprised by her sexual appetite; she certainly didn't conform to the stereotype of elderly ladies who prefer cocoa to sex. It made me wonder about other women of her age. Would they also like to have young men massaging them and giving them sexual pleasure? It was a subject I knew nothing about, but at least I could ask James.

A few days later I was summoned to see him again,

"Ann was very pleased with you," he commented, after greeting me at the door. For some reason this compliment embarrassed me and I remained silent. We moved into the living room. On the coffee table were two black robes but I made no comment about them as we sat down in our usual positions.

"Did you book up with Carol?" he asked.

"Yes I will be seeing her tomorrow evening," I said.

"Oh good," he said,

he was silent for a moment.

"How did you get on with your study of the Holy Grail myths?" he asked.

"I don't think I cracked any codes," I admitted.

"So you don't think you know the true meaning of the Holy Grail?"

"No, I don't," I said, wondering if he'd really expected me to solve such a massive riddle in a couple of weeks. "To be truthful, I found the stories confusing, especially the early stories about King Arthur and the ancient Celtic myths."

James waved his hand dismissively.

"It doesn't matter. The reason I wanted you to read up on King Arthur is because we're going to see a 'Holy Grail Mystery Play' tonight. If you didn't know much about the myths surrounding Arthur and the Grail Legends you might have had problems understanding it."

He picked up one of the robes.

"Put this on," he directed, handing it over to me.

It covered the whole of my body. Then came a hood with two eye holes, but since he had placed it over my head backwards, I couldn't see a thing.

"Yet again, I'm sorry I have to do this," he apologised, "but I'm not allowed to show you where we're going."

I heard him put on his own robe, then he led me to his car and we sailed off to an unknown destination. There was the usual routine of being led into a building, followed by a trek through interminable corridors. When I was told I could turn my hood around the right way, I did so and saw that I was in a lobby crowded with many more hooded figures. James was hooded as well, so I had no idea where he was until he spoke.

"Follow me."

I followed him through a door into a small theatre, where we both took a seat. Curious as ever, I tried to talk, but he put a finger to his lips to signify silence. Other hooded figures were entering. I looked up. There were balconies behind and to the side of us which were also filling up with silent people. I could see that the theatre was of a 19th century design and wondered where it was. Was it the place I had completed my first initiation? Did it belong to the organisation or was it a public building? Then music began to play and my attention moved.

On the stage were three women, elegantly dressed in long flowing robes, who were eating and drinking at a long oak table, waited on by male servants. A voice in the background announced that the three women were Morgan Le Fay and her two companions. Another male servant entered. He knelt in front of the women and waited for their attention.

Male Servant - Your ladyship. Three Knights of the Round Table have arrived. Should I allow them to attend you?

Morgan le Fay - Yes, you may bring them to us.

The servant left, returning quickly with three young, powerful-looking men. They appeared travel-weary but eager.

Male Servant - (loudly) Sir Galahad, Sir Perceval and Sir Bors!

The three knights bowed to the seated Ladies.

Morgan le Fay - You are welcomed. We have been expecting you. Please - take a seat.

She indicated an intricately carved settle. The three knights sat down.

Morgan le Fay - Now, gentle men -for what reason do we have the pleasure of your visit?

Sir Perceval - My Lady. For many long years we three have been on a quest, to search for the Holy Grail. Because we have been guided to this place, we believe that the Holy Grail must surely be in this Castle.

Morgan le Fay - Indeed - you have been brought to the fulfilment of your search. The Holy Grail is within this very room.

The three knights immediately began to look around the room. The three Ladies smiled at them in amusement.

Sir Perceval - My Lady, may we gaze on it? (He is unable to keep the longing from his voice)

Morgan le Fay - You have to earn that right. Unless you understand what the Holy Grail is, you will never look on it.

The three knights continued to search avidly around the room, examining corners and high places with piercing eyes.

Morgan le Fay - You may rise to assist your search if you wish.

The three knights immediately leapt to their feet and prowled about the room, much to the amusement of the three Ladies. After exhausting all possibilities, they abandoned the fruitless search and resumed their seats.

Morgan le Fay - You will not find the Holy Grail hiding in a corner somewhere. It is always where you may plainly see it.

Sir Bors - Forgive me for asking, My Lady, but if it is in view yet we cannot see it, then what is the Holy Grail? Can you give us a sign?

Morgan le Fay - You have been given signs on your journey to this castle.

The three knights began to talk quietly amongst themselves. Then they turned to face the ladies again.

Sir Perceval - On our way here we all shared the same vision one night. In our dream we stayed at a castle where we were shown a mysterious ceremony. The head of a King was displayed on a silver platter filled with blood. We believe that this was a symbol of the Holy Grail, though we do not understand its import.

Morgan le Fay - Gentle knights. You must discern for yourselves the meaning of this sign. Then you will realise what the Holy Grail is.

The knights once again turned to each other to discuss their vision, before facing the three Ladies again.

Sir Perceval - My mother told me that in ancient times the people sacrificed their king for the fertility of the crops. Would this be the purpose of the ceremony?

Morgan le Fay - Yes, it was.

Sir Perceval - (with a puzzled frown) Are you saying that we have to sacrifice ourselves before we can see the Holy Grail?

Morgan le Fay - (smiling) We do not expect you to chop off your heads. But you will have to understand the true meaning of sacrifice in order to drink from the Holy Grail.

Sir Perceval - Drink from the Holy Grail! But it is full of blood! (He pauses)

What would happen to us if we were to drink from the Holy Grail?

Morgan le Fay - You would obtain everlasting happiness.

Sir Perceval - Is this because it contains the blood of Jesus Christ?
Morgan le Fay - Perhaps.
Sir Galahad - But is it the blood of sacrifice?
Morgan le Fay - In your vision it was.
Sir Perceval - So Jesus Christ, like the ancient kings, sacrificed himself for the good of the people.
Morgan le Fay - Yes, such people sacrificed themselves for the sake of others.
Sir Galahad - Are we required to sacrifice ourselves?
Morgan le Fay - Nothing is required of you. Sacrifice has to be given in complete freedom and with no regret.
Sir Bors - But is it only through sacrifice that we will find the Holy Grail and drink from it to obtain everlasting happiness?
Morgan le Fay - That is so.
The knights appeared puzzled. They regarded each other thoughtfully for a few moments.
Sir Perceval - Are we required to allow ourselves to die in a sacrificial ritual?
Morgan le Fay - (sighing gently) Death would only be a sacrifice of the body. No. Once you are willing to devote your whole being; your mind, body and soul, to the Holy Grail, then you will be allowed to drink from it.
Sir Perceval - What more can we give if death is not enough! How is it possible for us to sacrifice our whole being?
Morgan le Fay - It is late, gentle knights, and you have travelled far to reach us. It is time for you to retire. The servants will lead you to your chambers. The Holy Grail will not be given to those who do not understand. Be sure that we will continue to aid you on the morrow.
The knights stood and bowed to the ladies. They were escorted from the room by servants.

Scene 2
The curtain opened on the same room, Morgan Le Fay stood at a window. The window showed a large painted scene of, a young, pale sun cast its watery light on the surrounding landscape. Among ruined buildings and the skeletons of dead trees, a green haze of new shoots carpeted the ground. When the three knights were ushered into the

room, she turned to join the two women in their woven chairs and waved the men to their seats.

Sir Perceval - My Lady. We pondered the meaning of your words long into the night and woke this morning with our hearts still yearning to drink from the Holy Grail. This is our thought. As Knights of the Round Table we swore an oath to protect the weak and poor against the powerful; to serve and protect all women. Is this what you mean by sacrifice?

The three ladies laughed. One rose from her chair to touch the hand of Sir Perceval as if to reassure him that their laughter was not unkind.

Morgan le Fay - No, gentle men. ( She looks gravely at them) As Knights of the Round Table you have served your King well, but the honour of drinking from the Holy Grail asks far more of you. What are you willing to give?

Sir Perceval -earnestly - Everything! Our minds, bodies and souls if such are needed.

Morgan le Fay - (smiling) Do you believe, in all honesty, that you are capable of sacrificing yourself completely?

The three knights looked at each other, unsure of her meaning.

Morgan Le Fay - Would you be willing to surrender yourself into total servitude?

Sir Perceval - Why must we do this, my Lady?

Morgan le Fay - To learn the joy of giving without thought for yourself.

Sir Bors - Do we have to become slaves to learn how to do this?

Morgan le Fay - A slave is constrained to obey and does not do so of his own free will. A man must become a willing servant.

Sir Perceval - Then it is different for a woman?

Morgan le Fay - Indeed. Women, in this world, are the creators of life. As such, they love their creations because all women are reflections of our spiritual Creator. Unless she has forgotten who she is, a woman cares for and nurtures her children, and feels united with all things. Over time, she has not forgotten how to love others unconditionally, since she remembers that we are all one. Women have sacrificed themselves for countless generations, putting the needs of others before their own because it gave them happiness to see others thrive and grow. A man as yet has seen no reason to sacrifice himself for others, and has accepted the love of women as his right.

Sir Galahad - Are you asking us to become like women?

Morgan le Fay - You cannot bear a child, but you can learn the charity, love and compassion of a woman.

Sir Bors - Please, my Lady. Tell us. What should we do?

Morgan le Fay - Do nothing. We seek nothing from you. Yet you cannot drink from the Holy Grail unless you desire more than anything in the world to surrender your whole life in giving, to learn the joy of service to those who have lovingly nurtured you in the past as you explored your desires.

Sir Galahad - Then the Holy Grail is something to do with women. Its sacredness is only revealed to those who truly wish to serve it. (He is becoming excited)

Morgan le Fay - (smiling) Gentle knight- you are right. The Holy Grail is only sacred to those who see it as such. It is made of no precious metals, adorned with no gems. It is not a relic of a famous person, revered by millions. Yet some details of the stories you have heard is truth. It is filled with blood.

Sir Bors - And it is in this room. My Lady, you are human and thus filled with blood. Are you the Holy Grail?

Morgan le Fay - (laughing) Your veins run with blood as mine do, Sir Bors.

Sir Perceval - There is only one answer possible. The Grail is your womb and the blood is menstrual blood. (wonderingly) My mother told me in secret, once, that before kings were sacrificed for the harvest, women blessed the growing crops with their holy blood. My Lady, are we required to drink menstrual blood?

Morgan le Fay - You are required, by your own need to serve, to learn unconditional love for others. Drinking from the Holy Grail is but one small lesson in this. The head of the king on a platter, which you saw in your vision, is not merely a symbol of sacrifice. It is also representative of a man worshipping a menstruating woman.

Sir Perceval - So is the ceremony our initiation?

Morgan le Fay - To a new way of life. One where that which was reviled is now revealed as sacred. One where the pleasure of giving and caring is discovered, a pleasure as yet unknown to most men. It is only by learning unconditional love that a man can obtain everlasting happiness. And his teachers are women, who will receive in great measure what they have already given to others.

Sir Perceval - We have to become your willing servants?

Morgan le Fay - Everyone's, though you will find that you are guided to those who are ready to accept your service. The finding of the Holy Grail is not an end, but the beginning of a completely new way of living. Look outside. See the new life springing from the dead ashes of the old. Then choose. Do you wish to commence this new quest, to learn about unconditional love for others?

The Knights - (together) I do.

Morgan le Fay - It is well spoken. We can begin. 'Tis only fair to start by allowing you to drink from the Holy Grail, which lay beneath our gowns the whole time you searched!

She smiled mischievously and raised her skirts. The men knelt before the simple altars of the women's willow chairs, positioned with their mouths on the sacred triangle. It is the Holiest of Holy places, from whence all human life emerges. The Knights drank the sacred blood of the three women and then a voice in the background told us they were led away to a life of willing servitude.

The curtain fell. A few seconds later the actresses and actors came on stage to receive their applause, while I remained in a state of shock. I was in a daze when James led me out of the theatre. Passively, I allowed him to reverse my hood for the return journey and we drove silently through the night. Back in his living room, I slumped into my seat.

"I think you could do with a drink," James suggested.

I took a large gulp before I spoke.

"Were those actresses really menstruating?" I asked, "Or was it just tomato ketchup."

"It was for real," said James calmly. "The production of the play was timed to coincide with the actresses' periods."

"How was it arranged for them to menstruate at the same time?" I asked curiously.

"The actresses live together," he answered. "Women who live together frequently menstruate at the same time." He shot me a penetrating look. "I can see that you were shocked by this."

"Yes, I suppose I was," I replied. "What got to me was seeing a religious and spiritual play suddenly turn into hard pornography."

James was unfazed by my accusation.

"It has to do with the culture you live in," he said calmly. "You've unknowingly been brainwashed into believing that everything to do with sex and reproduction is dirty or sinful. Or it's trivial and unspiritual. But if you look at the past, what you will find is an enormous amount of vaginal symbolism. The first male archaeologists who excavated Neolithic and Palaeolithic sites dismissed these images of the vulva as Stone Age pornography. What they didn't understand was that to those ancient people, the vagina was sacred. In fact it was the holy of holies simply because it was from there that the whole of animal and human life was born. For this reason, everything to do with reproduction was sacred, from the sex-act to breast feeding. Even women themselves were venerated as Goddesses because they are the creators of life. In those days, it was an enormous privilege for a man to drink from the Holy Grail, the source of all earthly creation. Of course, when patriarchy took over, this changed. Male rulers and priests found that women still had great power and respect as the creators of all life. So sex, menstruation, the vagina, childbirth and even breast feeding had to be devalued, to undermine the authority of women. For this to happen, a propaganda campaign was created to convince people that everything to do with reproduction was inferior and it became a taboo area. It's still at work today, even in our so-called liberated times. Many people feel ashamed of their sexuality and see it as completely divorced from their spiritual aspirations."

"I see," I said, I now remembered how my young teacher had forced me to sniff her panties. "Well perhaps I am brainwashed. I'll have to think about it. There is one thing I'd like to know, though. Who were the actors and actresses? Are they also initiates?"

"Just normal out-of-work actors and actresses. We pay them well, ask them to keep quiet. We have no problems finding volunteers as there is high unemployment in the acting profession."

"And do they all keep quiet?" It seemed unlikely.

"Most of them do," James replied, "because they want a repeat invitation. We also try to vet them in advance. Like you, they're brought to the theatre blindfolded, so they never know where they are. Many of the plays we do are pretty shocking, so those who do blab don't tend to be believed. As a matter of fact, the few who have talked exaggerated what they saw and made claims about black masses, Devil worship and similar nonsense. On the positive side, we've also picked up a few initiates from those who show an understanding of the roles they play."

Are you a Satanist Cult?" I asked directly. Now that the subject had been raised I might as well find out.

James seemed amused by the enquiry.

"We've been accused of that more times than anyone can remember," he said. "It's far easier to charge us with Devil worship than to understand our devotion to the Compassionate Goddess."

"So you don't worship the Devil," I repeated.

"Certainly not as a male god of evil."

"Are you saying you worship a Female Devil?" I asked relentlessly.

He laughed outright.

"The word Devil comes from 'Devi' which means 'Goddess' or 'women' in Hinduism and comes from a ancient Indo-European language. The word Satan derives from the name of the Egyptian god Set or Seth. What's not so well known is that the name of the Goddess Isis is a Greek translation of the Egyptian word As-Set. So Set was originally the name of a Goddess. Our opponents have always attempted to discredit us by turning our Goddesses into evil gods."

"Who are your opponents?" I wondered who these nebulous enemies were and why they would bother to hound a harmless group of Goddess worshippers.

"I'll tell you more when you're further along the road of initiation," James declared. I could see he was not going to be drawn.

He looked at me thoughtfully.

"I can see you're not impressed by the little drama you saw tonight."

"Perhaps it is because I'm brainwashed," I said. "I was genuinely shocked when I saw the actors lick menstrual blood from those actresses. It was just too much for me." I shuddered at the memory.

"The play was designed to disturb," James explained, "so the audience can gain access to their subconscious attitudes. It was pretty effective in your case. It exposed your fundamental belief that in some cases a woman's vagina is unclean - which is understandable. We've been told this for such a long time that we never question whether it's true. Now you can decide for yourself."

He paused, waiting for some comment from me, but I couldn't

think of anything to say.

"Before you were so appalled by the scenes at the end," he said, "did you understand the comments about male sacrifice?"

"I think so," I said hesitantly. "In order for a man to learn unconditional love, he has to sacrifice himself to women."

"No," he corrected me. "It's not a commandment, it's a choice. And it's not the only way for a man. It's just a easy way, for many men, because it uses the energy of his sexual desire to fuel change."

"I see," I said feebly.

We moved on.

"Have you ever heard of the expression; 'make love not war?" James asked me.

"Yes," I said, "It's a 1960's hippie slogan."

"And have you heard of the Bonobo ape?" he went on.

"Er, it's a sub-species of the Chimpanzee," I said, hoping the next question led somewhere I could follow.

"It's a species of ape that's closely related to both the Chimpanzee and humans," he informed me. "Have you read much about it?"

"No," I admitted. "I've only seen bits about it on a wildlife program."

"It's called the 'make love not war' ape by some people," he said. "Find out why, plus anything else you can dredge up about it, before we next meet."

He paused for a moment.

"Another thing," he went on, "what do you know about positive thinking."

"It is something my father used to lecture me about some times." I said defensively.

"Tell me your understanding of positive thinking."

"Its what sports stars and people like Uri Gellar talk about on TV." I stated, "My father believed in it, he claimed that illness was all in the mind and would get very impatient with me if I got ill. He even forced me to go to school when I was ill, no matter how bad I was."

James frowned.

"I see you have got a very bad introduction to positive thinking from your father," he said. "So are you now against positive thinking?"

"I can only say I have many bad memories as a child of not being allowed to show weakness or being allowed to complain, in case I was accused of negative thinking."

James sighed

"What would you say if I was to re-introduce you to positive thinking?"

"I don't know," I said uncertainly.

"We won't be doing it in the same way as what you father done it. I'm afraid he done a very bad job in the way he communicated his beliefs to you. We will try to do it with far more sensitivity and understanding."

"All right, I will have a go."

"Oh good. What I want you to do is find two positive thinking book in your library or local book shop and read then and tell me what you think next time I see you. You will find them in the self-help section."

"Right," I said with a sigh.

I went home feeling emotionally drained, idly wondering what on earth could be the connection between a Bonobo ape and the Holy Grail, as well as dreading the thought of having to read positive thinking books again. I wasn't all together convinced by his explanation about Devil worship. He seemed to have admitted to worshipping a Devil even if it was a female devil. Perhaps the government secret service I was spying for was right, they were a dangerous organization.

## CHAPTER SEVEN

The next evening I nervously rang the door bell of Carol the Dominatrix. After a minute the door opened. I was then confronted with a very tall black woman, a half a head taller than me.

"Are you Arthur," she asked.

"Er yes," I said

She invited me in and then let me down a flight of stairs to the basement. In it I found a large room with the usual Dominatrix equipment. The room was decorated far more tastefully than Liz's room and it felt more professional.

"Put my fee on that shelf," she ordered.

I quickly pulled out my wallet and put the money on a corner shelf. Meanwhile she unzipped her dress and took it off revealing a skin-tight red PVC cat-suit underneath.

"Kiss my feet," she ordered

I knelt down and done to do as I was told and realized why she look so tall, she was wearing very high platform soles on her boots.

"All right worm," she said as I kissing her boots, "what do you want to do?"

"Um, body worship," I said.

"Very well," she said, "raise your body but keep kneeling,"

I done as I was told and she turn her back on me and then pushed her bottom into my face.

"Kiss and lick my beautiful arse," she instructed.

I done as I was told, although she wasn't fat she had wide hips and a large bottom so I found I was licking over a large area. I found this very exciting and frightening at the same time.

"I bet you would like to lick and kiss my naked flesh," she said after some time.

"Oh, yes please," I said with an enthusiasm that surprised me.

"If you want to do that you have to earn it," she replied, "tell me how wonderful my bottom is and how much you yearn to worship it."

That threw me for a moment.

"You have a truly magnificent bottom," I stuttered and paused not knowing what else to say.

"Is that it?" she demanded.

"I am overcome and overwhelmed by your beautiful bottom," I said as an excuse. I then thought up a few more comments and said them, putting as much feeling I could into my words.

She let me continued for awhile until I began to repeat myself as I ran out of original complements. She suddenly took a step forward and looked down at me.

"Stay there," she said wagging her finger at me.

She then left the room I waited for a few minutes and became very aware of how uncomfortable my knees were knelling on the floor. Then she came back she was now naked. She held a pillow in her hand and threw it in front of me.

"You can kneel on this if you like," she said.

"Thank you," I said gratefully. I shuffled onto the pillow and she backed herself into my face once again. I was soon absorbed into licking and kissing her bottom once again when I felt a urge to kiss and lick her into the valley between her buttocks. I done this tentatively at first but then grew bolder and was soon licking all the way up and down her crease.

"I suppose now you want the ultimate to kiss my anus," she said suddenly.

"Um, I'm not sure," I replied.

"Oh," she said in a surprised voice, "Haven't you ever kissed a Women's anus before."

"No."

"But you want to."

"Not until now," I said, "I am also worried about the hygienic aspect of this."

"I've been a Professional Domina for nearly ten years now," she said, "And I never had a client who suffered ill effects by doing this. Don't you think it is a great privilege to allow a worthless male like yourself the honour of kissing my anus. If you want to do this, you have to earn the right to do it."

I wasn't sure how to respond to that. I realized I would once again have to give her many complements. I also realised that I did really have a powerful desire to go through with this.

"I didn't realize that I had a desire to kiss a women's anus, until now," I said truthfully. "But your bottom is so beautiful and magnificent that, that I am filled with a overwhelming desire to want to kiss it."

"Hold it there," she commanded, "That is the best complement you've made and you sound if you really mean it. Now lay on the floor with you head on the pillow."

I was also surprised at the emotion in my voice, I quickly done as I was told and she stood directly above my head, where I was able to look up directly between her legs. She held this position for a minute and then slowly began to lower herself on my face. I then realized she must have strong legs to do this so slowly, she then finished up in a swatting position. With her bottom inches from my face.

"Your tongue and lips are not to touch me until I tell you to," she commanded. "I want to hear from you how much this means to you, first."

I felt a strong urge to giggle at this bizarre situation, but I managed to suppress it as I knew it would be so inappropriate. I didn't know what to say so I got in touch with my feelings and tried to express them.

"I just have this overwhelming desire to kiss you there," I said, in a pitiful voice, "and I don't understand why."

She shuffled her feet and then lowered herself down closer to my face.

"You may have the great honour and privilege to kiss my anus," she said.

I fearfully reached out my tongue wondering what it might taste like, and was surprised to find it didn't have a bad taste. So I began to both kiss and lick it and soon found myself trying to push my tongue up her anus as hard as I could.

"Do you want to understand why you want to kiss my arse-hole?" she asked suddenly.

"Er, yes," I said between licks.

"To kiss someone's arse is considered to be one of the ultimate acts of submission. Do you feel that?"

"Um, I think so."

"You don't sound very sure."

"I don't know how I should feel, this is all new to me."

She laughed.

"Dominance and submission is a very masculine point of view. From a feminine point of view this would be about expressing deep love for the person you are doing this to. Do you feel this?" she asked.

"I don't know," I said in desperation, "I am completely confused."

"All right then," she said laughing, "I will leave you alone."

She held her position and seemed relaxed and comfortable swatting like this. While I just kept on licking until my tongue began to get tired. After what seems like a very long time she suddenly stood up.

"Right," she said, "You hour is nearly up, I want you out of the house before my next client arrives."

I was surprised how quickly the hour had gone and I realized I had spent nearly the whole time in just kissing her bottom. She made me quickly get dressed while she left the room then a minute later came back in the same dress as she first greeted me at the door.

"Aren't you finished dressing yet?" she asked as I was putting on my shoes and socks. "Get a move on."

I followed her up the stairs with my laces still undone.

"Can I ask you one question," I asked in the hallway.

"Make it quick," she said.

"Do your clients also drink your pee?"

"Yes, some of them do, and if you are worried about hygiene again, none of them have die on me because of this. In India they use urine as a medicine, they have a form a therapy where people drink their own urine every morning."

"Oh," I said in surprise.

I wondered if she was pulling my leg and decided to look this up on the Internet. She then pushed me out of the door and I was soon on my way, feeling emotionally shattered.

The following weekend I visited Ann again. This time she had no painting for me to do, so I was assigned housework. I discovered that Ann had hundreds of small ornaments distributed all over her house on display shelves. Apparently, she was fond of going to Antique

Fairs and buying little objects she considers beautiful. So I found myself picking up every one of them and dusting both it and the shelf it stood on, a task which took most of the morning. Variety came in the form of a little light vacuuming.

When it came to the time for Ann's massage, I noticed a slight change in my attitude, which I ascribed to the effects of the Mystery Play. I tried to imagine her body as sacred, the fountain of all life and found it had a strange emotional effect on me, which I could neither quantify nor name. My new feelings were powerful, but they were ones I could not clearly define.

I also went through the same routine of giving her a massage and cunnilingus afterwards before I returned home.

There was only silence from James, so I continued with my studies and my trips to see Ann. Slowly, I began to realise how much this new life was taking over the old one. My friends and family complained they never saw me, but when they asked me what I was doing that took such a large slice of my time, I was unable to give them a sensible answer.

After three busy weeks, James contacted me and I drove to his house the same evening.

"So what did you find out about the Bonobo?" he asked, direct as always.

"Let me think," I said, trying to put all my thoughts in order. "The Bonobo and the Chimpanzee are, genetically speaking, the closest relatives of humans. But the body of a Bonobo is far more like a human's than a Chimp's is, because the skeletal structure of a Bonobo is very similar to an Australopithecine, an early pre-human. Also, like humans it has a very lightly-built skeleton, whereas all other apes have stronger and more robust ones. The Bonobo is also unusual in that it can mate any time of the year, just like us. All other animals only mate for a short time when the female is in oestrus, and this includes the Chimpanzee and other apes."

James cleared his throat.

"Dolphins can also mate any time of year - another extremely intelligent mammal," he said, then paused for a moment. "I'm sorry for interrupting you. It was rude of me. Please continue."

"The Bonobo," I went on, "is a highly sexual ape and like a human being, it can mate either face to face or from behind. It's also been observed displaying homosexual behaviour. Females have been seen giving males sexual favours in return for helping to look after their young." I took a long breath then continued. "Sex seems to play an important role in the Bonobo's social behaviour. In any dispute they will defuse tension by having sex together and it doesn't matter if it's two females, two males or a male and female. Doing this will stop the argument escalating into violence. This is in complete contrast to the behaviour of the Chimpanzee. Violence is commonplace in Chimpanzee life; they've been known to commit murder and they have 'wars' with other groups of Chimps. That's why the Bonobo is called the 'make love not war' ape. Its promiscuous sexual behaviour makes sustained aggression well-nigh impossible."

"Nice lecture," said James, without a trace of sarcasm in his voice. "What effect does this have on the relationships between male and female?"

"It gives the female an advantage," I said. "Even though the female Bonobo is smaller than the male, it seems to be the females who rule Bonobo society. Females come together in a strong sisterhood reinforced by lesbian sexual behaviour. They use this unity to gang up on males, who can't co-operate with each other in the same way. Also, the lack of violence in their communities undermines the males' biggest advantage - their larger size and strength. It's really different from Chimpanzee groups, where males use aggression to control and intimidate females."

"Do these facts infer anything about human behaviour?" James asked me.

"It suggests to me that if we were more sexually liberated, there would be far fewer wars. Does this mean we should all be behaving like Bonobos?"

"There are no 'shoulds' about anything," said James, "If people prefer to live in a world riddled with conflict and killing, then fine! Mostly they don't get to choose. No one has told people that we can inhabit a society of unrestrained sexuality but no violence, or a world of suppressed sexual expression and unrestrained violence. The past tells us the story in graphic detail. In Palaeolithic and Neolithic sites we find a huge amount of sexual imagery, and no evidence of violence or war. But when we excavate Bronze and Iron Age sites, there are weapons of war, images of violence and bloodshed."

"So the people of the Neolithic age lived like the Bonobo."

"Very similarly," James agreed, "although human society was obviously far more complex, and we've behaved much more like Chimpanzees over the last five thousand years."

"Yes, but," I objected, "in the 21st century we're not anything like as violent as we used to be."

"That's a matter of opinion," he said wryly, "but certainly there are places where women have become less oppressed and violence has diminished. There seems to be a correlation between the two. If you look around the world, the fewer rights and respect women have in a community, as in many third world countries, the less peaceful it is."

I went on objecting.

"But most men today wouldn't see themselves as violent. We decide who the alpha male is through elections, not fighting, - we can even have an alpha female ruling us! You have to admit that war is not so commonplace as it used to be; politicians now do all they can to avoid it."

"You're right that outright war is no longer so acceptable in most Western countries, though it still is happening as we see in the Iraq war." said James. "Unfortunately, we still live in a very masculine society where political parties compete with each other for power, firms compete with each other for business and the individuals involved do their best to grab what they can from the other guy. Everything works on the basis of non-violent warfare. Admittedly, it's an improvement on direct bloodshed, but it still produces a society where aggressive behaviour secures an advantage, leaving many people out of the loop, powerless and poor. What's even more frightening is the increasing number of countries with nuclear weapons. It only takes one lunatic dictator or terrorist group with a nuclear bomb to start a new World War. I'd say we have a long way to go yet."

"Fair enough, there's a lot wrong with our world," I admitted. "We haven't even mentioned pollution, global warming and the mass extinction of animals. But I can't see people suddenly deciding that it would be better if women ruled the world."

"You're perfectly correct," James replied. "We can't bring about overnight change but we can accomplish it if we don't try to go too fast. This is what we've been doing over the last few hundred years. Bringing about alterations that have undermined the patriarchal slant in religions like Christianity and Islam. We've also encouraged and helped the women who wanted emancipation."

"Are you claiming your organisation engineered all that?" I exclaimed.

"Of course not. But we do work behind the scenes, helping and protecting those who try to bring about the social change we want."

"So how powerful is your organisation?" I asked. Maybe they had delusions of grandeur and believed themselves responsible for every change they approved of.

James was not to be tempted. He shook his head.

"That I can't tell you," he said, "not after half a step on the path of the initiate! Be patient."

He got to his feet and I followed suit.

"Now how did you progress with the compass and square symbol."

"I didn't get very far," I said. "I was told when I first became a Freemason that I mustn't try to work out what the symbols mean, I should just let them influence me subconsciously."

"Naturally," he said. "If masons did work out their true meaning, most of them would no longer want to be members."

"So they're about sexual perversion again." I joked.

"No, they are about the true meaning of love and compassion," he corrected me.

"Oh well, I hope I do better," I said feelingly, "I haven't been very good at finding hidden meanings in symbols."

He patted me on the back.

"You've done well so far," he said. "We don't expect you to be a genus. All we are trying to do is help undo the way you and everyone else have been conditioned. People are easily brainwashed because they accept what is told to them without question. We give you puzzles to get your mind working so you can challenge everything you have been taught."

"Is it all lies then?" I asked.

"No," he conceded, "but there are many lies and distortions of the truth in the media and in many history books you read. Now how did you get on with positive thinking books?"

"I brought two, one was all about how to become a millionaire.

The other claimed you can have what ever you want by repeating affirmations."

"From the tone in your voice, I gather you didn't think much of either of them."

"I'm sorry, but some of the things in the book are similar to what my father used to say to me. I found them hard to read."

"I see," he said with a sigh, "It seems that your father done you a great disservice by the way he introduce you to positive thinking."

"Well to be fair, I'm sure he had my best interests at heart, and was trying to help me. It was just that he made me feel I had committed a grave sin in becoming ill. In fact he seems to suggest that everything that went wrong for me, was all my fault."

"Yes, that is a heavy trip to put on anyone, is this a subject you don't want to study?"

"Um, I'm not sure," I said, uncertainly.

"Very well," he said and went to his bookshelves again. After a few minutes he came back with two slim volumes and gave them to me.

"These are two books that explain how positive thinking works," he said, "If you don't want to read them that is up to you, but they are books I would recommend."

The session ended. James saw me to the door and I drove off, considering the circle I had travelled in the last few months. I had begun by seeking the inner meaning of Freemasonry; now I was repeating my search. Maybe this time I would be able to make sense of its symbols in the light of the new perspectives I'd been given. We would see.

For the next two weeks I continued to visit Ann, settling into the role of weekend servant. I also booked another session with Carol but it seems she was fully booked up and I could only see her in a month time. Then I received a phone call from James summoning me to his house again.

As I expected, he dove straight into the subject of Freemasonry. What had my researches revealed?

"Well," I said, "I couldn't see anything at first. Then I noticed there was a similarity between Neolithic and Masonic artwork. Neolithic images contain a lot of triangles and 'v' shaped symbols that appear to represent the pubic triangle of a woman. They also use other shapes that look like vaginas. One of the most well-known Masonic symbols is the eye within a triangle. To me the eye looks like a vagina placed inside a triangle representing the female pubic area."

"Very good," said James, applauding gently. "Did you find anything else?"

"In the compass and square symbol," I said, "you have two 'v' shapes again. The way they are combined shows another vagina – to me, anyway. Then there's the beehive symbol that is so prominent in Freemasonry. A bee hive is ruled by a Queen bee; it's a matriarchal society."

"You are doing well." he said. "Anything else?"

"Only that I have notice just how many women there is in Masonic art," I said. "In some pictures, Freemasonry is represented by a woman or perhaps a Goddess."

"Very good," James commended again, "but I'd like you to keep on digging. For instance - the number 13 comes up frequently in Freemasonry. Find out the significance of this number."

As he spoke, James reached into a drawer and pulled out the hood I'd become so familiar with.

"Tonight," he said, holding it up, "you are going to meet your teacher again. Is that all right?"

It was a rhetorical question which required no answer. I stood patiently as he put the hood over my head, then endured another ride in total darkness. At our destination, I became Batman again. James went off as he always did and I waited in silence for my teacher. Dulled by the routine I'd become accustomed to, it took me some time to realise I was afraid. There was no telling what this girl might do with me. As the minutes passed, my imagination tormented me more and more so it was almost a relief when she finally came into the room. I bowed down and kissed her feet. She in turn, patted my head.

"So how is Rover?"

"Very well, thank you," I said inanely.

"Have you recovered from our last encounter?" she asked.

"Er, yes," I said, knowing I sounded like a fool.

"You don't sound very sure."

"I'm fine now. At the time it just brought up emotions and fears I couldn't handle," I admitted.

"Very well. I will be a little more gentle with you this time."

"Thank you," I said gratefully, then realised I was grateful. Because she was not going to be so cruel? Wasn't this one of the ploys of a torturer? What had I got myself involved with! She continued blithely,

"I can see there's a change in your attitude. You are more respectful in your behaviour. It seems it did you a power of good."

"Thank you," I repeated.

"I hear you are doing housework weekends," she went on. "How's that working out?"

"I don't mind housework."

"So if your girlfriend wanted you as a househusband," she said, "that would be acceptable?"

"More than acceptable," I said with enthusiasm, "because we'd be living together."

"And you would like that?"

"Oh yes," I said feelingly.

"Do you know, that's the first time I've had a positive response from you," she said. "I can see your little tail wagging and your tongue hanging out just begging for it. Now. What if she wanted children? Would you be prepared to look after them full time?"

"I've never done that sort of thing," I admitted, "but yes. I'd do that willingly."

"You're not so sure about it, though, are you?" she commented.

"I don't know how I would cope with it," I conceded. "It's the great unknown for me."

"As it is for many people," she said. "Many women have never held a baby, let alone looked after one, before they are thrown in the deep end as new mothers. The important thing here is, are you willing to learn?"

"Yes," I said stoutly.

"It would be nice if we could send you to somewhere to look after children, but the fear of paedophilia in recent times has made it harder for men to be accepted. Even the Sisterhood is now wary of men until they have demonstrated that they are capable of unselfish love for others."

"I think I would rather look after children than old people or the homeless." I commented.

"Did you bring back my knickers from last time?" she said

suddenly changing the subject.

I felt in my shirt pocket. took them out and handed them over. She examined them with interest.

"Yes, they're neatly folded, ironed and clean," she said. "Good. Did you sniff them when you got home?"

"I suppose so," I said, hugely embarrassed.

"What do you mean? Either you did or you didn't."

"Well, I did put them over my face," I admitted.

"And?" she asked.

"I've tasted and licked them as well," I confessed, in voice just above a whisper.

"There's nothing to be ashamed of," she assured me, "in wanting to taste and smell the panties of a Goddess. I expected you to give them all the adoration and veneration they deserve."

"Oh, I did," I broke in quickly.

"I'm glad to hear it," she said, mollified, she then stood up and pulled up her skirt.

"Take off my panties," she ordered.

I done as I was told, the last time I had done this it was so unexpected that had done it without thinking. This time I done it more slowly and enjoyed having my face only inches from her bare vagina. I pulled them down to her feet and she stepped out of them. She then handed me the panties in her hand.

"You can put these back on me."

I did it as reverently and gracefully as I could manage, having never dressed a woman before. When I'd finished, my teacher pointed to her used knickers.

"Do you realise that is a sacred object?" she said. "And do you know why?"

"Because they are the panties of a Goddess?" I ventured.

"Nice try, but a bit of an obvious answer. It's because they have been impregnated by the bodily fluids of a Goddess," she said firmly. "Because they are sacred I believe you should worship them."

I took the hint. Despite feeling a complete fool, I put my forehead on the floor just in front of them.

"I don't think you are putting enough feeling into it," she complained. "Go over to the other side of the room. Quickly!"

I scrambled to obey her.

"Now crawl towards them slowly," she ordered, "keeping your nose to the floor."

I had problems. It took all of my self-control not to shriek with laughter at the insanity of what I was doing. As soberly as I could, I crawled forward until my face was above the panties and I could smell the womanly aroma emanating from them.

"You may now kiss them," she said, "and I want you to put all the devotion and adoration you can into it."

I began immediately, smelling and tasting their delicate fragrance. As I lost myself in the pleasure of the task, a huge involuntary sigh escaped me.

"What was that for?" she demanded.

"I don't know," I admitted, "somehow I just had to."

"I think you're starting to get it," she said after a pause. "We'll stop for today. You may thank me."

I kissed her feet and expressed my gratitude towards her.

"Because of your devotion, you may have my panties to worship at home," she said, and got to her feet. As she walked through the door, I could see by her body language that she had far more confidence and arrogance than the giggly teenager I first encountered only a few months ago. Had I changed as much in that time?

When I reached home that night I removed the panties from my pocket, wondering what I should be doing with them. I tried to worship them again, but without my action being witnessed by my teacher the gesture seemed empty. In the end I lay back on my settee, draped them over my head and simply enjoyed their delicious smell.

Maybe there was no connection, but the loosening I felt as a result of the sigh drew me closer to Ann. On my next visit I found myself telling her all about my relationship with Mary. She turned out to be a sympathetic listener. Her only comment was that Mary should consider herself lucky to have a young man like me who was willing to wait for her. If there was a note of wistfulness in her voice, it was well controlled, but I noticed that she didn't ask me to penetrate her, only allowing me to give her oral sex. I would have to ask James whether I'd stepped over some invisible line and offended her. Women were still a mystery to me.

# CHAPTER EIGHT

A few days later, James phoned again and instructed me to come to his house that evening. When I walked into the living room, I saw the hood on his coffee table. It wasn't clear to me whether I was frightened or excited at the sight of it, but a jolt of emotion passed through me.

"How have you been getting on with the Masonic symbolism?" he asked as soon as I was seated.

"I did find out a few things," I said. "Hiram Abiff is called by the Brotherhood - the son of the widow. I just wondered if there was a hidden message in that title. Does it mean he lived in a society where people were not referred to by their father's name but by their mother's? Another thing I dug up is that modern Witchcraft was started by a man called Gerald Gardner who also happened to be a Freemason. It was modern Witchcraft that first introduced present-day people to Goddess worship."

"Did you discover anything about the significance of the number 13?"

"No I didn't," I admitted.

"Keep on digging," he said, then looked at his watch.

"We have a bit of time to spare. Do you have any questions?"

"Yes," I said quickly. "You claim that the people of the Neolithic age were matriarchal. Yet there's Goddess imagery and artefacts found in Palaeolithic sites as well. Were human beings matriarchal right through the Stone Age? That's 95% of human existence! If it's true, it would suggest human beings are naturally matriarchal."

"I'm afraid that's something we can't be definite about," James replied slowly. "We can say for sure that human society was matriarchal during the Stone Age at certain times but we can't claim it was true all of the time. The evidence is that human beings probably went through cycles of both matriarchal and patriarchal consciousness."

"Earlier on, you said you'd talk to me about these cycles," I said, "and my teacher mentioned it in connection with the Tarot. Is now a good time?"

"Why not?" he said. "Shall we have a drink first?"

When he had supplied us both, he settled down comfortably in his leather chair.

"Very well," he began, " you're familiar with the theory of evolution and the - survival of the fittest."

I nodded.

"When people talk about the survival of the fittest," he said. "The image that's generally given is of powerful Stone Age men who could fight off sabre-toothed tigers and kill mammoths. This may have happened now and again, but it completely leaves out the role of women during the Stone Age. Human beings lived right through the last Ice Age and through times of rapid warming and cooling, which caused mass extinctions of various animals. Some of the ones that became extinct were species of hominids, the most well known being the Neanderthals. To put it bluntly, we are the only species of hominids to survive the Ice Age and even then we did it by the skin of our teeth. According to genetic information, the whole human population is descended from a handful of people. The odds against us were enormous." He took a gulp of his drink before continuing.

"What you don't read about in theories of evolution is that the most important figures in the survival of any animal species are females who can bear young. If most of the men in a human group are killed, it doesn't matter, because one man can father hundreds of children. Whereas if too many women die, then the tribe has little chance of survival, because a woman can only produce one child a year. On top of that, you have to remember that it takes about fifteen years of care before a child reaches full maturity. It means that a tribe with only a few women in it, would take a long time to recover from disaster, if it does at all."

"What we've learned by observing animal groups where males are the dominant sex is that alpha males get to feed first. In a situation where there are severe shortages of food, only the alpha males will survive. Females and young, being at the bottom of the pecking order, will die first. But if females are dominant, they and the young will be fed before the males, ensuring at least a chance of the species surviving. It seems to us that matriarchal tribes were more likely to survive hostile conditions than rigidly patriarchal ones. When the ice melted and we had stable weather conditions once more, it's hardly surprising that matriarchal civilisations were the ones that thrived."

"That makes sense," I agreed, "but what about this patriarchal and matriarchal cycling you mentioned. Are you saying that a sexually equal society has never happened in human history?" I asked. It seemed the logical conclusion of his ideas.

"Only when we were changing from a patriarchal to a matriarchal one, as is happening now," he said, "or vice-versa, at the end of the Neolithic age."

"I don't think the feminists would like to hear this."

"Perhaps," he said, "though even feminists admit that equality is very difficult because we live in a masculine society, designed by men exclusively for men. There's little provision even today for women who have both a career and children. If a woman has children she has two stark choices. Pursue a career while simultaneously caring for her family, which is enormously stressful, or leave work for a number of years, thus reducing her promotion prospects. It can be done if the woman has a househusband, but that can't be called equality, because the male then has to sacrifice his own career. We also live in a highly competitive society that favours aggressive men rather than co-operative women. If we change our society so that the feminine virtues of co-operation and caring are rewarded, this would help women, but it would severely disadvantage the average man. Equality between the sexes becomes very difficult to sustain over many generations. What helps men, disadvantages women and vice-versa."

He paused but I didn't have nothing to say.

"How did you get on with the positive thinking books?" he asked.

"One them I found incomprehensible, but the other I found explained things very clearly." I said.

"So what was your understanding?"

"Well both books treat the human mind like a computer. With the unconscious mind being the computer itself and the conscious mind being the programmer. They claim the conscious mind programs the unconscious by repetition. It's a bit like learning to drive a car; the person at first drives the car using the conscious mind and then as he become familiar with the controls the unconscious mind takes over leaving the conscious mind free to think of other things. This can be a great help, as the conscious mind doesn't have to think about every single thing it has to do. But it also means that our lives can be dominated by habitual thinking, that we have previously programmed into the unconscious mind."

"Very good," said James, "how is this connected to positive thinking?"

"Only that, if you have negative thoughts about yourself," I said, "like you can't do certain things, we assume it to be a fact. Whereas it is only a negative program we have accidentally programmed into our unconscious mind. So it means if we have certain behaviour patterns we want to get rid off, we can do this by reprogramming our unconscious mind by repetitive behaviour or repetitive thoughts by the conscious mind."

"Yes you seem to have grasped the principles of the idea," he said, "very good."

"Well I only wish my father explained it like that," I said with feeling.

"Your father may of not fully grasp what the science of mind is all about."

"So what am I suppose to do with this?"

"Nothing at present, except to continue to study the subject."

"So how does positive thinking relate to Goddess worship, dominant women and secret societies?"

"The science of mind is one of the most important secret of many secret societies. This knowledge is not new, it is very old. Ruling elites have kept the secrets of mind power to themselves and fed the masses concepts like fatalism so they would be powerless and easy to control."

"How would fatalism make people easy to control?" I asked.

"Its simple enough, if people believed everything that happens is the will of Allah or God then, they have no reason to change the world they live in. So if they happen to live in poverty, that is the will of God, so they are encouraged to accept their lot and not to challenge the power of the ruling elite. The same is unfortunately true of atheism. The atheist believe everything is the result of evolution, and just good or bad luck. So although the atheist has more confidence to question the status-quo than the fatalist, he is still restricted by the belief we live in a material world. The people that bring about big changes in our world are those who know we live in a world of the mind. It is these people the ruling elite fear."

"So does your group use mind power?"

James laughed. He stretched his arms and legs before standing up.

"I think that's enough for one evening."

I rose as well.

"Are you still seeing Ann every weekend?"

"Yes."

"It's time for you to move on to a sterner test," he informed me. "We're going to get someone to take your place with Ann. You're going to be with another woman who is more demanding. Is that all right?"

"I suppose so," I said uncertainly.

"You'll be fine," he reassured me. "I'll arrange a meeting. Just visit Ann on Sundays for the moment. We'll see how she gets on with the new initiate."

He picked up the hood from the table.

Tonight's mystery tour was different. James suddenly accelerated his car at various times and went around a number of corners at speed.

"Sorry about that," he said, after a time of throwing me violently around in the car seat until I began to feel sick, "I thought a car might be following me. Fortunately it doesn't seem to be the case, but we'll drive around a bit more to make sure."

The result of our detours was that we arrived at our destination much later than expected. When we finally stopped, James led me into the house as usual, but took me to another room. My hood stayed on.

"Wait here," he whispered, "and don't say anything. Someone else is now having an audience with the Goddesses because we were delayed. I don't know when it will be possible for you to see them."

I heard him leave the room. Waiting in silence, I wondered why I had to remain blindfolded. Surely this was just another bare room with a couple of chairs. Then finally, after a very long wait, the door opened. Someone grabbed me and guided me out of the room, down a corridor then into another room. It was James who took my hood off.

"You don't have to bother about undressing this time," he said. "We mustn't keep the Goddesses waiting. Just crawl through that door when I open it."

I crept awkwardly into the room to find the three veiled women seated in its centre. As usual, I kept my nose to the floor.

"We don't have much time for you today," came a female voice. "Come over here as fast as you can."

I must have looked stupid as I executed a speeded-up crawl to reach them. I quickly kissed their feet then took my usual position, sitting on the cushion with my head bowed.

"How did your session go with Carol?" asked another voice.

"I felt she is a far more powerful dominatrix than Liz," I said, "I had got similar feelings from her as I get from all of you."

"Did she try to psychoanalyse you?"

"She did tell me that dominance and submission was an expression of love."

"We agree, it is a pity we cannot invite her into our group."

"Your teacher thinks you are starting to move - emotionally that is," said another voice, "True?"

"I think so," I said uncertainly.

"You're not sure, then?"

"My feelings of devotion seem to be becoming stronger."

"Good. Now what we want you to do is to take those feelings of devotion and apply them to your everyday life. Do you understand?"

"Not really," I confessed hesitantly.

I heard an exclamation of impatience, followed by a shushing noise.

"We really don't have the time to spell it out," she said. "You are learning to see women as sacred and holy. We want you to take this feeling of sacredness and apply it to the whole of life. Now do you understand?!"

"Um, I think so," I said. I was lying.

"I don't think he does," another female voice joined in.

"All right," said the first female voice with a sigh, "do you have a pet?"

"No, I live in a flat, we're not allowed pets where I live," I said.

"Do you look after anything! A garden, or even a house plant?"

"Er, no, nothing," I said desperately. "I live on the third floor."
"Are you allowed window boxes?"
"Yes, I think that would be all right," I said.
"Very well. Invest in a window box or house plants and learn everything you can about looking after them. Then apply the feelings of devotion you have learnt from us to your plants. We want you to talk to the plants; try to form an emotional relationship with them. Learn how to nurture and care for another life form and see how this affects you emotionally. Is that clear!"
"Yes," I said confidently.
"You are dismissed!"
I thanked them for agreeing to see me and backed out of the room as fast as I could.
On the journey back to James' house I asked him.
"One of the Goddesses said they cannot invite Carol to their group even though they would like to. Why?"
"It seems she has her own religious views and opinions that doesn't include our Creatrix is a Goddess or even feminine in nature. It seems she is a committed Christian."
"Oh, I see," I said, "Isn't it a paradox being a committed Christian and also a dominatrix?"
"It would seem that way at first sight," admitted James, "but there is nothing in the bible that forbade being a professional domina."
"Yes, but I am sure there is something in the bible about being a prostitute."
"I don't think Carol would see herself as a prostitute, because she doesn't have sex with any of her clients."
"Yes but," I objected with some exasperation, "if she goes to church every Sunday I bet she doesn't tell the rest of the congregation what she does for a living."
James chuckled.
"I'm sure she claims she is a therapist or even a psychologist" he said calmly.
"Well that is my point," I said getting at bit worked up now, "she must be as different as chalk and cheese to normal Christians."
"No, I can't agree with that," said James smoothly. "Many Christians believe that homosexuality is a mortal sin, yet we know there are many homosexuals in the church including the priesthood.

Gays can quote lines in the bible that suggest that homosexuality is perfectly all right. Some go as far as claiming that Jesus himself was homosexual."

I gave a brief laugh.

"I never heard of that one," I said, "how can they justify that idea?"

"I can't quote you chapter and verse," said James, "but in John's bible he claims to be Jesus favourite disciple and in his version of the last supper he suggests having a physical relationship with Jesus."

"Oh I see," I said in surprise, "I don't remember being taught that at Sunday school. I might look that up. Do you think that might be true?"

"I really don't know," said James dismissively, "You can get all sorts of meanings out of the bible, to fit in with what you want to believe. I wouldn't be surprised if Carol can give you quotes in the bible that support her profession as well."

"Do you really think so?"

"I'm only speculating," he said in a voice that told me he was now bored with the subject, "and I don't want you to question her about this, to her you are just a normal client. She doesn't know we send her some of our trainees and we don't want her to know either."

"Don't worry I won't." I said and dropped the subject.

# CHAPTER NINE

I visited Ann the next week, but only on the Sunday. The new arrangements left Saturday free, so I visited my neglected mother. I wondered how Ann was getting on with the new initiate and whether my new mentor would be as kind as her and Liz. There certainly seemed to be a big difference between the women in the Organisation and those who trained the men from outside it. It hadn't been made clear to me whether I was being moved on to another outsider, but it seemed likely. Maybe it would be someone young this time, but less scary than my teacher. Maybe it would be a scholar like James. I had no choice but to wait and see.

It was another two weeks before James phoned me again. He told me to bring my massage table that evening.

"I finally worked out the significance of the number '13'," I claimed enthusiastically as we both sat down in his comfortable living room. "Apparently, in the past, there were thirteen months in the year. A month originally described one complete cycle of the moon and there are thirteen of them in one year. It made far more sense than the nonsense we have today. You had thirteen months lasting exactly twenty eight days each, then you divided them into four, seven day weeks. Simple. Why on earth it got changed I can't imagine."

"The twenty eight day month isn't perfect either," James pointed out, "because one month had to be twenty nine days long to make it 365 days a year. There was also the problem of the extra day every four years, just like today." He smiled at me. "But yes - it was a much more logical system than our present twelve month year. Do you know why the calendar was altered?"

"No," I sighed. "I can only guess. The thirteen month calendar reflected the cycles of the moon, which in turn determined women's periods. So it was dominated by feminine rhythms. This would give it a link to the ancient Goddess religion of Neolithic times. I suppose it was dumped to break this link to the past."

"Yes. A woman's menstrual cycle is an average of twenty eight to twenty nine days," he said, "the length of the old month. It was too potent a reminder of women's importance to be retained. It also had to do with astrology, which was also changed, but we'll leave that aside for now. The main thing is that the alterations in the calendar were part of widespread reforms aimed at destroying all knowledge of the past."

He took a US dollar note from his pocket and showed it to me.

"Look at this image of the eagle," he said. "There are thirteen stars above the eagle, who also carries thirteen arrows in one claw. In the other claw is an olive branch with thirteen leaves on it. Yet America considers thirteen an unlucky number, so much so that many hotels in the U.S. don't have a floor numbered thirteen; they prefer to call it 12a. So why does a country like the USA have an unlucky number on one of its banknotes?"

"I don't know; it is a bit strange I suppose."

"I would imagine," I said, "that there was thirteen states when USA declared their independence."

"That is true," said James, "but the number thirteen was important number in Freemasonay before the USA was created. The Freemasons at the time saw it as a important omen that there was thirteen states at the start of independence."

"Oh I see," I said.

"And on the other side," he said, turning the note around, "we have a pyramid with the eye in the triangle representing the Sun Goddess. Can you guess what all this is about?"

"No," I said firmly. In my opinion, nobody ever looked at banknotes except to see the denomination. There might be rabbits and elephants dancing on the ten dollar note for all I knew – or cared.

"I'll give you time to think about it," James said encouragingly. "Perhaps we might talk about it next time you come."

I took a Tarot pack out of my pocket.

"I looked at these cards you asked me to bring," I told him, "and I can't find anything to do with history on them."

James picked up the pack and sorted through the cards.

"It would be very difficult with a pack like this," he explained.

"Over the years, people have changed the images and even the order of the cards. So the original meanings have been distorted or completely lost. You would have been better off if you'd bought a copy of a medieval pack."

"Well, you didn't tell me that," I complained sullenly.

He looked briefly at his watch.

"It doesn't matter. I think we have time to run through the pack quickly, just to get you started," he said. "Wait here."

He left the room and about five minutes later came back.

"I'm not allowed to show you a very early pack," he said, "but this is a copy of a medieval one that is now in the British Museum."

He shook the cards out of their box onto a nearby table and then remained silent for a minute.

"It's been a long time since I last picked up a Tarot pack," he explained. "I'd forgotten how powerful they are."

He picked through the cards, selecting certain ones, then came to stand beside me,

"Right," he said. "The Major Arcana goes in pairs of male and female cards."

He placed two cards on the table.

"The first two are The Fool card and The World card. These two cards signify the beginning and end of a cycle. They are also called the 'Adam' and 'Eve' cards, the Fool being Adam and the World being Eve. This duo describes the Golden-Age of innocence, when society is united and untarnished. You can see that the fool wears medieval costume, but in older packs he is nude."

He put another two cards on the table.

"The next two are The Magician and High Priestess," he said. "This would relate to the Silver age in Greek mythology. The pair are not so innocent now. The High Priestess is a sort of shaman and spiritual leader of the community. She has been teaching some of her skills to the Fool, who has become a Magician. He thinks he is very clever, and is moving towards seeing himself as equal to women. This is related to the time when Eve tempted Adam to eat from the tree of knowledge and when Pandora opened her box."

Another two cards were laid on the table.

"The next two cards are The Empress and Emperor. The Emperor is a man who has broken away from the control of women and rules an empire through fear and brutality. But women haven't completely lost their magical powers over men. They are still revered and respected as the creators of life and have great power in the community. It's the very beginning of the patriarchal age."

Another two cards came out.

"Here we have The Pope with The Lover. This shows men creating their own masculine religion, worshipping a male god and claiming it was a male god who created the world. The 'Lover' card depicts the stage where women come to love and worship patriarchal men."

James looked enquiringly at me before resuming. I must have looked as if I understood, because he moved straight on.

"The next two cards are The Chariot and Justice. The 'Chariot' card shows men who are so confident that they are pressing forward to conquer others. This would represent people like Alexander the Great. The 'Justice' card presents a woman. She has accepted the rules of male religions and believes in masculine concepts like right and wrong, good and evil."

"What do you mean?" I interrupted. "How come good and evil are masculine ideas?"

"Because of the difference between feminine unconditional love and masculine conditional love. The masculine part of the psyche exacts conditions before he will love. You also have to behave a certain way to keep his love. If you don't, then his version of love comes to an end. It's from this limited love that judgements about what is right or wrong, good or evil come. Feminine love, on the other hand, is total and unconditional. The feminine has no concept of good and evil and will love others no matter how they behave."

"Oh," I said, "I have to think about that one."

"The next two cards are The Hermit and Wheel of Fortune," James commented. "Men have now created a male monotheistic god, like we have in Judaism, Christianity, Buddhism and Islam. They have also destroyed all knowledge of the last matriarchal age and the religion of the Great Mother. So man is almost completely alone, cut off from the Great Mother and the unity of all life. Even the sense of there being something beyond the realm of the senses is disappearing for many of them and they are turning to atheism and Science. Dispensing with a god leaves man as the only intelligent life in the universe. Wonderful for his ego, but terrifyingly lonely at the same time. The Hermit is the complete individual, cut off from all real contact with others by his own choices. He is as far away from the Great Mother and the One as he can get. The feminine card is the Wheel Of Fortune. It shows women who are now totally powerless to control their own destiny. They are completely at the mercy of men and fate. This is woman at her lowest point; she has descended as far as she can go and the Wheel of fortune is beginning to take her up again."

James looked at me again, to see if I was keeping up. I was so riveted by his narrative that I waved him on impatiently. I wanted to know what happened next. It was where society was today.

"The next two cards are Strength and The Hanged Man. The Strength card is somewhat controversial as it shows a woman holding open the jaws of a lion. This represents women who are mightily fed up with being second-class citizens and are willing to challenge the patriarchal power structure - like Mary Wollstonecraft who wrote; 'A Vindication Of The Rights Of Women' back in 1792. It's about the beginnings of the Suffragette and Feminist movements. The Hanged Man no longer believes in a male god or patriarchy but he doesn't know what else to do, so he is literally just hanging around. He is often the passive mate of the powerful and active woman. We begin to see some reversing of sexual roles at this point, though it's still within a male-dominated world. If you read Jane Austen's `Pride and Prejudice` there's an excellent example. The proud and snobbish Darcy allows himself to be taught humility by the strong- willed Elizabeth Bennet."

"Wait a minute," I said. "You told me that the Tarot pack was created in medieval times. Yet you're talking about events long after that period."

"That's true," James agreed, "but I'm not allowed to tell you too much until you are fully initiated. What I can say is that whatever is happening now has also occurred in the past, in previous cycles. Not exactly, of course. Each time we go round we've learned a little more."

We moved on.

"The next two cards are the Death card and Temperance. The Death card concerns what happens when you marry the power of modern technology with male aggression. You end up with inventions like machine guns, torpedoes and nuclear weapons. During the Cold War, men came very close to committing global suicide via a nuclear war. At the same point in the last patriarchal era, a nuclear war did happen; fortunately it wasn't world-wide. The card also warns us about other forms of racial suicide – killing our environment through pollution and other irresponsible uses of modern technology. That's not the end. It also signals the death of the super-inflated male ego. Men have spent the whole of the patriarchal age developing a sense of importance as an individual, a male and a member of the dominant species on the planet. They feel completely secure in that importance. Some of them believe they are the most superior life form in the universe! Now this ego has to die, as all things must, to make room for fresh beliefs."

"The Temperance card is a vital balance to the Death one. It depicts those who are attempting to moderate male excesses. These are people who oppose war and the terrible weapons it spawns, as well as environmentalists, who are trying to alert the public and influence politicians about the dangers posed by unthinking or selfish uses of modern technology. At a more subtle level it represents those who seek balance in other ways by eliminating sexism, racism and all the other 'isms' that divide us from each other."

"What exactly do you mean," I queried, "about men not needing the ego any more?"

James put his hands together as if he were praying. He remained silent for some time.

"The concept of the ego is the cause of great misunderstanding," he said eventually. "In eastern religions and in the New-age movement the ego is seen as an enemy, because it's the cause of all suffering. However, we all need one, to feel that we are individuals and worthy of love. There's no way to give up or transcend the ego until we have a secure sense of self, at which point we can reach out to join with others and become One with everything but still retaining our ego."

He might as well have spoken in Serbo-Croat. I tried something more concrete.

"And what about this nuclear war in the last patriarchal age? Surely we were in the Stone-age then, before the start of civilisation."

"You'll learn more, later in your initiation," he replied. "but for now you can read about it in ancient Indian Sanskrit texts like the

Mahabharata. Somehow, fragments from the history of the last cycle have survived in these writings."

We moved to the next pair of cards.

"We now have The Devil and The Falling Tower. The original pack shows a female Devil. She is the sadistic Dominatrix type, who has a lot of suppressed anger against the male sex. What she wants to do, as the Americans so crudely put it, is 'kick ass'. As well as revenge, she wants power, especially power over men. No way is she a Feminist, looking for fairness and equality; men's place is on their knees, begging for forgiveness and a chance to make it up to her. In the older packs the Devil is nude. I haven't time to explain, but this is a coded message signalling the beginning of a new matriarchal age. The `Falling Tower` represents the end of patriarchy, which will be destroyed quickly and dramatically."

He pointed at the tall building on the card.

"The Tower is of course the erect penis. In modern packs it's lightning that demolishes the Tower, but in more ancient ones the Sun obliterates it, the feminine sun used in Masonic symbolism. On the American dollar note, you have the unfinished pyramid of the present patriarchal age reaching up to the feminine sun shown by the eye within the triangle."

I was struggling to understand his allusions.

"So the pyramid and the tower represent the same thing?" I asked. "They're symbols of what patriarchy has built?"

"It depends," he replied. "The pyramid is masculine and active and the inverted triangle is feminine and passive, a pretty good description of the role of the sexes in patriarchy. But there's also an active feminine principle as well as a passive masculine one. If you have an eye with the sun's rays coming from it, within a pyramid shape, you're depicting the active feminine in her role of Sun Goddess. The unfinished pyramid of the Masons symbolizes the progress of the patriarchal age. The pyramid has to be completed before it can end."

"I'll have to think about that one," I said, mouthing my usual euphemism for 'I don't understand a word of what you just said'.

"Then there are The Star and The Moon cards, "James went on blithely. "The Star shows a naked woman healing the Earth with water. It represents those who will undo all the damage that masculine technology and industry has done to the Earth. The Moon card shows two dogs baying at the moon. If you reverse the spelling of god you get 'dog'. The god-like male is now reduced to the role of a dog. Some men have reached this stage today and are paying back what they see as a karmic debt to women for the way they treated them in the patriarchal age. The male moon is also the lesser light of the female sun as we'll see in the next card.

"The next pairing is of The Sun and Judgement cards. What we see now is the female sun in all her glory, represented, like in Masonic symbolism, as an eye with the sun's rays streaming from it. The Statue of Liberty by the way, is also the Sun Goddess. Her head-dress emits rays of light, as does the torch she holds. Look at the happy boy on a horse, basking in the sun's warmth. This is man after he has been forgiven by women; they no longer wish to chastise him, nor does he feel the need to be punished. All debts have been paid. The Judgement card gives the same message. All wrongs have been righted and there is a clean slate for humanity to write on.

"And so we return to the World and Fool cards. People now live in a female-led world containing much more harmony and oneness. But it is a world that still needs to evolve. The masculine need for separation and individuality has not disappeared. When it resurfaces, the feminine looks to the masculine to lead it into a new cycle, and off we go again."

James turned away from the cards to look at me. It was obvious he expected some reaction. Inside, I could feel myself reeling at all this potent information, but I needed time to assimilate it. At the moment, all I could do was ask a simple question.

"Is this repeated cycling inevitable then; there's nothing we can do to stop it?"

"No," James answered, "we can stop it if we want to, once we've become aware of it. But why should we? Once you have all the facts and know the real history of humankind, it's hard to see an alternative way to progress, unless there's a radical change in the nature of both men and women. And don't forget that we're tracing a spiral, not endlessly repeating a cycle. Each time we begin again we know more of who we are. That way we can avoid the worst mistakes of the last cycle."

He glanced briefly at his watch then stood up.

"It's time we left," he said, quickly dropping the hood over my head and leading me to his car. I was still asking questions.

"You said that some of what's happening now has happened before," I reminded him as we drove along. "Are you talking about Atlantis?"

"We're talking about a world-wide civilisation, " he replied, "but no one country was dominant. The period we're talking about was in the Ice-age so the effects of global warming were far more devastating than they will be for us. But yes - many of the mistakes we made in the past we're repeating now. That's why the suppression and destruction of ancient knowledge is such a horrendous crime. If the past is lost to us, how can we see and avoid our previous errors? Admittedly, the Roman Catholic Church, the Moslems and the Chinese Emperors did their best to prevent the return of science and technology. On the surface it looked like a refusal to accept new truths, but the ruling elites have often retained knowledge of the past, so they knew what would happen if science was allowed to flourish before men were mature enough to cope. They failed to suppress it and, as they say, the rest is history. Off we go again with a mission to destroy ourselves and everything around us."

"Well if your organisation has all this knowledge," I protested, "why didn't you warn everybody?"

"We did," was his rejoinder, "and we still do today. Unfortunately we're limited in what we're allowed to reveal. Our opponents are totally ruthless. I know you don't believe this, but they have absolutely no qualms about murdering us, or creating false evidence to put us in jail, so we are always forced to work underground and behind the scenes. You're not wearing a hood for fun, I do assure you. At the moment we have a truce with our opponents, but it can end at any time. If it does, people like me will probably be the first to go, but the main organisation will survive."

"So who are your opponents?" I asked.

He laughed. We both knew he wasn't going to tell me.

"Sometimes it's hard to know," he said resignedly. "We've been part of a secret war that's endured for thousands of years, but it's been a war of spy networks, double agents and traitors. It's commonplace for people to switch sides, so in the end you can trust no one. Look at Freemasonry, for instance. It was founded by us, but over the years it has been infiltrated so much that we've lost control of whole sections. But to answer your question: essentially, our opponents are people who want power for their own personal gain and for that they need to keep the patriarchy going. Only under a patriarchal system can a small elite group rule the world. It would be an understatement to say they don't like us because we do our best to undermine that system."

"Hang on," I said testily, "you claimed that most of what's happening is inevitable - whatever anyone does, a new matriarchal age will still come about. If that's true, why is there a secret war? It makes no sense if there's nothing you can do to change anything."

"You're right," James agreed. "We can't change the broad picture - but we can influence many of the details. The patriarchy will ultimately fall, but how that happens and what damage the Earth sustains meanwhile is crucially important. I don't want to sound over-dramatic, but we could avoid beginning a new matriarchal age with a barren planet, blasted by war or a major environmental disaster. We prefer a planet that is still thriving, so there's a lot at stake."

It was a chilling image – a desolate and denuded planet if patriarchy continued. I remained in thought for the rest of the journey.

At our destination, James led me to a familiar room, where I slipped on my Batman mask. When my veiled teacher came in, I silently kissed her feet. This time she accepted my homage without a snigger and gravely ordered me to sit on the floor below her chair.

"Has your girlfriend in America contacted you?" she asked. It seemed she always began with this question. I shook my head.

"That's a shame," she commiserated. "Are you upset?"

"Very," I said, "but it's something I've had to get used to."

"Have you got yourself a house plant or window box yet?" she went on.

"Not yet," I confessed, "but I have got some books out of the library about plant care. I don't know anything about keeping them indoors or maintaining a window box."

"Amazing," she commented sarcastically. "Do you have to read a book on everything before you try it?" I opened my mouth to speak, but she made a dismissive gesture.

"Never mind! Did you ask James about the Tarot?"

"He gave me a run-down just before I came here," I explained.

"You should get him to go into it deeply," she said enthusiastically. "It's fascinating. Has he mentioned the Kabalah as well?"

"Not yet."

"Oh, the Kabalah tells the same story, but in a different way from the Tarot. Both are about the spiritual journey of men and women. What people don't realise is that the spiritual evolution of each sex is very different. During a patriarchal age the lesson for men is to learn to love themselves unconditionally and for women to learn to love others unconditionally. In a matriarchal era, the roles are reversed. Women learn to love themselves and men to love others."

She looked at me for a second before deciding,

"It would be a really good idea for you to start looking at the Kabalah, then James or I can explain its hidden meanings."

There was a sudden change of subject as she scanned the room.

"I see you brought your massage table," she said. "James claims you're very skilled, so I thought I'd try you out. Set it up in the middle of the room."

As I obeyed her instructions, she began to remove her clothes until only the veil in front of her face remained. She had a lithe, taut body with honey-coloured skin. Highly distracting.

"You're very furtive in the way you look at me," she commented.

"I'm sorry," I blurted out, immediately averting my eyes.

"Don't be," she retorted sharply, "I like men looking at me and admiring my body."

She climbed on to the table and I began massaging her back. Though I'd brought some oil, it wasn't necessary; her skin was supple and easy to manipulate. At first I could feel a slight tension in her body that was mirrored by my own nervousness, but within a few minutes it eased into complete relaxation. Neither of us spoke until I had massaged her whole body, which must have taken over an hour, so it was slightly alarming when she finally broke the silence.

"Have you finished?

The question was a difficult one. As far as I was concerned it was for her to decide when the massage was over, but I had come to the point where I would normally stop.

Undeterred by my stuttering attempts to formulate an answer, she went on,

"Have you ever kissed a woman's arse?"

"No." I lied.

"Oh goody," she breathed rapturously, "so I'll be your first one again."

She turned back onto her face and opened her legs.

"Off you go," she ordered. "Kiss my arse."

I bent down and covered the two cheeks of her bottom with kisses, knowing from her tone that there must be more to it than this. After a minute she raised her head from the table.

"You're not going to get away with just doing that," she said scathingly. "Get a cushion and put it under me."

It elevated her bottom considerably. I waited for the next command.

"Now lick my arse hole."

At first I licked between the cheeks of her buttocks, and then plucked up enough courage to put my tongue in her anus.

She laughed to herself.

"Get your tongue in as far as it will go," she yelled. "I want to really feel you do it."

The surprise was how much I was becoming turned on by what I was doing. It made no sense, yet it felt somehow exciting and satisfying and comfortable all at the same time. She kept me at it until my tongue began to tire before finally instructing me to stop, then moved off the massage table back to her chair. I had to kiss her feet. Again it felt like something I could dive into and lose myself in; lose track of time and any sense of where I was. It was both enjoyable and terrifying.

"Have you been worshipping my knickers?" she asked, smirking down at me from above.

"Oh, yes," I said fervently.

"Well, well, you are improving," she said approvingly. "I even noticed a hint of enthusiasm in your voice. Now put the clean knickers with the rest of my clothes - you can have my used ones to worship - then you can help me get dressed."

"Um, er," I said feebly.

"Um, er, what?"

"Nothing."

"I know what Rover wants," she declared, grinning widely. "You want a drink don't you?"

"Er, yes," I mumbled.

"What do you mean; er, yes," she scolded. "You need to show a lot more passion than that, if you want to drink my golden nectar."

"Oh, yes, yes, please, please," I begged, completely surprised by the desire in my voice.

"That's much better," she giggled. "We'll try it another way. Lie down on your back."

When I was in position, she straddled my face.

"All right. Get your mouth ready."

With a sigh of pleasure she urinated into my mouth. The flow was not as copious as on the previous occasions and I found myself slightly disappointed, though I had no idea why. I licked the last drops carefully and slowly, then helped her to dress. When I thanked her for her time, there was no pretence in my voice. I was genuinely grateful to be given the chance to serve this immature girl, because somewhere behind her or inside her I could sense a greater being, of which she was the emerging representative.

After she'd left, I packed up the table and waited for James to return. As I did, I reflected on what he had said about the Devil card in the Tarot. Clearly my teacher enjoyed having power over a man. I wondered if she also had sadistic tendencies, as Liz had. It dawned on me slowly that although I'd been able to refuse Liz the opportunity to inflict pain on me, it might be different with my teacher. I had the feeling that a refusal would mean the end of the initiation process and I would never find out about the organisation's secrets.

When James came into the room I was laughing – the same nervous panicky laughter I'd exhibited before.

"What's wrong with you?" he asked in a concerned voice.

"I don't know," I said.

"All right," he said with a knowing look, then put my hood on my head and steered me to his car.

As the return journey progressed, I managed to calm the urge to laugh and deal with the questions that the session had thrown up.

"Do you know anything about the Kabalah?" I asked.

"Yes," James said slowly, "I learned about it when I was being initiated."

"My teacher wants me to study it."

"Well if that's what she wants," he said, "you'd better start tomorrow."

"Judging from the tone of your voice," I commented, "you don't approve."

"Different teachers have different approaches," he parried. "When I was initiated nearly forty years ago I learned about the Tarot, Kabalah, coded teachings within the Bible, Shakespeare, Tao Te Ching and alchemy. There's so much more available now that censorship has weakened, that each initiate can be guided in a different way. Personally, I'd skip the Kabalah."

He didn't have to argue the point. I was already fastening onto a new direction for my questions.

"What's this stuff about coded teachings in the Bible and Shakespeare?"

"Very well," James sighed. "In any major religion, those who control it are generally consummate politicians with a desire for power. They're unlikely to be deeply interested in spiritual matters and in many cases are pretty poor scholars, though there are exceptions. So when the Bible comes up for its periodic editing or translating, you get the phenomenon of good scholars or genuine believers having to do the rewriting whilst disagreeing with the content. As a result you often find heavily veiled messages in the text, that point towards the truth for those who can decode it."

"Like what?"

"Take the story of Jonah, He was swallowed by a giant fish. Now in ancient symbolism the fish is drawn to look like a vagina."

"I don't quite see that." I interrupted.

"Have you seen the way the fish are drawn in the astrological sign Pisces?"

I thought for a moment.

"Oh yes, I see it now?"

"The vagina of women also smell like fish," said James continuing, "so the coded message of this story is that Jonah was swallowed whole by fish representing the Great Mother. So the real story is that Jonah went astray because was tempted by male priests to worship their new male gods and everything went wrong for him. Then when he realized this, he returned to the religion of the Great Mother and everything became right for him. So it become a similar story to the prodigal son. Which is the opposite sentiment to what the men in charge of rewriting the Bible wanted to convey.

"Wait a minute, didn't the early Christian also use a fish symbol?"

"Yes, because Christianity in its original was full of goddess teachings. This is why later, when it became a state religion, they discarded the fish symbol."

"Oh, I see,"

I was quiet for a moment.

"And what about Shakespeare?"

"His writings also contain esoteric messages. He was a member of a secret society and because he was popular and a genius, his work was used to dispense secrets to the public."

"What sort of ideas and information?" I asked curiously. As far as I could remember, Shakespeare's work was only used to alienate and frustrate successive generations of bored schoolchildren. What hidden jewels had we all missed?

"Have you read Shakespeare?"

"Well, no," I confessed. "just what was taught to me at school."

"Do you remember any reference to the 'dark lady' in his sonnets."

"Er, yes."

"The dark lady is a code name for the Goddess Isis."

"Oh", I said in surprise, "I can't see the connection."

"In some Southern European counties they have what is called black Madonnas. These are ancient statues of the Virgin Mary in Catholic churches that have been painted black. Which is a real mystery. The explanation for this, is that all these churches were built on the ruins of Isis Temples. When the Romans adopted the Isis religion they worshipped her as a black woman. Because the religion was originally African. Then when Christianity became a state religion, in many places the new Christian priests were forced to compromise with the people to avoid a up-rising against the new religion. So they painted the Virgin Mary black, like Isis, to satisfy the many people who still wanted to keep the Isis religion."

I was quiet for a moment, thinking about this.

"What else?" I then asked.

James had had enough of my idle curiosity.

"If you were really interested in Shakespeare ," he said tightly, "then I could answer you. But because you don't know anything, the information would make no sense. I would rather you read Shakespeare and find out for yourself" It was the closest he had ever come to a rebuke.

"What about alchemy then," I asked in my meekest voice, "what's the secret message there?"

"That's simple enough to answer," he said. "Alchemy is about transmuting lead or another base substance into gold. That's at the physical level. Spiritually, it concerns the transformation of the individual ego through various testing processes until the divine gold shines clear. It's at the heart of the Ancient Goddess religion."

"In what way?"

"You don't stop, do you," he sighed.

"Sorry."

"No, it shows you are interested," he said, "but you have to remember that it's often far easier to ask a question than understand the answer. Let me see." He was quiet for a moment. "At the root of many patriarchal religions is the concept of good and evil. This gives the religious elite enormous power because they get to define which is which. You can say your enemies are evil, women are inherently evil, the supporters of other religions are evil, anyone who disagrees with you is most definitely evil, eating pork is evil, contraception is evil......need I go on! The possibilities for excluding people's common humanity are enormous. You can commit genocide, bomb countries into oblivion, colonise whole continents while massacring the original inhabitants if they resist, or burn women as witches in an orgy of misogyny if you are so inclined. All this is right and good because 'the other' is evil. The concept is so ingrained in our collective psyche that even today, most people do not question the belief in good and evil. Yet the logic of it is fatally flawed, because to judge anyone as evil is to dehumanise them, to put them in a category labelled 'not me' and discard them. It's a classic patriarchal ploy to separate out people who do not fit in order to deny them their souls. After that, it's generally customary to consign them to Hell when they die."

"I know about that one," I interrupted. "My father told me that my cousin Lauren was going to burn in Hell for eternity because she's a lesbian."

"Exactly!" James said fervently. "It's so easy to judge and condemn in a patriarchal society that it soon becomes second nature. We start off with the murderers and child-molesters, then before we know where we are, people who wear orange shoes or dance badly end up in the eternal flames."

"Well I can't imagine a society without ideas of good and evil or right and wrong," I said. "How else do you stop people from stealing or murdering or whatever?"

James sighed.

"Yes I know it's difficult. All we know is our patriarchal society so it's hard for us to imagine a world run on completely different lines. The problem is that if we judge, condemn and punish others we create a vicious cycle of fear, hatred and violence. Punishment works very well in the short term but eventually it makes the situation far worse than it was before."

"You can't give up punishing criminals," I said. "That would be far too scary to be acceptable."

"If it was brought in overnight, yes," he agreed, "it wouldn't work. Yet it's beginning to happen now. Back in the 19th century it was accepted that to keep children in order you beat them with a strap or a stick. Husbands could legally hit their wives. Today that behaviour would be seen as child abuse or domestic violence. Within a hundred years, we have moved to a position in most Western countries where an adult who hits a child is seen as guilty of assault. So how has this come about? Why are we in a situation where a hundred years ago it was perfectly acceptable to use violence to keep children in order and now it's a crime?"

"I don't know," I said, waiting to be enlightened.

"It's tied in with the rise of feminine power," James explained. "A hundred years ago women didn't even have the vote. Here in England they had no legal existence after marriage, which is hard for us to believe. There have been dramatic changes since then, as we know. Women now have much more power and influence in our society. As a result, we have begun to move over to the feminine way of doing things, which means you try to teach children with encouragement and praise rather than threats and punishment. You attempt to understand the roots of anti-social behaviour and correct the causes instead of always relying on fear of consequences as an aid to discipline. I know this is a piecemeal process and not all children respond to kindness, but it's the direction society is heading."

"Maybe," I conceded, "but there are those who would say society is changing for the worse because we can't punish children and we're far too soft on criminals. I know this was my dad's belief."

James laughed,

"I can sympathise with your father," he said. "The problem is that we have a largely masculine way of seeing the world colliding with the incoming feminine. They naturally oppose each other. We live in confusing times. If a man sees that selfishness and ruthlessness are still heavily rewarded, he's unlikely to relinquish them without being forced to. Only when those qualities go unsupported is he likely to contemplate changing. As yet, the feminine way of being has only lightly scratched the surface of our society. The doubt and confusion will only end when it permeates every aspect of our world."

He was silent for a moment.

"Now to get back to your original question," he said, "Alchemy is the feminine way to deal with problems like crime. Femininity is not about punishment, but reform, and alchemy is the symbol of this. So to reform a criminal, is like turning lead into gold, it is a alchemic process.

"Is it your organisation that's been bringing about the changes?"

"I wish we had that sort of influence!" he said feelingly. "No. Most of what happens is quite unconscious; society moving to accommodate shifts in the human psyche. All we can do is support the feminine as much as possible."

"There is another thing. You said when you were talking about the Devil and the Moon card, that women will punish men in the future. Yet now you're saying women will give them support and understanding."

I heard him sigh again. I seemed to have that effect on him.

"You're touching on something that is enormously complex," he began. "It will take me more than one session to explain it, so be patient."

He re-settled himself in his seat and drove silently for a while.

"Women are different from men. For one thing they have a deeper interest in human nature. Masculine society hasn't been all that interested in why people behave the way they do, but if you live with a woman you become very aware that she is observing you all the time and will eventually get to know you better than you do yourself. It means a feminine society will dig deep in an attempt to understand human behaviour, which is fine until you encounter aspects of it that people don't want to know about."

He paused for a moment.

"Do you know what the root cause of sadomasochist behaviour is?"

It seemed an odd diversion, but I did my best to answer him.

"From what I have read," I said, "psychologists claim it comes from a lack of self-esteem. Sadists have a feeling of inadequacy which they try to avoid by inflicting pain on others. A masochist also has a sense of being inferior but believes he deserves to be punished because of this."

"That's certainly the psychologist's point of view," James agreed. "But we look at it from a spiritual perspective. To us it ties in with the spiritual quest of each person to learn about love – for both others and oneself."

"My female teacher and Carol talked about this," I interrupted. James was silent for a moment and then continued.

"Do you remember when I talked about the masochistic behaviour of Jesus?"

"Yes," I said. How could I forget?

"Not only did he allow himself to be betrayed, whipped, humiliated and crucified," he said, "much of his teaching was as passive. He said - love your enemies; do good to those who hate you. If struck by a blow turn the other cheek. If someone takes your coat give him your shirt as well. Give to everyone who asks. Lend and expect nothing in return. If someone forces you to carry a load one mile, carry it two miles for him. A modern psychologist would assess Jesus as someone who lacked the courage to stand up for himself or see that he had value. It's not seen as healthy to behave this way; even women who espouse these ideas are seen as devaluing themselves. Yet if we were able to do this, all wars, conflict, violence, poverty and suffering would disappear from the face of the Earth."

It seemed to me he must be joking.

"Are you saying we should be masochists?" I asked. "That makes no sense. All you'd get would be selfish people taking advantage of your good nature and laughing at your stupidity."

"No, I'm not," James answered me, "but we do need to learn unconditional love for others whatever they do. Masochism is one way to do this."

"But I don't understand how suffering pain can help us spiritually. Surely it's a barbaric anachronism we should be getting rid of, not encouraging?"

"So you've been told! But you only think that because the reasons why people chose voluntary suffering as part of their spiritual path have been forgotten. Only the behaviour has been left behind and on its own, yes, it makes no sense. There are a few places where holy men torture themselves to gain enlightenment, but in general, pain is now seen as something to be avoided at all costs. Like sex, it has become unspiritual; if you're suffering, you must be getting it wrong. What our society doesn't remember is that willing sacrifice and the courage to suffer can be a step on the road to wholeness. It's not about devaluing yourself but surrendering that self in service to others."

As usual, I said I would have to think about what he'd said. It was flying in the face of everything I'd been taught about self-worth.

"What about sadists though – have they got some spiritual justification to sanctify their cruelty?"

If James noticed my sarcasm he didn't let on.

"The problem with masochism," he said, "is that it requires the partnership of a sadist. No other kind of person would accept the extreme expressions of sacrifice offered by a masochist. And just as submission can be necessary for someone's spiritual growth, so can the experience of complete control of another person. I'm not saying this happens in every case, but it is a possible avenue to self-love."

"So you're not saying that to progress spiritually we all need to be involved in sadomasochism."

"Oh no," he said, laughing. "There are a myriad ways to evolve. It's just that sadomasochism is a part of human nature which can be used in a constructive way. If it is seen as an alchemical process, which transforms potentially destructive emotions into something very positive, then it's entirely helpful."

"Yes, but," I objected, "most sadists force pain on people against their will. You can't tell me that school bullies, Nazis and the Inquisition are a good thing."

"True enough," James agreed. "The problem is the old one, that patriarchy separates sexual desire from the expression of love. Sadists, who have an overwhelming need to be loved, can have problems finding it in a patriarchal age. They turn towards power, which becomes a substitute for love. Sad though it is, they believe that inflicting pain and suffering on others, hurting them against their will, somehow completes them. All that happens, of course, is a temporary reduction in their own pain, so they have to repeat the sadistic behaviour to gain any kind of satisfaction. It's a far cry from the love they really want." He again paused before going on.

"Also, revenge has become mixed up with sadism, so we have to be clear which is which. If the victim welcomes the suffering, as masochists do, then the desire for revenge is completely unsatisfied. It doesn't bother a true sadist one bit to have a willing victim; if it does, then there's more than one need being fulfilled."

James drove silently for a while before picking up the thread of his narrative again.

"It's all so complicated to explain, because we are talking about different levels operating simultaneously. Take the example of a man going to a Dominatrix, for example. There are so many possibilities. One man may feel that he still controls the situation completely. He has chosen to go to the woman, who dresses in a way he finds sexy, not her, decided on his punishment for himself and is free to stop whenever he feels like it. Because he pays, then he's obviously the boss as far as he's concerned. He is giving extremely limited love and service to the woman, whom he sees as meeting his needs. Another man may be entirely incapable of saying 'no' to the woman. He is surrendering himself entirely at the emotional level, so she will make all the decisions, including the one to stop when she is fully satisfied. He is giving much more love than the first man because he places far fewer limits on the woman."

"I see," I said after a while. "It can certainly get complicated. Though surely, sadomasochistic behaviour only involves a small minority of the population."

"Most people would like to believe that," he said. "Unfortunately it's not true. As you point out, school bullies are sadists, and every school has them. Every society contains men who beat their wives in great numbers, if it's condoned by the culture. Many countries even today, still practise the genital mutilation of women, which makes sexual intercourse painful for them. What are we to think of a man who has sex with his wife knowing it hurts her? Or the wife who still loves her husband even though he inflicts pain on her through rape and beatings. In China they once practised foot-binding on girls for hundreds of years despite the fact that it's painful and crippling. Wherever you look, all you have to do is scratch below the surface of society to find vast amounts of sadomasochistic behaviour. It's much more common than most people would like to admit. For this reason, it seems far better to try and understand why people behave like this, than to push it aside and pretend it's not happening."

I had no idea what to say after James had finished speaking so I kept quiet for the rest of the journey.

"Did you do any more research of the science of mind?" he asked as he took of my hood when we reached his house.

"Yes," I said, "I have come across the concept that we all create our own reality."

"From the tone of your voice," he commented, "It doesn't sound you agree with this."

I sighed.

"I don't know what to make of it," I said, "what I find disturbing is that if it is true that we all create our own reality. Then it means that everything that happens to us is our fault. So if I happened to be assaulted by a mugger and was left brain damaged, it is my fault and not the muggers."

It was James' turn to sigh.

"I am aware that some people do use this concepts like this," he said, "So some rich people can claim that poverty is always self-inflicted and so they don't have to feel guilty because they have so much money and others have nothing."

He held out his hand in a invitation to sit down and he poured us both a drink.

"Now," he said, sitting down himself, "In our world today the accepted reality is that many of the things that happen to us, happen as a result of pure chance. So if you was assaulted by a mugger, it was your bad luck. Now this also can be true in science of mind. This is because if you are unaware that what you think continually does create our reality. Then by chance you can create a reality that makes it possible to be mugged. This is because it is the unconscious mind that creates our reality. So for anyone who has not control of their unconscious mind, then what the mind can create can be very haphazard to say the least."

"So are you saying we only create our own reality," I said, "when we consciously take control over our unconscious mind."

James frowned.

"You are partly right," he said, "the way I would put it is; that the degree we create our own reality is the degree we take control over our unconscious mind. So a person who has only just began to learn science of mind has less conscious control over their reality than the person who has been practising for a large number of years."

"So how do you learn to practice science of mind?" I asked.

"The simplest way is the practise of affirmations," he said.

"So if keep on affirming to myself that I am a millionaire, will that work?"

"It would, but I wouldn't advice that affirmation."

"Why not?"

"How well a affirmation works depends a lot on what is in your subconscious mind already. For instance if you have a unconscious belief that only crooks get to become rich, this affirmation will push you into the direction of crime. Another unconscious belief may be that you have to work really hard to obtain money, so you might find yourself in a stressful situation of working really long hours. Or if you had read a story of someone who had a bad accident and sued a company for a million pounds, then your subconscious may bring the money that way. So it would be better to also affirm how you will get this money. Or state is will come in a harmonious way."

"I see, so what affirmation would you suggest?"

"I would like you to think about it yourself, but one general affirmation you can try is, 'I live in a compassionate and caring world'. If you practice that consistently you will find it will greatly help with your general well-being and your relationships with other people."

"Yes, but, as we don't live in a compassionate and caring world," I objected, "I would feel silly affirming something, that is so different from reality."

"The reality we live in," said James patiently, "Is the reality that we all have created both individually and collectively. Whatever we accept is true becomes our reality, so if you believe that we live in a world of conflict and aggravation, then that becomes your reality. A positive affirmation like the one I suggested is a way to change that reality, if you want to."

"It still feels ridiculous," I said stubbornly.

"Very well, shall we try it out? Repeat after me; I live in a compassionate and caring world."

Feeling foolish I done as I was told.

"That wasn't so bad, was it? He said encouragingly. "Now repeat it a number of times."

I did as I was told, and I admitted the more I repeated it, the more comfortable I became with it.

"When in company," he interrupted me, "you can repeat to yourself; 'we all live in a compassionate and caring world', which helps to bring harmony to the group you are in."

"So you are saying," I said with still some disbelief, "that all I have to do is keep on repeating his and my life will magically become better."

"Yes," said James, he seem immune to my provocation, "I want you to be a happy person all you need to do is continue affirming you are happy! Affirmations can also smoke out many of your unconscious beliefs. If say you have been brought up to believe we live in a hard and tough world, or you always have bad luck. Then this affirmation will hit negative programs in your unconscious head on, and bring them out into the light of day. This is the time when you really need to question your beliefs, so you don't accept them as a fact of life, but just as programmes within you unconscious mind."

"So are you saying," I said in a puzzled voice, "that beliefs are the same as unconscious programs."

"Yes," replied James, calmly, "beliefs are what has been programmed in our unconscious mind, change your unconscious programming and you change your beliefs."

"I see," I said uncertainly.

He patted me on the shoulder.

"I think you have had more than enough for one night it is about time you went home."

I droved home in a thoughtful mood.

# CHAPTER TEN

It was a few days later. James called to give me the name and phone number of the woman who would give me a sterner test, whatever that might be. I dialled her number immediately; after a few rings I heard the phone being picked up.

"Yes, who is it?" asked a female voice.

"Is that Janet?"

"Yes."

"My name is Arthur. I am a friend of James Ashe. He told me to phone you."

"Oh yes, you are the gigolo, masseur, slave person," she said. Her words surprised me.

"Yes," I said eventually, "I suppose you could say that."

"James assures me you are good," she said briskly, "but I'd like to check you out myself first. Can we meet somewhere?"

We arranged to meet in a pub we both knew that evening. I described my general appearance to her so that she could recognise me, then she hung up. Later, I drove to the pub, ordered a drink and waited at the bar, curiously scrutinising any woman who came in. Eventually a short, slim woman aged around thirty entered, scanned the bar and quickly hurried over to me.

"Is your name Arthur?" she asked pointedly.

"Yes," I managed to say. "Are you Janet?"

"Yes of course," she snapped, then said more softly. "I didn't have any trouble in recognising you."

"What are you having?"

"I'll be ordering my own drinks," she said firmly.

When she'd bought her drink we sat down at a small table by the window.

"Now," she began in a very business-like way, "I prefer to be with men who do as they are told and know their place - which is under there."

She pushed her thumb on the table and turned it backwards and forwards a few times.

"I like men under my thumb. Is that acceptable to you?"

"I suppose so," I said feebly. It wasn't something I'd ever really thought about before.

"You suppose so," she said sharply. "Look. You either do or you don't. I'm not interested in any man who wants to crawl out from under. I want a firm commitment from you and no backsliding."

"Well, yes," I said. "I'm sorry. I just I find you a bit overpowering."

She glared at me and stood up.

"If you're going to criticise me," she said coldly, "I might as well go home now."

"No please, I'm sorry. I didn't mean to criticise you. I'm just a bit flustered."

"Yes I can see that," she relented and sat down again. In a gentler voice she asked, "All right then. How would you describe yourself in relationships with women?"

"I suppose I'm laid back and easygoing.

"Would you describe yourself as very passive?"

"Yes, I probably am."

"Are you prone to passive aggression?"

"I don't know what that is," I said, confused again.

"It's when a man obeys a woman," she explained, "but does it with reluctance or bad grace. Sometimes he'll pretend he didn't hear the request, or deliberately misunderstand what he's been ordered to do. That sort of thing."

I thought about it. It was a new concept.

"No," I concluded. "I don't do those sorts of things."

She stared at me intently. I had a feeling she didn't believe me.

"All right," she decided, "I suppose I'd better try you out. Do you live in a house or flat?"

"A flat."

"Is it a bedsit?"

"No," I said. "It has a kitchen, bedroom, bathroom and sitting room."

"Do you live on your own?"

"Yes," I said, wondering how many questions were left.

"Do you have noisy neighbours?" she continued the interrogation.

"No, they're mostly really quiet."

"Right!" she got swiftly to her feet. "We'll go to your flat now and I'll find out just how good you are at massage. Let's go!"

About ten minutes later I was showing her into my flat.

"It's not very tidy," was her first comment.

"Well, I didn't know you'd be coming back here," I explained.

"So this is how you normally live?" she went on. "James said you were good at housework. I don't see much evidence of that here."

I tried to defend myself.

"When you live on your own," I explained, "you don't bother too much unless you know someone is coming to visit. I put more effort into it when I do housework for other people."

"Fine," she said, "we'll see if that's true. Get to work. Tidy your flat and we'll see if you're telling the truth."

I began to clear up while she wandered around my flat taking an interest in everything it contained.

"You have a lot of books," she commented, "Why isn't there a bookcase?"

I couldn't explain to her that some were James's books and others I had bought recently to keep up with the studying he required of me.

"I just haven't got around to buying one."

"I suppose it's because no one has told you to." It was an odd comment to make, which I didn't dare challenge. Instead I got out my vacuum cleaner.

"Put that back," she ordered. "I don't want to hear that row. Your flat's a lot better than it was, so you can set up your massage table. Do you have a dressing gown?"

"In my bedroom."

"Go and get it."

I hurried to fetch it as she impatiently drummed her fingers on a nearby vase.

"I'll get undressed in the bathroom."

She seemed less confident as she slipped off the dressing gown and took a prone position on the table. Assuming nothing, I tentatively began to knead her back and after receiving no rebuke, continued over her buttocks and legs. Her skin was very dry and I found myself apologising for the pauses while I tipped more oil into my hands. She said nothing, but I could feel the release of tension in both her body and manner in an almost palpable way. By the time she turned over to expose the front of her body, I could see she was relaxed and enjoying the sensuality of the experience.

"Well you are a good masseur," she said languorously, after I had finished massaging her face. "Let's see what you're like at licking me."

"Can I take my shirt off?" I asked nervously. "You've still got oil on your legs." She looked at me suspiciously.

"Okay, but don't start taking anything else off unless I tell you to."

I put my face between her legs and was surprised at how quickly she came to orgasm. The only sound she made was the release of breath as she shuddered.

"I can see you've done this before," she commented. I took it as a compliment.

After she'd dressed, she opened her purse and shocked me with her next question,

"How much do I owe you?" I was stunned but managed to recover enough to tell her there was no charge. I found myself feeling insulted by her assumption that I wanted money from her.

"I'm not having that," she said with finality. "I know what you men are like. If you start doing things for free, later on you start expecting something in return."

"I'm not like that," I protested.

"I don't know you well enough to decide," she said, "so until I do I'll pay."

She took some bank notes out of her purse and placed them on my computer table.

"That's far too much," I said, beginning to panic slightly, "you don't need to give me that amount."

"I can do what I like," she said firmly. "You certainly don't tell me what to do. Is that clear!"

I mumbled some sort of reply before she rapidly moved to the next item on her agenda.

"Are you free next Saturday?"

"As far as I know."

"Right! You can come over to my place at eight o'clock in the morning and we will see how efficient you are at housework,"

She took a card out of her purse with her address on it and gave it to me. Then she left while I was still gawking at my unwelcome fee.

The following Saturday I drove to her house. The moment I walked through the door, my work started; tidying, cleaning, washing, sweeping, vacuuming. It was exhausting. Her place was far untidier than my flat and much larger, giving me a sense of never-ending labours. At first she stood over me, continually issuing orders and instructions, but after a while she tired of this and wandered off. Late morning she came back again.

"Can you cook?"

"Yes," I said. Though I was hardly cordon-bleu, I was proud of my culinary skills.

"Then we'll see how good you are. You can cook me a meal."

Leading me into the kitchen, she pointed out where everything was, then asked,

"Will you want something to eat as well? You haven't brought any food with you."

I was ravenous after the morning's hard graft. Of course I wanted something to eat! Doubling up the quantities I'd cook to serve one person might not be enough to fill the growling hole in my stomach.

"Please."

"There's some bread in the bread bin," she said. "Use the loaf that's already been cut - it's yesterday's bread and I want it used up. I think there's some cheese in the fridge or you can have jam if you prefer."

With that she left me. It seemed highly provocative of Janet to expect a complicated hot meal yet only allow me stale bread and cheese. I could see why she was a bigger test for me than Ann. My assumptions about the way women should behave towards men were being challenged again. Could I cope with my new role as menial or would pride intervene?

The meal was deemed satisfactory and I was allowed a brief rest before beginning work on her garden. It was as large and untidy as the house. Clearly Janet either had very little time to spend on its upkeep or simply ignored its overgrown state. My ignorance about plants meant that I could only do the most obvious tasks, but it felt good to liberate some of the shrubs from entangling weeds. I hoped I would be recalled to the garden in future visits.

By late afternoon it was too dark to work outside. I was sent to get the massage table from my car and spent the next hour relaxing Janet before tonguing her to two orgasms. Though she clearly enjoyed the experience, she was silent throughout, It was unnerving not to receive any feedback; women are always grateful for any pleasure you give them - in my experience anyway.

"Right," she said, after recovering from her second orgasm. "Are you free next Saturday?"

I nodded.

"Good. Make it the same time."

She picked up her purse and paid me. I put the money in my pocket without looking at it, vaguely ashamed. As I moved to leave, she blocked me, and wagged a finger at my face.

"Just a minute," she said. "Next time, if you want something to eat, bring it yourself. I'm not in the habit of feeding the hired help and I resent your expectation that I will."

When I got back into my car I found myself grappling with mixed emotions. One part of me was angry at the way she treated me, but another found it amusing and sexually exciting.

# CHAPTER ELEVEN

There were two more Saturday visits to Janet before I heard from James again. Maybe I was being given time to accustom myself to the new demands on me, which were pretty tough. Janet seemed to regard me as a service rather than a person and I found that difficult to cope with. The fact that she was paying me should have made me grateful – I'd whinged to James about my relative poverty on several occasions, hadn't I – but instead I was resentful and I wasn't sure why. Perhaps James could spell it out for me.

"Janet, is a very strange person," I said as we sat down together.

James frowned.

"I think there is something you should know about her," he said, "she has a hatred for men. She has had a few bad relationships with men who have abused her and taken advantage of her good nature. So she now thinks, all men are nasty brutes . She also has women friend who think the same way, so they encourage this hatred for men among themselves."

"Oh," I said and the thought crossed my mind; what is James doing sending me to a woman like her. Then as if he read my mind, he answered me.

"Many men are unaware of the anger women feel towards men. Women don't express this anger because they are frighten of men's violence or ridicule. Also many women still love men, and this creates in them a love/hate emotion which many find hard to deal with. So Janet is a good teacher, she will teach you a lot about the unexpressed hatred women have for men."

"Oh," I said again, I didn't like the sound of this. "What about my teacher does she also hate men?'

"Not in the same way, because of the way she was brought up, she has become very aware of the mess men are making of ruling our world. She would have been aware that poverty is, man-made long before Bob Geldof told this to the world. She would also know about the insanity of war and the patriarchal propaganda need to justify it. So she would be angry with men for a different reason."

"So why pick on me?" I complained, "I don't create poverty and war."

"You are still a man and to her you represent all men. Though you may not realise it, you are being a great help to her. Our organization has strict rules about not wanting hatred to contaminate the Sisterhood. This is because hatred and revenge are very negative emotions that not only will distort a person's judgement. They can lead to unhappiness for the person nursing the feeling of hate. So you are helping your teacher by getting these negative feelings out of her system. She has been given a change to express them with you and hopefully she will learn to understand how negative they are, and reject them. If she cannot do this, she will not be invited to join the Sisterhood. She is also enjoying the power she has over you and we need her to explore that as well."

I opened my mouth to ask what about me. Then I realised what he would answer. I was giving her an important service, and this is what I needed to learn. How to help and service others. So I closed my mouth and changed the subject.

"For the life of me I can't find a medieval Tarot pack," I complained. "These New Age shops only seem to sell modern ones."

"I might be able to help you there. I'll arrange a copy of the pack I showed you."

"Thank you," I said and paused. "There's another thing. Do you know how old the Tarot is? I can't find anything definite in the books I've been reading."

"We don't know ourselves," he answered, "but we can trace it much further back than the official history. Pictorial images of The Eternal Cycle were saved from the Alexandria Library before the Christian mobs burnt it and some were rescued from libraries in Rome. Further back than that, we don't know. Turning the information into a pack of cards came later, as a way to carry secrets from lodge to lodge. It was also Christianised to conceal its true meaning; it took a long time for the Church authorities to work out what the cards really meant. When they did, they called them Devil cards and started to destroy them. Fortunately, there were so many in circulation by then, that they continue to survive outside secret societies ."

"What about the Minor Arcana? Do they mean anything?"

"They do, but I'm not a Tarot expert so I can't tell you much. As with most codes, the meaning is not obvious. You'd have to have it explained by someone who understands it more than I do. The same goes for other esoteric writings like the I Ching and the Kabalah."

"Talking about the Kabalah," I said, "I couldn't find any sensible histories of it at all."

"You're in luck," James grinned, "I have something to show you."

He took a rolled up chart from the table in front of us, looped the string at its top over a hook on a nearby bookcase and unrolled it, revealing the Kabalah.

"Voila!" he said with a dramatic flourish. "Seriously though, the Kabalah is essentially the journey of the Prodigal Son. I'm sure you're familiar with the New Testament story. It's symbolic of the journey of everyone away from the Oneness of the Great Mother into individuality and suffering, then back again into peace and harmony. Naturally, the Bible turns the Great Mother into a Father."

"The trick to understanding the Kabalah is the realisation that the spiritual paths of men and women are utterly different. The journey for a woman begins at Kether, where she is still united with the Great Mother, and travels down the Tree to Binhah, Geburah, Hod, and finally to Malkuth. At this point she is as far away from the Great Mother as possible. Then she returns through Netzach, Chesed and Chokmah to reach Kether again. Men travel in the opposite direction; from Kether they go to Malkuth via Chokmah, Chesed and Netzach, coming home to the Great Mother through Hod, Geburah and Binah."

I could see what he meant. One sex went round the circle clockwise, the other anti-clockwise. But why? James continued,

"The journey away from the Great Mother for both men and women is into a patriarchal society. We lose our feeling of unity with everything and experience individuality, a sense of being separate from others and alone. Men can take this to extremes, denying the rights and needs of anyone but themselves, while women stay in touch with their love for others. As a result, they are left to maintain society emotionally and physically, without the assistance of men, at a high cost. They lose self-love and eventually see themselves as inferior to men. Only masculine ideals and philosophies are respected, leaving women oppressed and undervalued. Then comes the matriarchal society, which starts when we reach Malkuth, the furthest distance we can travel. Which we are all experiencing now. We all have begin our return to the Great Mother, our source, to re-experience Oneness. Since we are moving towards the Divine Feminine, women become the valued sex and men look to them for their learning. Like I said, it's basically the story of the Prodigal Son. The son leaves his loving father but is robbed and suffers great hardship. Recognising his misery, he swallows his pride and his fear of being unwelcome to return to his joyful father."

"What about Tiphereth and Yesod in the middle?"

"That's the beauty of the Kabalah," he said. "it caters for everyone. The centre path is the spiritual path for those who don't fit into the neat categories of male and female, like homosexual men, lesbians and hermaphrodites. It is also the path of matriarchal communities that have survived throughout the patriarchal age. Mostly they live in isolated areas and have had to compromise with the patriarchal communities around them, like the Minangkabau people in Western Sumatra. There are about four million of them. They've survived by becoming strict Moslems and yet still retain their ancient traditions of matriarchy."

"I didn't realise there are any matriarchal communities left." I said in surprise.

"There are about 150 all over the world," James said. "Many more lasted until the 19th century but didn't make it into our technological age. Governments tend to keep quiet about them; they're seen as an embarrassment. But they exist in Africa, South America, China and India they even have survived in Europe in historic times."

"I've never heard of matriarchy in Europe!" I exclaimed.

James shrugged his shoulders.

"The Basque people of France and Spain were matriarchal in historic times, and their matriarchal customs were finally destroyed by the Inquisition and the Medieval witch-hunts. The Czech people were matriarchal up until the sixth or seventh century. Where after the last matriarchal ruler, Queen Libuse had died, there was a patriarchal take over. In this legend, the women fought back led by two women warriors called Vlasta and Sarka but they were finally defeated. The Lapland people were also matriarchal up until recently. There also have been communities who have remained matriarchal by keeping it a secret."

I stared at him for a minute before returning to the picture of the Kabalah in front of me. "What about the paths that go across the Kabalah, like the one from Hod to Netzach?"

"Shortcuts," he said succinctly. "The majority of people sleepwalk through life, remember. They are the sheep who just follow traditions and conventional thinking. They go around the Kabalah on the outer paths. Then there are the goats. They devote themselves to various spiritual disciplines and in doing so can take short cuts across the Kabalah. We all go to the same places, but the shortcuts save time."

"I see." Pause. "What's this about journeying from Oneness into individuality and back again?"

"The feminine is the One," James explained slowly. "When we lived in the Great Mother we were all One. We had no sense of being individuals. All of us basked in the love of the Great Mother and gave it back to her unreservedly. There was no concept of difference or separateness; it hadn't been conceived of as yet. I know it's hard to understand this; we are so used to the idea that we are alone in our bodies that it seems impossible to accept that there might be another way of seeing ourselves. Anyway, that's how it was. Then we decided to experience the Masculine, which involves individuality and separation. So we had a patriarchal age. Once we've explored being on our own fully, which is largely through the experiences of men, we go back to unity via a matriarchal age, which values everyone as part of a whole."

"So you're saying we need the patriarchal age," I asked, "it's not just a mistake?"

"That's right. We've all suffered in the patriarchal age because it separates us from each other and the Great Mother. We're lonely, afraid and in pain because we've locked ourselves into a body and seen it as the limit of our reality. We've created hatred, violence and selfishness in our quest to experience individuality, but we felt compelled to do it because of our desire to be independent. Once we become confident in our sense of individuality, then we set off home again, back to union with All That Is. Just like the Prodigal Son."

"Both matriarchal and patriarchal ages are necessary then?"

"Yes," James nodded, "For the moment anyway. In a completely feminine world we would lose all sense of individuality. In a totally masculine one, society would dissolve into chaos because no-one would care for others. The human race would quickly die out."

"Can't we experience the masculine and the feminine at the same time?" I asked, depressed by the thought of this endless circling.

"Of course," James said reassuringly. "It's what we're learning to do, even though we haven't yet succeeded. Uniting the opposites, bringing the masculine and feminine together in ourselves, is where we're headed. It's symbolised in alchemy as the Sacred Marriage of a King and Queen or as a hermaphrodite. Once we've done this, we can leave this plane of existence and move to higher planes. But it takes time and willingness to do the Great Work, whatever the cost. You don't achieve it by reading a few books and saying the odd mantra, but through immense courage and a soul-desire to be whole."

"Surely you can't do it in one lifetime!" I protested, feeling daunted by James' words.

"No, you can't," he granted. "If you think in terms of a separate individual, the journey of the soul continues through many incarnations. If you admit we are connected to each other, then we all learn together."

"I read we can reincarnate as male or female," I said. "You seem to be suggesting we stick with one sex. Do we?"

"There's no simple answer to that," James explained. "What you have to remember is that any powerful sense of being a individual or being male or female is lost when we leave the body. As the memory of existence in matter fades, we find that we have immense freedom to join with others or to express aspects of ourselves as somehow separate from each other - we can fragment ourselves to widen our understanding. Because the lessons associated with incarnating as a male or a female can be so different from each other, many souls split into two halves. Each half experiences what it is like to be male and female in both a patriarchal and a matriarchal society and attempts to achieve balance through this . Not all souls do this. After lifetimes as a male they may incarnate as female, for example and find it difficult to cope. It's all about choice."

"Do the ones who split into two become soul mates?"

"In a sense," James said slowly, "though that concept has caused great misunderstanding. If you look at it from a matriarchal perspective, we're all soul mates. If you think in terms of separate souls, then the other half of you is not your perfect lover but just 'you' having a different experience. You can hate your soul mate or find them as bland as blancmange. It depends. I certainly don't agree with this concept of finding your soul-mate."

He looked at his watch for the tenth time in our conversation.

"Time to go." He hooded me and I meekly accompanied him to his car, but I wasn't finished questioning him.

"Are the matriarchal and patriarchal ages about the same length of time?"

"We don't think so," he said. "Humankind seems to be more matriarchal than patriarchal"

"How do you know?"

"We can tell this from the our physical weakness. We have a much slenderer skeleton than Gorillas and Chimpanzees, who live in groups dominated by alpha males. In a masculine-led society, males fight to see who is the strongest and the winner gets to mate with the females. Over time that would lead to increased physical strength as the winning males passed on their genes. We'd end up with very chunky human beings! But it hasn't happened, which suggests that females have been able to choose their mates, at least some of the time. Strength and physical prowess might still have been a factor, but not the only one."

"When you think about it, giving a choice to females has allowed us to select for characteristics like intelligence instead of focusing entirely on big muscles and a loud voice. I know there are other reasons, but if you look at it objectively, we are pretty puny. A chimpanzee is smaller than us but is three times as strong. While animals like deer of about the same size as us, can run up to five times faster than the quickest man. We don't have size, teeth or speed on our side, just brains and flexibility. When the going gets tough, we can adapt and that's how we survive. That is why the Neanderthals died out instead of us."

"I don't see the connection."

"All right. The extinction of the Neanderthals is something of a mystery; it's been puzzled over by palaeontologists for years. The Neanderthals had the same size brains as us, they had the same tool technology and they were far stronger physically. Yet it was they who died out, not us. We don't know for sure what wiped them out. Some scientists have suggested that they depended too heavily on a meat diet to survive hard times, others that we bumped them off, directly or indirectly. But it may be that they went the way of other male-dominated apes in an Ice Age. The alpha males fed themselves, leaving the females and young to die. End of story. End of species."

"I don't understand,"

"All right. The way we are taught about evolution always puts the empathise on the male and forgets about the role of the female. Whereas in the survival of any species the most important sex is the female. This is because the young has to develop inside her and then when they are born the females generally take most responsibility in caring for the young. This means that in a situation where a species faces extinction if it is male dominated then the males will feed first and the females and the young will die first of starvation. So even though the alpha males might survive without females there is no way the species can breed and so will come extinct. Whereas in a female dominated species the females will feed first ensuring the females and the young have the best chance of survival. So even if only one male survives, he is able to impregnate hundreds of female ensuring that the species can keep breeding and survive."

"I never got told anything like this at school or university," I said aggrievedly. "It was always something to do with climate change or other 'environmental challenges' as they called them. Nothing to do with how women were treated."

"Of course you weren't," James replied patiently. "Until recently, women have been historically invisible. I think they were allowed to have children and collect a few grubs and tubers, but apart from that, they didn't count. When the possibility arose that they might be past leaders of society, the idea was ignored, censored or suppressed. It still is."

We were quiet for the rest of the journey.

At our destination James removed my hood, revealing the familiar, bare room. I donned my mask and waited. This time my teacher arrived within a few minutes of James' departure and I greeted her as usual by kissing her feet.

"Did James teach you about the Kabalah?" she enquired brightly.

"Yes, he gave me a quick lesson before we came here."

"Oh good," she chirped. "Now I noticed you were a bit resistant about kissing my arse last time. How do you feel about it now?"

"I realise it is a great honour and privilege," I said solemnly.

"Oh, good boy," she said, patting my head in time with the words, "you're starting to learn. For being such a good boy, you get the same honour again."

"Oh, thank you very much," I said feelingly.

"You're welcome, but don't expect to receive this privilege every time you see me. I only give it as a reward for progress and hard work."

Even though she wore a veil over her face I could still detect a smirk in her eyes and the tone of her voice.

"All right Rover," she went on. "Set up your massage table."

I moved to obey her as quickly as I could, but when I turned round after erecting the table she was already naked. On the floor lay only a dress and panties. Was she trying to avoid being ogled as she undressed? It seemed unlikely, but who was I to speculate? I got on with the massage. Today she was talkative.

"Has James discussed the sacrificial drama of Jesus Christ?"

"He did suggest that Jesus was a sort of sacred masochist," I said, She laughed.

"Do you know that a lot of the symbolism surrounding Christianity is sexual?" she giggled. "Think about a church steeple."

I thought briefly. I'd always been taught it represented our striving upwards towards heaven. I never thought it had a sexual meaning, but thinking of it in those terms the meaning become obvious.

"I suppose it's a giant penis."

"Of course," she said, still giggling. "Many pagan religions worshipped the penis. Some sects of Hinduism still do. What about a Gothic arch?"

"The vagina?" I ventured. This was easy.

"Right again! Did you know that on some Churches they even have carving of a clitoris on the top of these arches."

I looked at her is surprise and disbelief.

"Surely the church wouldn't allow that!" I exclaimed.

Her giggling briefly turned into outright laughter.

"If the Church authorities were not aware that the Gothic arch represented a vagina then they wouldn't put two and two together, and realise the carving at the top is a clitoris. It is only when you realise what the arch really represents, that it become obvious."

"I see."

And what about the Cross?" A little harder, but if it was sexual, then,

"Is that another penis? Two penises?"

"Partly right," she said more soberly. "The Cross is a very ancient symbol going back well into the Stone Age, but the Christian cross comes from the Egyptian Ankh. At the top of the Ankh you have an oval vagina shape. Below that is an upright shaft symbolising the penis. Between them is a horizontal bar which divides them. It describes a society with women on top and men at the bottom. That's the way it should be, don't you agree?"

"Oh yes," I said quickly.

"Christians don't realise just how perverted their religion can seem," she said earnestly. "Every Sunday they worship a near-naked man on a cross who has been whipped and tortured. If another religion was to worship a whipped near-naked woman on a cross, there would be an uproar! "

She laughed and her whole body shook.

"They say Christianity today is more popular with women than men," she continued. "I bet some of those sexually starved women get a thrill, seeing a tortured, half-dressed man on a cross every Sunday."

"I suppose they would," I said, not knowing how to react to her. She seemed to have a low opinion of churchgoers, not to mention seeing everything in sexual terms.

"As I was saying, a lot of spiritual symbols are really about sex," she said, echoing my thoughts. "Have you worked out the meaning of the rosy cross of the Rosicrucians?"

"I suppose the rose is the vagina and the cross the penis." I said. Following on with the same theme, it wasn't hard to work out. I remembered the pop group, Guns and Roses, had a similar meaning.

"Correct! Another one you should know about, because it comes from Freemasonry, is the cross inside the crown. That symbol's been adopted by Christian Science and Seventh Day Adventists,. Isn't it interesting that sects like these adopt an image that is both sexual and comes from Freemasonry?"

"Why would they do that?"

"I thought being a Freemason, you'd know all about this," she said sulkily.

"In my lodge they hardly tell you anything."

"One of the founders of the Seventh Day Adventists was a ex-Freemason," she informed me, "and Mary Baker Eddy, the founder of Christian Science, her first husband was a Freemason. Also a number of Freemasons helped get her sect started."

"I see," I said gamely.

"The Star of David and the Pentagram are also symbols of sexual union," my teacher continued.

"Are they?" I said in surprise. It seemed highly unlikely.

She laughed at the shock in my voice.

"Can't you work it out?" she mocked. "The Star of David contains two triangles that are joined together. Both are the pubic triangles of a woman, Get it?"

"Er, no."

"It represents two women joined together in sexual union, so it represents Lesbian love."

"Your joking." I said.

"The hexagram is far older than Judaism. It goes back to the last matriarchal age. Has James told you about how women then held power over men?"

"By a powerful sisterhood."

"Yes and this sisterhood was reinforced by lesbian sex. Most women then were bi-sexual. So it is a symbol of sisterhood power."

"If that is the case why did Judaism adopt this symbol?"

"Because it is a symbol of power. Patriarchal religions do this they have taken over our symbols and rituals and changed their meanings."

"What about the Pentagram. That doesn't have two triangles in it."

"Agreed there is only the female triangle. The other shape is more like an arrow and represents the male gentiles."

"I can't visualise it."

"Draw a Pentagram when you get home," she instructed me, "and you'll see both the pubic triangle and a penis."

"That's all very well," I objected, "but aren't we in danger of seeing penises and vaginas in everything. Perhaps they weren't originally intended to be seen that way."

"Are you disagreeing with me?" she said angrily.

"No," I hastily denied.

"Yes you are. Hasn't James taught you that you should never disagree with a woman?"

"He hasn't mentioned it."

"Okay," she said, drawing out the word. "Then it's James' fault. He should have told you. Now tell me you're sorry and beg to be forgiven!"

"I'm truly sorry," I said. "Please forgive me."

"Say it again, and put more feeling into it!"

With all the regret I could muster I repeated the words to her.

"That's better. I wasn't going to allow you the honour of kissing my ass a moment ago, but I've changed my mind. But if you do it again, I won't be so forgiving, Is that understood!"

It was.

"For your information," she went on through gritted teeth, "all religions before Judaism, Christianity, Buddhism and Islam had the sexual act at the centre of their rituals, because the joining of the male and female created life. Sex was a sacred act. Temples were full of sexual imagery. It was only the later patriarchal religions that banned sex from their rituals and demonised it. But they kept the ancient symbols and avoided saying what they really mean."

"Thank you for informing me," I said humbly.

"That's all right. It's a pleasure to inform those who are ignorant."

The rest of the massage was carried out in silence. When it was over, she lay quietly on the table. I wondered what she wanted me to do.

"Do you know that the success of a massage depends on how much love the masseur puts into it?" she suddenly said.

"No."

"It's the same with cooking," she went on, "how delicious the food is, varies according to the amount of love the cook invests in the preparation."

"Oh, I see," I said. Another snippet I would have to ponder.

"Now as a reward for giving me a wonderful massage, you can kiss my bottom." She turned over on her face.

I made for the valley between her buttock cheeks.

"I didn't say my arsehole," she said. "I know you're keen to get your tongue in there but I want my cheeks pampered first."

"Sorry," I said and kissed and licked her buttocks.

"Now you can lick all the way up my crease," she relented after about five minutes.

I obeyed, careful to do exactly what she said.

"Now you may have the great honour of putting your tongue into my asshole," she said.

I was soon pushing my tongue in as hard as I could.

"Are you holding back on your emotions?" she asked after a few minutes.

"I don't think so," I said in surprise.

"Yes you are," she insisted, "and I know you can do better. I want to feel all the devotion and reverence you're able to give when you kiss my arse."

I set to work again, doing my best to summon up a feeling of devotion to my task, but after a few more minutes she raised her head from the table.

"What is the matter with you?" she spat crossly. "I've given you the opportunity to worship a Goddess and you don't seem to appreciate it."

"I'm trying my best," I said lamely.

"It's not about trying," she hissed. "Just get in touch with all the feelings of ardour you have and let them express themselves."

I tried again, without much hope of success and gave up on it. To my great surprise, once I'd given up, an enormous passion swept over me, sucking me into a helpless feeling of yearning for a connection with my teacher. My body shook as I released the emotions in a frenzy of kissing and licking. Time was suspended until my teacher finally ordered me to stop. She seemed as shaken as I was, but said bravely,

"Now, how much love and devotion did you put into that?"

"A lot," I admitted. "The feelings took me over completely."

"And so they should. You should never restrain the desire to worship a Goddess." Is that understood?"

"Yes," I said, glowing with the pleasure of my experience. "Thank you for allowing me the honour of adoring you.."

"I don't think you deserve it," she said, surprising me. "You held back your feelings, so I won't give you a drink this time. It will remind you never to do it again."

Immediately I felt a pang of disappointment and watched numbly as my teacher hopped off the massage table. The glow began to fade.

"Have you got my clean panties?"

I took them out of my shirt pocket and kneeling before her, helped put them on. I was allowed to assist with her dress as well.

"On the floor," she ordered. I sat down at her feet.

"That's better. Did James tell you that another mystery play is coming up?" I shook my head.

"Doesn't he tell you anything?" she sighed. "It's about the Journey through the Netherworld by the Goddess Inanna. Do you know anything about her?" I shook my head again.

"You'll have to research it then," she said, "it'll help you to understand the play."

Scooping up the hem of her dress, she left, leaving her used panties behind. Nothing had been said about them, but I assumed they were a consolation prize for the loss of her golden nectar. I pocketed them anyway. Half an hour later James strode into the room, hooded me and led me to his car.

"Who is the Goddess Inanna?" I asked him as soon as we moved off.

"Ah. Your teacher told you about the coming mystery play." He didn't wait for a comment but moved swiftly into his answer.

"She's an ancient Sumerian Goddess. The tale of her sojourn in the Underworld comes from one of the oldest texts officially ever discovered. If you'd like I can lend you some books about it."

"Thank you." .

I was silent for a few minutes before I thought of something else I wanted to know.

"What you told me about the Kabalah wasn't from a book, was it?"

"No. It's very old knowledge, but never published. I'm afraid it would have met with censorship until very recently," he said. "Any references to the feminine as in any way powerful are forbidden in a patriarchal era. It would have had to be encoded or diminished in some way to make it acceptable. Mind you, it's not universal. More feminine spirituality has survived persecution within Hinduism than in any other major religion."

"I still don't understand," I said. "What exactly is so dangerous about Goddess spirituality that it has to be censored or destroyed? I can't see it as a threat to multinational corporations or the military-industrial complex of Western society!"

James gave a quiet chuckle at my attempt to be sarcastic.

"It's to stop the peasants from revolting," he said. "If you knew for a fact that people were much happier in the past under a matriarchal system, if you knew that war and poverty were unnecessary and that it's not divinely ordained that a few people prosper while others suffer, what would you do? You'd remove the boot from your neck and overthrow the present elites. Lots of people would join you too. That's why the evidence of peaceful and prosperous societies has to be suppressed, censored or derided as myth. It's far too threatening to the status quo of male rule through fear and aggression. Best to say it's all a wishful fantasy, dreamed up by malcontents who don't want to live in 'the real world'. If it was accepted as real historical fact, then it would give people hope, which is always a bad thing. They are much more likely to accept the yoke of oppression if they see no alternative."

"Does this mean places like Atlantis really existed? What do you know about it?"

"I'm afraid I can't tell you anything," James said regretfully. "I can only say that we're not the first civilisation to produce advanced technology on this planet."

"So why is there no evidence?"

"Because most of it is underwater. An ancient society flourished at least twelve thousand years ago. Like today, most cities were either on the coast or in river basins. The melting of the ice caps, which were far greater than today, caused the rising oceans to flood the coastal towns and cities. The sudden melting of glaciers in mountain ranges washed away towns and cities next to rivers. There was massive destruction. In spite of this, some evidence of past technologies has been discovered. Naturally, it's been censored."

"If they were so advanced," I said, "surely not all knowledge was lost. Why didn't they recover?"

James was quiet for a minute.

"For many reasons," he said eventually. "Most of them I can't reveal to you, but I can tell you one thing. There has been many patriarchal and matriarchal ages in the past. The civilization that was destroyed was a patriarchal civilization that was slowly becoming matriarchal. Unfortunately it was destroyed for the same reasons we are likely to destroy our civilization. Women took over too late to save it. These women then became frighten of a patriarchal backlash, of men re-taking power through violence. So they suppressed what technology that was then available because they didn't want men to use it and make destructive weapons with it."

"So are you saying the same will happen to our civilization?"

"We hope not, this is why we are trying to speed up the change towards matriarchy."

"Well if the environmentalists are right about global warming then you are far too late already."

"I'm afraid we can't go too fast," he told me. "There's been dramatic change in the last hundred years – and we're now moving in the right direction. We can't alter things too quickly; it has to be at a rate that people can cope with or there's a backlash later on. Overnight revolutions are dangerous. They destabilise societies and unless you're careful, you get chaos and anarchy followed by despotic dictatorships as people look to a strong leader to provide certainty. Just look at the French and Russian Revolutions to see what I mean."

"So is your group in control of the rate society is changing?"

James laughed.

"I wish we were," he said. "But as I keep telling you, it's a natural process; it takes care of itself. All we can do at the moment is to block the efforts of those who are attempting to put society in reverse gear so their little empires won't disappear."

"So you don't try to drive society in the right direction?"

He was silent for a minute.

"You've hit on one of the few controversies in our organisation. Some of us want to push forward, but we know there are risks. It's a delicate balancing act requiring intuition rather than intelligence. In the past it was easier, believe it or not. We were instrumental in the rise of Protestantism, which curtailed the power and corruption of Roman Catholicism and we nurtured the beginnings of Parliamentary Democracy. It was easy to see what needed changing back then; grey areas didn't really exist. And we were careful to go slowly so as to avoid anarchy and violence. Now it's much trickier. There are no easy targets and plenty of areas where, if we interfered, we might do more harm than good. So we tread carefully, argue with each other and consult the few women and men who have an intuitive sense of the best way forward."

"Oh," I said. So they were just human after all. "Where you involved in the French and Russian revolutions?"

"Yes we were involved," he said, "but I admit we did lose control of events. These revolutions were taken over by violent men only interested in personal power."

When we arrived back at James house, he went straight to one of his bookshelves. It took him a while, but eventually he chose a number of books which he handed to me.

"These are not only about the ancient Sumerian legends," he told me. "They also explain how the story of Inanna's Journey to the underworld was rewritten by the Mesopotamians. There's also information on similar legends in ancient Egypt, Greece and Rome and some books about matriarchal communities that have survived till now, bless them."

He patted me gently on the shoulder.

"I think you've had enough for one evening. Go home and relax. You can save the world tomorrow."

# CHAPTER TWELVE

The following Saturday I went to Janet's house as usual. She was in a capricious mood. Firstly I was instructed to undress and do her housework in the nude, then I was told that there were to be two guests for dinner. As I was making the meal, I heard the door bell ring followed by the sounds of Janet inviting two other women in the house. After about ten minutes of murmured conversation, she brought them into the kitchen where I was slaving over a hot stove.

"This is my servant Arthur," she introduced me. "So far he's been very subservient and a good worker. He's also very cheap."

They all laughed. I began to feel very vulnerable, standing naked while three clothed women examined me.

"Oh look," said one of the women, "his face is going red. I think he's actually blushing."

They seemed to think this was very funny and laughed even more.

"We'd better leave him," said Janet, "I told him I want dinner served in ten minutes time. We can have some fun with him afterwards."

As I served food to the three women, they took turns pinching and groping me. Although I felt slightly anxious about their antics, my penis was enthralled; soon I had an erection which they all commented on in graphic terms. Then came dessert, which had to be placed in the centre of the table. I was at full stretch, both my hands occupied, when one of Janet's friends delivered a stinging slap to my rear. My erection grew harder as the pain filtered through to me, causing general hilarity amongst the dinner guests. After that, I was given a hard slap whenever my erection threatened to go down.

After the meal, we retired to Janet's living room where I served tea and coffee. One of the women told me to bend over. I expected another slap, but instead felt something being pushed up my ass. As I cautiously straightened up, the women began to laugh all over again.

"Will it fall out?" This was Janet.

"No," explained the woman who'd inserted the object. "It's a special rubber dildo with a large knob on the end. I doubt if it will drop out very easily."

"Good," said Janet, before turning to me. "Arthur, you are to keep it inside you for the rest of the afternoon."

"Yes Madam," I replied, without thinking.

The women burst into fresh peals of laughter at my unconscious deference.

"Did he call you Madam?" one of the women tittered.

"So he should," Janet decided. "It's right that he should call me Madam."

They played with me the rest of the afternoon whenever the fancy took them. At one point a woman grabbed my erect penis and determinedly milked me into a bowl. The effect of ejaculating with a dildo inside me had a strange effect which was hard to catalogue as unpleasant or pleasant. It was just different from any previous experience I'd had.

After that they lost interest in me, the dildo was removed and the two women went home. I did the washing up, cleaned the kitchen and collected my fee from Janet, who sent me home without a single word of praise or thanks. I wondered if the sensation of the dildo, which stayed with me for hours, was a kind of bonus payment in lieu of applause for my fortitude. It was hard to work out what was punishment and what was a gift these days.

Halfway through the next week, James summoned me to his house. As I entered the living room I saw robes laid out on a table. I knew what that meant.

"Did you read about the Goddess Inanna?"

"I managed to get through one of your books," I said apologetically, "but I only had time to flick through the others."

"Never mind. At least you'll have some idea of what the play's about."

"There is one question I'd like to ask you," I began hesitantly.

"Ask me whatever you like." James waved his hands expansively and I began.

"When I first became a Mason, I found that one theory of their origins claims that they were originally Knights Templar who survived being persecuted and were forced to operate underground. When Philip IV of France set out to destroy the Templars, they were put on trial. One of the charges brought against them was that they worshipped a Horned god called Baphomet and that the Knights were required to kiss the bottom of this god during their rituals. When I read this, I assumed it was something that was invented to discredit the knights, because it's so bizarre. Then recently you got me to research Freemasonry again. I found that modern Witchcraft was started by a Freemason, and because of that I did a bit of research into mediaeval Witchcraft. When I looked at the details of Witch trials, there was the accusation again, except this time it was the Devil's arse being kissed." I paused to quell a feeling of embarrassment before continuing, "In my initiation sessions with my teacher I've been told to kiss her bottom. Is this all connected?"

"It is indeed," James said slowly. "What you have to remember is that both the Devil of the Witches and Baphomet of the Knights Templar are really Goddesses. The Church changed them into evil male gods, as it always does with female deities. We could hardly call them liars without risking a bonfire ourselves, so they made claims like this with impunity. The fact that secret Goddess religions existed has been suppressed, but they flourished underground. It was vital to avoid exposure, so the sects devised elaborate initiations to weed out spies and possible traitors. One of the more obvious tests was to see if a supplicant would kiss the bottom of a woman playing the role of a Goddess. A true believer from a patriarchal religion would never do anything like that."

"I see," I said, light beginning to dawn in my confused mind. "So if I'd refused to kiss the bottom of my teacher, I'd have failed my initiation."

"We are not so strict today, but you would needed to be tested perhaps in a different way if you refused."

That silenced me, but only for a moment.

"So are you Witches, were you once the Knights Templar?"

He smiled his usual patient smile.

"I'm afraid it's not that easy," he said. "Our history is very complex, full of breakaway groups and splinter sects. There's always been disagreement about how best to effect change, so you often had a split resulting in rival groups with different names. Multiply this many times to cover the whole era of Christianity in the West, minus a few factions discovered and killed and you're describing our past precisely. It's only relatively recently that we have been able to liase with each other co-operatively to share information and insights. We're not a united organisation under one authority, nor have we ever been like that."

"If that's the case," I said, puzzled, "how on earth did you survive so many years of persecution?"

"With difficulty. We've come close to being wiped out a number of times, sometimes because of treachery and other times through our own carelessness and downright stupidity. Our opponents often thought they'd completely finished us off, only to find we popped up again at a later date. What helped us is the fact that the patriarchal church and its rulers made a lot of enemies by behaving so repressively. We used that to boost recruitment. And we also became very skilled at the spy, traitor and double agent game. On the whole we've been better at infiltrating their organisations than they have at penetrating ours."

"I still don't understand why you have to play the spy game in the 21st century," I said, genuinely perplexed.

"Because there's still a lot at stake," James insisted. "007 types with - a licence to kill - do exist. They murdered both Princess Grace and Princess Diana in fake car accidents, both successfully covered up in spite of being bungled jobs."

I'd heard about this before. The books I'd read had lots of detail about the accidents then went very hazy and complicated about why the Princesses were killed.

"Were the Princesses members of your organisation?"

"I can't say," he said firmly. "Does it matter?"

"Only if my own life might be in danger because I've joined your organisation."

"That is a point. If they were full members of the Sisterhood then they would be still alive today."

"Do you have the power to protect them?"

"I have said too much already. People like you and me are far too unimportant for them to worry about. The reason why Princess Grace and Princess Diana were murdered was because anything they said or did would be reported all over the world. This gave them great power to help any cause they supported. They'd both been held in shackles by the family they married into, but decided to break out. Both were strong and compassionate women who wanted to use their authority to make the world a better place. Princess Diana had already demonstrated her influence by changing people's attitude towards Aids and highlighting the suffering caused by the trade in land mines. It made her highly dangerous in the eyes of our opponents. She was no longer under the control of the British Royal family and was free to use her immense personal power to promote any cause she felt strongly about. Princess Grace echoed this; she was inspired by Diana and wanted to emulate her. It was for this reason, rather than any secret society they might have belonged to, that they became marked women."

"So are the conspiracy theorists right?" I asked curiously. "Is there a secret organisation that rules the world."

"Partly right," he said. "Men of power do get together and carve the world up between themselves. Fortunately for us, their capacity for ruthless treachery means any agreement is short-lived, because they will always compete with each other for power."

"What about the idea that the Freemasons or the Illuminati rule the world?"

"The Freemasons are not a united organisation," James answered, shaking his head, "though they do have great power. Many decisions are made behind closed doors in a patriarchy, remember. You don't have to be a member of a secret cabal to do this; you just have to be willing to bribe, kill, outmanoeuvre or coerce whoever opposes you. You might be just a politician, a religious leader, a corporation or the head of a military force. As long as you have power you can get what you want."

It was a depressing thought. I had to remind myself that there had been progress, that there were glimmers of light here and there in the world. James must have read my mind.

"It's not all bad you know. We have our own conspiracies. For instance, the United States of America was created as a new country to lead the world back to the matriarchal age. All sorts of influences were brought to bear on its birth, from the Constitution down to its very name. Although our ideals have been distorted by the strength of our opposition, we still think we did pretty well. Just at the moment our opponents are in the ascendant in the U.S. but we know that's only temporary."

"Who decided that the USA was to lead us back to a new matriarchal age?"

James thought for a moment.

"I'm not allowed to tell you," he said finally. "Trust me that there's a good reason. Now we have to be quiet. I have to prepare myself for the play."

It was the same theatre, small but richly decorated. I was admiring its restrained opulence when the curtain opened and dramatic music began to play. On stage were two women dressed in sumptuous robes and a dark-skinned man stripped to the waist. One of the women stood on a balcony above the stage; the other, clothed completely in black, sat on a throne in the middle of the stage. The man was between them, on a staircase leading from the balcony to the stage. The woman on the balcony spoke first.

Inanna- I am Inanna, Queen and ruler of both heaven and earth and of the peoples and creatures who live therein.

The black-clad woman spoke next.

I am Ereshkigal, Goddess of the Netherworld.

I am the Gatekeeper to the Netherworld.

Ereshkigal - Come, my sister. It is time for you to visit me.

Inanna begins to descend but after only three steps her progress is barred by the Gatekeeper. An unseen voice gives a commentary.

Storyteller - Inanna arrives at the gates of the Underworld displaying all the symbols of Her rank and position: crown, lapis necklace, a double strand of deep blue beads, a jewelled belt around her waist, gold armband. She is holding a lapis measuring-rod and wearing Her royal robe. To begin the descent to the Underworld she must pass through seven gates, surrendering one article at each gate.

The gatekeeper removes her crown.

Inanna -(angrily) Why has my crown been taken from me?

Gatekeeper - Be satisfied Inanna! The Me of the Netherworld is being fulfilled. You must not open your mouth against its sacred customs.

Storyteller - When the Crown of Inanna was removed from Her head, the warlike patriarchal Indo-Europeans invaded the peaceful matriarchal peoples further south. They conquered these societies and became their leaders. The Queens and High-Priestesses were stripped of their positions and forced to co-operate with the new rulers.

Inanna walks down another two steps. She is again stopped by the gatekeeper. He takes off her necklace.

Inanna - Why have you taken my Lapis necklace?

Gatekeeper - Be satisfied Inanna! The Me of the Netherworld is being fulfilled. You must not open your mouth against its sacred customs.

Storyteller - The necklace symbolizes the ability of Inanna to express herself. Although the new patriarchal rulers had political power, the people they dominated were still matriarchal in their attitudes and ways of living. The despotic dictators began to curb free-speech. The women who had previously held power were silenced by the threat of death from criticising the new patriarchal rulers.

At the third gate, Inanna is stripped of the double strand of blue beads that hung between her breasts.

Inanna - Why have my beads been taken from me?

Gatekeeper - Be satisfied Inanna! The Me of the Netherworld is being fulfilled. You must not open your mouth against its sacred customs.

Storyteller – For a woman, the breast represents her ability to love and nourish others. When the patriarchal rulers first took control, the women were initially angry about losing their status and power. Slowly, they had a change of heart and began to co-operate with and even love these patriarchal men from the North.

As Inanna passes the fourth gate, she is deprived of her jewelled belt,

Inanna - Why have you taken my jewelled belt?

Gatekeeper - Be satisfied Inanna! The Me of the Netherworld is being fulfilled. You must not open your mouth against its sacred customs.

Storyteller - The jewelled belt signifies wealth. In matriarchal societies all possessions were inherited through the female line, concentrating wealth in the hands of women. It gave them great power. The patriarchs wanted inheritance to come down the male line. This was impossible at first, because women were still free to choose their sexual partners. There was no reliable way for a man to know who his children were. To overcome this, the male rulers and priests introduced the concept of marriage in which a woman had to be faithful to one man. A husband would then know that the children his wife gave birth to were definitely his. At last, inheritance could be from father to son and women could be stripped of all their property.

At the fifth gate, Inanna's gold armband is removed.

Inanna - Why have you removed my golden band?

Gatekeeper - Be satisfied Inanna! The Me of the Netherworld is being fulfilled. You must not open your mouth against its sacred customs.

Storyteller - The hands and arms denote our ability to act - to make things happen. For a long time, women were still farmers, builders, traders and even warriors. They remained capable of creating wealth and power for themselves. Slowly, these activities were denied to women and placed entirely in the hands of men. Resistance came in the form of Amazons, who made a last attempt to fight off the patriarchy, but in the end even they were defeated. Eventually, the only roles left for women were as wife, mother or prostitute. Any power a woman possessed derived from her attractiveness to men, her ability to bear sons or the status of her father and husband. Of herself she had none.

At the sixth gate, Inanna's lapis measuring rod is taken from her.

Inanna – Why have you removed my measuring rod?

Gatekeeper – Be satisfied Inanna! The Me of the Netherworld is being fulfilled. You must not open your mouth against its sacred customs.

Storyteller – In the past, women had been scholars, priestesses and rulers. They had skills which allowed them to use tools such as the measuring rod. The patriarchs began to bar women from education, to deny them the respect and status which comes from knowledge. All of that would now be given to men alone, leaving women dependant entirely on men for all skills except those of a wife and mother.

At the seventh gate, Inanna is stripped of her royal robe and left completely naked.

Inanna - Have you no respect for me? Why have I been rendered naked and defenceless by my own sister?

Gatekeeper - Be satisfied Inanna! The Me of the Netherworld is being fulfilled. You must not open your mouth against its sacred customs. Kneel before your sister, the Goddess Ereshkigal!

Storyteller - Even though much had been taken away from women, traditional customs and beliefs still gave them respect and an unacknowledged status. They could be midwives, healers and seers. The fact that they created life could not be denied either. To counter this, patriarchal religions began to disseminate propaganda about the inherently evil nature of females. They became the cause of all men's suffering, exemplified in figures like Pandora and Eve. They were also unclean, particularly during menstruation and after childbirth and could contaminate a man who touched them. He would have to be cleansed of this impurity through a ritual of the male god. Deep hatred of women led to the persecution of healers and seers as Witches who were seen as being in league with the Devil. Soon, ordinary women became the victims of widespread orgies of torture, Witch burning and drowning. No woman was safe from accusations of witchcraft, nor could she prove her innocence once charged. Male-dominated institutions attempted to eradicate the last vestiges of respect for women within society and any lingering belief in their own value that women still clung to. At this point, women had nothing left. All sense of worthiness had disappeared and Woman was left naked and defenceless before the might of the patriarchy.

Ereshkigal – Sister. You are no longer a Goddess but an ignorant, stupid woman, of value to no-one. You are condemned to be whipped, raped and abused by men who will have only contempt for you. In return you will love them unconditionally and surrender your life, serving them as their slave.

Two men came on stage. Inanna was tied up and whipped with great savagery. It looked quite shocking, but I had no way of knowing how much of it was an act. The actress was then thrown to the floor and raped by both men. At the same time they abused her verbally, calling her a worthless whore, and appeared to kill her with a series of vicious kicks and blows. It was deeply disturbing. When she had been slung into a coffin and the curtain came down, I nearly ran from the theatre in my distress. It was only James restraining hand and his whispered 'it's all right' that prevented me.

Five minutes later the curtain rose again. Ereshkigal and the Gatekeeper had been joined by a man who stood on the balcony. He began to descend.

Gatekeeper - Who dares approach the Goddess Ereshkigal, Queen of the Netherworld?

I am Enki, the God of wisdom. I humbly beg for an audience with the Goddess.

Gatekeeper (looks towards Ereshkigal who gives a brief nod) - A brief audience is granted, but you are warned that if you stay too long you will be subjected to the sacred customs of the Netherworld.

Enki comes down to the stage. He kneels reverently before Ereshkigal.

Ereshkigal - What do you want of me?

Enki - I have come to beg for the return of Inanna. Since she left the upper world it has become a wasteland. Great forests are cut down and turned into desert. Animals are becoming extinct. The oceans, lakes and rivers are over-fished and polluted. The atmosphere is clouded with poison which is causing the Earth to heat up. Vast ice-caps are melting, causing the oceans to swamp our cities. Toxins have been carelessly dumped, leading to disease and infertility. Men continue to fight each other but now they have terrible weapons that can destroy whole cities. Can't you see that we are lost without Inanna. Only She can save us from our misery by returning to rule our world.

Ereshkigal - And what will you give me in return for Inanna? Think carefully, Enki. Do not insult me by offering anything less than her worth.

There is a pause while Enki considers his answer.

Enki - The only replacement I can give you which is worthy of Inanna, is myself.

Ereshkigal – I will agree to this. I will allow Inanna to leave if you will take her place in my realm.

Enki goes to the coffin. He removes Inanna's body, which is brought to life again by Ereshkigal and begins to lead her through the seven gates. At each one her belongings are restored to her until she is once more Queen of Heaven and Earth.

Storyteller - At the Seventh gate, Inanna receives her royal robe. Women move towards respecting themselves and the patriarchy responds in agreement, however slight.

At the Sixth gate, Inanna is given back her measuring rod. Women are deemed worthy of education. It soon becomes clear that they are as intelligent as men and they are allowed into a limited range of jobs and professions. They begin to move into the wider society and their ideas and skills open more doors for them. They can be respected by men as well as themselves.

At the Fifth gate, Inanna is given her golden armband. Women move back into becoming self-sufficient instead of relying entirely on men for money and power. They are allowed into higher education, to become doctors and scholars. During the First and Second World Wars, women began to work in factories and on farms doing jobs normally reserved for men. They proved they were capable and resourceful, but when the men returned from war, they were expected to go back to being housewives. They refused. Slowly women move into more and more areas of employment, reducing their reliance on men. Ordinary women become capable of supporting themselves financially. Though they are still restricted by motherhood and discrimination, they are beginning to be in charge of their own lives.

At the Fourth gate, Inanna's jewelled belt is returned. Women are not only able to earn a living, but some are becoming wealthy. At one time the only way this was possible was by being the widow of a rich man, inheriting property from a father without sons or becoming a successful courtesan. Now, a sprinkling of successful business women are millionaires, while others are taking the top jobs in many professions. Feminists complain that women are prevented from reaching the top by ingrained sexism, but slowly the glass ceiling is collapsing.

At the Third gate, the double strands of deep-blue beads are returned to Inanna. In the patriarchal age, it wasn't only patriarchal religion that kept women in bondage, it was also their sacrificial love for men and children. As we move towards a new matriarchal age, women are learning how to love and value themselves. So the beads that hang between Inanna's breasts and over her heart now symbolise a wider sense of love for women, one that includes a recognition of their own worthiness to be loved.

At the Second gate, Inanna's lapis necklace is returned to her. In many countries, women become free to speak out in public without the fear of reprisal. Some have moved on from demanding equality into a desire for dominance over men. This is disliked by Feminists, who see it as unfair and unjust to men, but it gains popularity. Soon, young women will forget about ideas of fairness and see that a society guided by women is the only true option for growth.

At the First gate Inanna receives her crown. This is the symbol that women have now resumed their rule. The Earth begins to flower again, as its manifold life-forms are respected once more. We can see the beginnings of this in the plethora of environmental organisations such as GreenPeace, concerned at the damage patriarchy is doing to our world. As women take over, this concern will grow until widespread practical steps are taken to correct the problems. The wasteland created by men will be healed by compassion and care, now free to be expressed in a matriarchal world.

Inanna is warmly greeted by Enki, who kneels and worships her.

Inanna, (loudly to the audience,) "I am that I am. The Me has now been returned to Me. I am a Great and Wonderful Goddess. Once more I know it to be true."

Enki quietly surrenders to the Underworld. He is stripped naked and presented to the Goddess Ereshkigal.

Ereshkigal – Enki. In the absence of Inanna, you have been an unworthy ruler of the earth. You have abused and raped its beauty. In spite of your wisdom and your power you have learned little and harmed much. The task before you now is to learn how to love others unconditionally, as Inanna did throughout the years you ruled. You and your brothers will now become the servants of women, tendering them the same care you once received from them. If women so choose, it is within their power to abuse you as cruelly as you abused them. You will submit to all their desires.

Two women enter from the left. They restrain Enki, accuse him angrily and whip him in a slow, lascivious ritual of degradation. He offers no resistance to this, nor to their next actions. He is tied to a cross which is then raised upright. The curtain comes down. A few minutes later the curtain rises again to reveal the cast, who bow to the applauding audience.

James wasted no time in hustling me out of the theatre and into his car. Unusually, I was quiet for the whole journey, going over the implications of the scenes I had just witnessed. Back at his house, though, I began the questions he knew I would have.

"How real was that whipping?" I quizzed him, as soon as he'd divested me of my hood.

"It was probably authentic," James replied. The performers who took the roles of Inanna and Enki are known to be heavy players in what's called the BDSM scene."

"Why do you have scenes in your mystery plays that are sexually explicit and involve sadomasochism?" Even after James' previous explanations I found it difficult to understand.

"It's just another way of finding out about our initiates," he said. "Let's say a person has real problems with sex or sadomasochism. Usually it's an indication they won't be comfortable with much of the secret knowledge we possess. We can only initiate people who are willing to question the propaganda that patriarchal religions has spread about sexual expression, and can accept that they have sadomasochistic desires within themselves."

"You're saying that all people are sadomasochistic."

"To a lesser or greater degree, yes." James agreed. "Obviously it varies a lot between individuals. Some people are only satisfied by extreme expressions of their desires, while others are very mildly sadomasochistic."

"How can you be sure everyone's like that?" I asked. "What's the evidence?"

"There's a sadomasochistic theme running through most comedies and dramas, for a start," James began. "Slapstick humour is all about people having unfortunate accidents, yet we laugh at them! We do the same to those who play the fool in comedy shows. If we did this in real life, we'd be accused of cruelty and callousness. The comedians themselves play the role of a masochist - show themselves up as idiots or losers - to get a laugh. On the flip side there's the sadistic comedian whose tactic is to attack and ridicule other people for fun. Sometimes they have a foil or 'stooge' - a partner who is always the butt of the humour."

"You mentioned drama as well," I reminded him.

"In comedy, the sadomasochist themes are fairly obvious," he continued, "but they're also tucked away in most dramas. All good stories have to have both victims and persecutors. In the past it was often women who were the victims – the classic 'maiden in distress'. The main thrust of the tale was in the relationship between the female victim and the sadistic villain. The hero only comes into it to sanitise the story, to make sure that good triumphs over evil. Now we can see that image disappearing, replaced by men who are the victims of sadistic women. And even where you still get a female victim, the rescuer might be another woman!"

"Just because people read books or watch films like that," I protested, "it doesn't mean they're like that themselves."

"If the themes in comedy or drama didn't chime with feelings inside you," he stated calmly, "you wouldn't bother to watch the film or read the book. People identify with the characters, often at a very deep level, and if the drama is powerful enough, they can release emotions they couldn't access in normal life. It's one of the earliest functions of drama. The Greeks called it 'catharsis', but whatever it's called, it's real, and it's usually about inflicting or suffering pain."

"Let me get this straight. If you watch comedies or dramas with victims and persecutors in them, then you must have sadomasochistic desires yourself."

"That's pretty accurate. It starts in childhood, with Fairy tales of Big Bad Wolves and never stops."

"I can see what you mean," I said earnestly, " but you could just as easily claim these stories are about the fight between good and evil rather than our sadomasochistic desires."

"Of course you could," James agreed, "and it's a far more acceptable explanation for most people. It allows them to kill the villain, slay the dragon or whatever without acknowledging what's really going on."

"Which is?"

James took a long breath and resettled himself in his chair. I knew it was time to concentrate.

"I've told you that we're all sadomasochistic. We all have desires, conscious or unconscious, to suffer pain and to inflict it. Sometimes we incorporate our fantasies into our sex life, sometimes we concentrate on power issues alone. Everyone's different. But one of the commonest things we do is to deny one half of the equation. We admit to being a victim, but not to our sadistic side, or vice versa. When we encounter a villain in a story, it's easy to project our unacknowledged sadism onto him, then punish him for it. The hero kills him or put him in jail, he's removed and we breathe a sigh of relief. Good has triumphed again. But what has actually triumphed is hatred and the desire to hurt another human being. Just because we've dehumanised him by calling him 'bad' is irrelevant. We've punished him for our own deep-seated desires, ones we disapprove of and suppress. The same goes for the victim. If we refuse to accept our masochistic tendencies, we identify with the aggressor. We have nothing but contempt for the weakness of the person suffering at the hands of a sadist. That way we beat up our own capacity for sacrifice and suffering instead of dealing with it honestly."

"What makes you say we dehumanise the villain? Surely we see him as a human being who is evil and has to be stopped."

"Agreed," he said. "There are intelligent adult and children's books, films and TV shows out there with deep spiritual truths incorporated in them. At the same time, we have plenty of Christians and Muslims rooting for a god who supposedly sanctions the wholesale slaughter of others and tortures 'sinners' in the fires of Hell. Sadism is alive and well. "

Undeterred, I tried again.

"Another thing. Surely you could argue that fictional books or films exist to entertain. No-one would be interested if they just tried to inform and educate us."

James erupted into laughter.

"Sorry Arthur. Sometimes your naiveté just strikes me as funny. Writers and storytellers have been manipulating people's belief systems since we lived in caves! Even then they knew that a gripping storyline was the best way to involve us in looking at a cause they advocated, whatever it was. Look at the novel "Uncle Tom's Cabin," for example. It gave a powerful message to the 19th century American public about the suffering caused by slavery. Charles Dickens, meanwhile, was awakening the social conscience of Victorian Britain. All over the world, and at all times, writers use their work to promulgate their ideas. That's why the issue of who controls the media is so important. Being able to communicate whatever you want to large numbers of people bestows enormous power. Preventing others from doing the same helps you hang onto it?"

That shut me up for a second or two before I moved back to the original issue.

"What would happen to an initiate who claimed he or she didn't have any sadomasochistic desires at all?"

James just smiled.

"We'd be very suspicious. It could be true, of course, but it's far more likely to show a lack of self awareness. If that person is still stuck to this claim after we'd shown him or her all the proof, then they would probably have to go. Wilful blindness is not encouraged in our organisation, and it can be dangerous.."

"You're being a bit hard," I objected. "People are taught that if they have these desires they're sick and perverted. You're turning accepted wisdom completely on its head and saying it's so widespread it's normal. It might be difficult to swallow for some people."

"Like I said," James insisted, "we're looking for people who are open-minded. If an initiate resists new ideas, then he's not prepared to change. There's no shame in it, nor would it be right to insist that they believes us. They are simply not ready, and until they are, we'll leave them alone."

"One other point," I said suddenly, remembering. "In the Sumerian translations I read, it was Inanna's husband Dumuzi who takes her place in the Underworld. Why did they have Enki in your version?"

"Because it's a older account," James explained. "We possess older tellings of this legend than is officially acknowledged. In these versions Inanna doesn't have a lover or husband; they're added on later. In the oldest story we have, it is Ereshkigal, representing Everywoman, who takes the journey through the Netherworld. Other characters like Inanna, Enki, The Gatekeeper and Dumuzi were brought in later to make a more complex drama out of the story."

"Why are there so many versions of the same story?"

"Because ideas change over time. Each generation tinkers with the archetypal story a little, so it fits current beliefs. The tale evolves with society. If it didn't do that it would be discarded."

I had my next question ready.

"Is Enki a sort of Christ figure? He was put on a cross in the final scene."

"Well done!" James congratulated me. "I hoped you'd pick that up. Yes, he's the original Jesus, or to be more accurate, the first sacrificial saviour we know about."

I waited for him to continue.

"They retained some of the original myth in the Bible. Like many saviours, he died on a cross or tree, went to hell and three days later was resurrected ."

"In the books you gave me," I said, "there are a lot of death and rebirth stories, like the one about the Phoenix rising from the ashes of a fire, or Osiris being brought back to life by Isis after he'd been killed and cut to pieces by his brother Set. Or Odin, who is hanged on the tree of life. Are they just different versions of the same story?"

"To an extent, yes," James said, "but it's more complicated than that, really. In the past there were many mystery religions attempting to save ancient knowledge about the cycle of matriarchal and patriarchal ages. They had a complex system of outer and inner mysteries. The outer mysteries could be shared with anyone; they were innocuous enough to avoid censorship, they didn't ask for total commitment from a believer, nor did they require deep understanding of spiritual matters. The inner mysteries were different. They were powerful truths that might be seen as dangerous by the authorities and they required a high level of spiritual development to be understood by an initiate. The outer mysteries involve stories of gods or Goddesses making a journey into the Underworld, dying and returning to life. They were often taken to be actual events by the unsophisticated believers of a particular religion. The inner mysteries are what I'm beginning to teach you. Most academics assume the inner secrets of the mystery religions have all been lost, since they were never written down. Fortunately it's not the case. Much of the esoteric knowledge is coded into the stories of the outer mysteries. You just have to be able to see it."

An idea hit me.

"I suppose the inner mysteries are feminine, since females have hidden sex organs," I said. "And the outer mysteries are masculine, as the male has external sex organs."

James was impressed.

"That's right. Well done - you are starting to catch on."

"But I'm still confused," I confessed. " Are you telling me that the Tarot, the Kabalah and all these death and rebirth stories are more or less saying the same thing? About the cycles in human history, matriarchal and patriarchal ages and all that?"

"That's right," he said. "You can even find it in Revelations at the end of the Bible."

"Oh," I said. "I suppose you want me to read it and see if I can find the hidden meanings."

"I'd like you to try, but it will be difficult for you. You don't have much knowledge about religions."

We were silent for a while. I was doing metaphorical jigsaws in my head and James was unhurriedly sipping a drink. When he spoke it took me a second or two to tune in.

"You're now aware we worship a Goddess," he said, "but have you thought about the implications?"

"Not really, but you seem to be suggesting that women will soon rule the world instead of men."

"That's true," he said, "but I want you to think more about the psychological effects of believing we were created by the Great Mother, by a female. If you look around the world, you can see what happens when there's a belief in a male Creator. What would be different if people believed in a female deity as the Creatrix?"

"How could I possibly know that?" I asked, baffled.

"By looking at and comparing the feminine and masculine mind."

"I think you've mentioned this before," I said resignedly. I was tired and still attempting to assimilate today's experiences. I couldn't cope with yet another demand on my overtaxed brain. James seemed to sense this, or maybe he saw the look on my face and took pity on me.

"Good. You remember," was all he said, then, "now go away, have a rest and then you can think about it with a clear head. Just one last thing how have you been getting on with the affirmation I suggested?"

"I still find it really silly," I admitted, "I felt all right saying it with you, but when I went home I felt really stupid saying it and gave up."

"It must be hitting against many of your deep seated beliefs," sighed James, "Try and use it as a tool of self-awareness and see what happens when you say it."

He then showed me to the door and I was soon driving myself home with no thoughts at all beyond the need to sleep.

# CHAPTER THIRTEEN

I was stunned to receive a phone call from Mary the following evening. She was in England visiting her parents and wanted to see me before she flew back to the USA. In the morning I called work and told them I was sick, then waited nervously for her to arrive, pacing restlessly about the flat to relieve my anxiety. When she finally rang the door-bell it was late morning, but she gave no apologies. The first thing she noticed was my indoor plant.

"Since when have you been interested in plants?" she demanded.

"I just thought it was a good idea," I said defensively.

"It is," she agreed, "but you've never thought of it on your own. Who suggested it?"

"Nobody," I lied.

She stared at me until I felt very uncomfortable, then suddenly changed tack.

"I've only got two hours to spare," she said. "You mentioned that you'd learned massage, so you can give me one before I catch my plane."

It was clear she was in a hurry and had no time for pleasantries.. I set up my massage table while she undressed, gave her a long and thorough massage, then brought her to orgasm with my tongue. After she'd climaxed, she instructed me to light a cigarette for her.

"You have changed," she said, drawing on her cigarette. "What's been happening since I last saw you?"

Her questioning put me in a difficult position; I wasn't allowed to tell her about the organisation, so I just smiled and shrugged my shoulders.

"Nothing much."

"Have you got another girlfriend?"

"Oh no," I said hastily. "I haven't had one since you went off to America."

"Something's changed," she said firmly.' "Do you massage many people?"

"A few."

"Are they all women?"

I nodded reluctantly.

"And do you go through the same routine you just did with me?"

"More or less," I confessed, terrified of her reaction.

She frowned, but there was no explosion.

"Perhaps that's it," she said. "Do you enjoy massaging women and giving them oral sex afterwards?"

"I suppose so," I admitted. It felt like I was stepping through a minefield. Any false move and my legs would be blown away.

"And you don't have normal sex with them?"

"Not really," I said, hoping the vagueness of my answer would save me.

Mary looked at me suspiciously. I could see that she didn't believe me, but for some reason she let it go.

"All right," she said, drawing out the words. "I don't mind what you're up to because it seems to be doing you a lot of good. You're a million times more soft and caring than before. Sometimes, when I knew you at university, I felt you resented the way I treated you and you were even angry with me. That's why I didn't ask you to come to America. Now all that suppressed anger seems to be disappearing. It's great!"

She laughed in amazement.

"Do you know, I even felt you were worshipping me when you went down on me!"

Then a frown crossed her face.

"Like I said - I don't mind you giving these women oral sex, but that's where it stops. If you need to relieve yourself, then use your hand. Is that clear!"

"Yes Mary," I said, faint with relief.

She looked at the clock on the wall, swung herself off the massage table and began to dress.

"It's time I left to catch my plane," she said mildly. "You can come to the airport if you like."

"Oh great, thanks," I said enthusiastically, pleased that I had a little more time with her.

She gave me another suspicious stare, then relaxed.

"You really have changed, you know. You seem to be able to express your emotions more freely. Are you sure there's nothing you haven't told me?"

"No," I insisted. I hated lying to her but I didn't seem to have much choice.

I drove Mary to the airport. While waiting for her flight, we shared the most companionable conversation I could remember since we were together at university. Just as we were about to leave, she kissed me warmly on the cheek.

"It's been very relaxing being with you," she said. "Have you taken your annual holidays yet?"

I shook my head, wondering where this was leading.

"Would you like to spend a couple of weeks with me in the States?"

"Yes, I would," I said, with all the joy of a small child.

"I've taken my leave already," she explained, "but you won't mind giving me a relaxing massage when I come home from work will you?"

"No of course not." Was she kidding?

"There's work to do on the house," she went on. "That should keep you occupied during the day. I'll send you an email about the best time for you to come over." She paused. "I'll also pay your fare, because I can see you don't have much money; I always knew it was unlikely you'd get a decent job."

While I was still reeling from her words, Mary hurried through to the boarding lounge, giving me a wave just before she disappeared behind a screen. I returned to my flat in a daze. I was now seeing the benefits of the training the Sisterhood had given me. Mary seemed to like me more, she wanted me to visit her in America, and on top of that, pay my fare as well. It was all so different from before.

It was back to Janet for the next two Saturdays. I thought about the mystery play and the god Enki as she ordered me about and smacked my naked ass whenever she felt like it. I knew I wasn't a heavy player, like the actors I'd seen on stage, but I now realised I must be mildly masochistic to endure the way Janet treated me. Every week her behaviour seemed to get worse, though I made no protest. I cleaned her house, tidied her garden, gave her a massage and oral sex then left silently with an aching rear.

Then James rang. I went to see him the same evening.

"Have you thought about what a society would be like that worshipped the Great Mother?" he asked as we sat down. With James there were few preliminaries.

"I have, yes," I said. "I'm beginning to realise that our belief in a male god affects us unconsciously. We make all sorts of assumptions because of it."

"Give me an example."

"I know it's not a good one," I said, "but it hit me the other night when I was watching a old episode of 'Star Trek'. There's a common assumption in these programs that if we come across Alien civilisations they will generally be armed and some of them will want to conquer us. I really doubt if that's true. If there are aliens out there, they may be utterly different from us and completely uninterested in anything we have. I really think that an advanced civilisation wouldn't have any reason to overrun other intelligent life forms. It seems to me that popular Science Fiction stories on TV just project our own belligerence onto aliens so we can have the same old storyline of `baddies and goodies` set in Space."

James nodded encouragingly so I went on.

"I think a Science Fiction writer has the same problem as we have in imagining a society where there's no warfare or violence. How do you construct an interesting storyline if everyone lives in peace and harmony? I suppose that brings up the question of whether we'd find a co-operative and loving society so boring that we'd go looking for a fight to relieve the monotony."

"That, I would say, is another assumption," James reproved me. "It's possible to live an interesting and stimulating life without incessant conflict."

I was quick to take him up on this.

"Are you talking about sex here?" I said. "Sexual liberation can replace aggression?"

"It would help a lot," he agreed, "but it certainly wouldn't be the complete solution. There's no doubt it could improve our relationships with others and reduce frustration and anger. Love and human relationships can also be interesting to human beings, as we see with the many popular love songs and romantic stories."

"What about sadomasochism in relationships?"

"That's also an important issue. Sadomasochism is very dangerous when it's pushed underground into the unconscious. As a society, we'd be far better off if it was brought out into the light of day where the desires could be expressed without inflicting great suffering. We need to be able to see that it can be used positively as part of our learning experience on how to love. But to go back to the original question. There's something that male gods do that is even more damaging than encouraging conflict."

"I remember," I said quickly. "You've mentioned this before. Judgement. Male gods judge, condemn and punish."

"They do," James said gravely. "Jesus said, 'judge not', but he was ignored by most Christians, who have carried on deciding that someone else doesn't deserve to live or have any rights, throughout the history of the Church. The belief that it is somehow justifiable to judge and condemn others is the most damaging idea we hold. Not only has it led to genocide and oppression, cruelty and hate, it offers a spurious sense of superiority to those who judge. In every way possible, it divides us from each other instead of allowing us to unite."

"I still don't see how you can stop judgement," I said desperately. "If someone goes around mugging or raping others, it's natural to see him as evil and lock him up for life."

"You're living in a patriarchal community, so it's difficult to think in any other way. But it's possible in a society led by feminine values, where you can say 'no' to such a person without demonising him. The first step is to see every problem, every difference, from the perspective of the whole rather than the individual. That goes for the aggressor as well. He has to understand that he is part of humanity, not a separate unit clawing for individual advantage and satisfaction. After that comes acceptance of others as being just as valuable as you are. Once you saw that, you'd want to help the mugger to regain his love for others instead of hating and fearing him so much that you banish him forever."

It seemed to me that James was being outrageously naïve.

"Feminine values!" I protested. "I know plenty of women who'd administer a lethal injection tomorrow to a mugger or rapist if they could. They can be every bit as vicious in their judgements as men are!"

"That's why I said 'feminine values', not women," he said calmly.

"In a patriarchal society women are brainwashed by masculine thinking. If by a miracle all the countries of the world were ruled by women tomorrow, you wouldn't see many differences. After a generation you would, because women wouldn't have to behave like the worst kind of patriarchal man to get anywhere in the world. Think about it. If a woman decides to go into politics or business, she has to play by male rules of arrogance, ruthlessness and competition. If she doesn't, she never gets past first base. It's far easier to swallow masculine attitudes than insist that the rules are changed, even if you had the confidence to challenge them, which most women don't. By the same token, it's likely that most women will sit in judgement on men for some time to come and hate them with a passion. Men are evil oppressors who must be punished for their treatment of women and so on. There's an irony in that isn't there – men teaching women to judge and punish, then being hoist by their own petard!"

It was an interesting thought, but I had no time to consider it. James had consulted his watch and was pulling me to my feet.

"Time to go," he said. "Here's your hood. We'll talk about it in the car."

"So these women who will condemn and punish men," I asked as soon as James had settled into the journey, "are they the Devil from the Tarot pack?"

"They are," he said, "but the card doesn't just cover women who consciously want revenge on men for their crimes; it includes those who derive sadistic pleasure from inflicting pain. The Devil woman in the Tarot is the Sumerian Goddess Lilith who reappeared later as a Hebrew demon. To understand this archetype better you need to read about the Hindu Goddess Kali."

"Isn't she a sort of female Devil as well?"

"That's how Christian missionaries described her, but she's far more than that. I'll lend you some books about her when we get back."

More reading! I groaned inwardly before I remembered how much I'd enjoyed some of James' esoteric tomes. Maybe the Kali stuff would be equally riveting.

At the unknown house, I didn't have to wait very long for my teacher to arrive. She was carrying a cane. I wondered fearfully what it was for, hoping unrealistically that it wasn't for use on me. I couldn't avoid glancing at it while I kissed my teacher's feet. If she noticed my nervousness, she gave no indication, brightly enquiring,

"Has your girlfriend in America contacted you again?"

"Yes," I said with some enthusiasm. "She came to my flat for a couple of hours and then I saw her off at the airport."

"That's nice!" she exclaimed. "How did it go?"

"She said I'd changed for the better," I said joyfully, "and she wants me to spend two weeks with her in America."

"Wonderful! Now do you see how our training is helping you?"

"Yes I do," I admitted.

"I really hope it works out for you two," she said. "I think she's probably invited you over there to see how you might get on living together. You never know."

She patted my head. I was Rover again.

"And did you enjoy the mystery play?"

"Oh yes," I said, nearly adding 'mistress' but holding back at the last second. Now why had that popped into my head?

"Did you realise the significance of Enki's sacrifice?"

"Yes, Enki is the original Christ – the first sacrificial redeemer."

"Yes, yes," she said a little impatiently, "but why did Enki come into the Underworld to plead for Inanna's return, and why was he willing to take her place?"

"Because the world had become a wasteland without Inanna." I wondered what she was driving at with these questions. Clearly I hadn't come up with the right answer because she hissed at me in frustration.

"Yes, but what's the message to men of Enki's actions?"

This time I had to think before answering.

"Would it be," I said hesitantly, "that Enki -or Jesus- represents all men? To save the world, they have to sacrifice themselves to women."

"At last," she sighed. "The point of the play was that we are in a similar situation now. We're turning the planet into a wasteland. Unless men realise the harm they're doing and surrender their power to women, we're lost."

"But most men are totally unaware they need to do this. Either they don't see the problem, don't care or think they can fix it themselves – without women."

"Agreed. On the whole men are too blinded by arrogance and selfishness to be much use. Neither do they have the humility to realise that listening to women can save the situation. Is that correct?"

"Yes, mistress," I said. It felt right this time.

"You were a typical arrogant male when I first met you," my teacher mused as she patted my head again, "but under my tuition you're starting to change. Don't you agree?"

"Oh yes," I said. "Thank you. Thank you for everything you have done for me."

"You're beginning to understand," she said thoughtfully, "so I think it's time I gave you a lesson in sacrifice. Do you agree?"

I was suddenly afraid, but I could see no way out. I nodded my head dumbly and waited.

"I want to experience what it feels like to cane a man's bare ass. I know you don't like pain, but the question is, are you willing to sacrifice yourself to me so I can have the pleasure of caning you?"

I didn't know what to say. There was a war going on inside me, between the part of me that feared and resisted pain and the part that wanted to serve my teacher, please her in any way I could. My teacher picked up on my distress.

"You're really frightened aren't you? But you can't refuse the desires and wishes of a Goddess."

"I suppose not," I said miserably.

"You suppose not?" she repeated mockingly. I realised she was enjoying my fear and discomfort. "You should be ecstatically happy to do the bidding of a Goddess!"

"I'm sorry," I said, trying to stop myself from crying. "You're pushing me beyond my limits."

She leaned forward in her chair.

"I know," she gloated. "Isn't it fun? Well fun for me, not necessarily for you."

She got to her feet and picked up her cane.

"Right," she said. "Take off your pants and bend over."

I obeyed in a daze. Though I didn't want to fail my initiation tests neither did I want to be caned. Why couldn't she pick on someone who enjoyed it? Why me? A feeling of mixed humiliation and anger swept over me as I leaned forward.

"On second thoughts, get the shirt off as well," she instructed. "I don't want it hiding your ass. I want to see what I'm doing."

By now I was almost paralysed by my fear. I couldn't believe that this was happening but I managed to bend over, with my hands on my knees.

"Arch your back," she ordered, tapping me with the cane.

I did my best. When she was satisfied with my position, she moved with blinding speed, hitting me so hard that I fell forward onto my hands. The pain was terrible. I wanted to snatch the cane from her hand and fling it across the room, but a sense of powerlessness kept me in position.

"Keep your back arched," she said sternly, as I resumed my stance." I want your bottom nice and tight."

Somehow I managed to obey her. Time slowed down as she applied the cane another five times and it was only by detaching myself from the pain that I had the discipline to remain in position. I could feel tears sliding down my cheeks when she lowered the cane with a satisfied sigh.

"Six of the best," she said cheerily, "is enough for you. I might have needed more if you'd enjoyed it, so think yourself lucky."

She paused for a second as I started to raise my body and then realised she hadn't given me permission to do this, so I stopped half-way. She then struck a pose of mock anger as she pointed to my erection. Ignoring my profound embarrassment, she teased.

"Well, well! Where's your manners? Aren't you going to thank me for turning you on?"

"Thank you," I managed to say. The words were dragged from me by the fear of retribution if I remained silent.

She whacked me again.

"That's for not thanking me quickly enough."

"Thank you for correcting me," I blurted out, terrified she would hit me again.

"Correcting you?" she said testily, "I'm not correcting you, I'm doing it because I enjoy caning you. So what should you be saying?"

Fear made me think quickly.

"Thank you for the honour of giving you pleasure."

"Not bad," she said, "and what about the fact that I gave you the chance to sacrifice yourself to me?"

"Er, thank you for teaching me the true meaning of sacrifice."

"Much better," she mocked. " Now straighten up."

I levered myself upright and wiped the tears from my eyes.

"You really don't like pain, do you?" she said, with a slightly sympathetic tone in her voice.

"No," was all I could say, as fresh tears welled up.

"Well it's over," she said quietly. "Set up your massage table and relax. I've had my fill for today."

I spent the next hour massaging her, slowly releasing both my teacher's tensions and my own. The ache of my battered flesh began to diminish.

"I think I'll try a little suck," she instructed me after I had finished the massage. "Caning you has really turned me on."

I moved to obey her and found it was true. She was slick with moisture under my tongue.

"You remember what I said about massage and cooking?" she interrupted after a few seconds.

"Mmm," I said, briefly looking up.

"It applies to cunnilingus as well. The more a man expresses love and worship when he's sucking her off, the better the woman enjoys it. So I don't want you holding back on your feelings."

I reflected on my current situation. I'd been caned for no reason except my teacher's pleasure, used as a masseur and for oral sex and I was now expected to display love and devotion. I certainly felt I was being severely tested. Her words stirred two different sets of feelings. One was a powerful feeling of devotion and sexual desire, the other was resentment and anger at the way I'd been treated. For a while there was an internal war between these conflicting emotions until I somehow managed to push the anger to one side and concentrated on my feelings of devotion. After that it was easy. My teacher soon reached a shuddering orgasm, but waved her hand imperiously for me to continue. There were three more climaxes before I was allowed to stop, bone-weary and with an aching tongue. Then I had to thank her for the privilege of giving her pleasure and kiss her feet again.

"Did you feel you were giving me love and devotion?" she asked languidly.

"I hope so," I replied.

"It was there," she admitted, "but you were angry as well. We need to explore that sometime."

I helped her dress before she left the room. Part of me hoped I'd never see her again.

When James came back, he looked at me with concern.

"Are you all right?" he asked, bending over me to examine my drawn face.

I felt tempted to tell him the truth, but stopped myself.

"Yes I'm fine," I said wearily, accepted my hood and walked out with him to the car.

It was uncomfortable sitting down again. The fresh pain provoked me into expressing some of my fears to James.

"Do you have to be a heavy BDSM player to pass this initiation?" I tentatively asked.

"No, of course not," James answered. He seemed surprised.

"Then why was I caned?"

"Where you caned!" he said in surprise.

"Yes," I said, "and it really hurt, I can still feel it,"

"Did you ask to be caned?"

"No," I said firmly.

"I see," he said in a troubled voice.

"So will I get more canings?"

"I can't say," said James. Suddenly he seemed as powerless as me, despite his wealth and erudition.

"Were you caned or whipped when you were initiated?"

"No," he answered. "It only happens to a few of our male initiates, the ones who need to see their own internal attraction to violence and bring it out into the open."

"That doesn't apply to me," I said confidently, "I've never hit anyone in my life."

"I'm sure you haven't, but that's not the issue. You spend a lot of time watching martial arts films and Hollywood stuff with lashings of gun battles. You read books about War…."

I jumped in before he could finish his sentence.

So what! It's just harmless fantasy."

"No such thing, dear boy. It's what excites you. Tell me, who do you identify with in these films?"

I had to think.

"The hero, I suppose." I shrugged. What did it matter? No way did I take the stories seriously, anyway.

"And he's a man who solves a problem, or rights a wrong through the use of force."

I thought he was missing the point.

"It's only because he has to; there's no other alternative!"

"Isn't there? The director wants you to see it that way, to collude with him in believing that violence is justified in certain circumstances, that it solves problems and leaves the perpetrator with only clean hands and a righteous glow of satisfaction."

Not for the first time, I was astonished at James' unworldly attitudes.

"Right! So it wasn't okay to defend ourselves against Hitler and rescue Kuwait from Saddam Hussein." I couldn't keep the contempt entirely out of my voice, but he was unmoved.

"It's not about that, Arthur, it's about your preoccupation with violence, and the thrill you get from identifying vicariously with an aggressor. You do it over and over again, because you're addicted to the feelings it gives you. Your teacher turns the tables on you and it still excites you."

I felt a hot blush of shame rise to my cheeks. How had he known that the caning gave me an erection?

"Whatever you do, don't deny what's happening or suppress it. Accept yourself honestly. It might be uncomfortable, but it's the only way to grow."

It took me some time to calm down and by then I needed to change the subject. Hearing a few details of James' initiation had sparked my curiosity, so I plunged in with fresh questions.

"Can you tell me more about what it was like for you when you started?"

"It was nearly forty years ago. An awful lot's changed since then."

"In what way?"

He steered us round a few sharp curves before speaking again.

"When I was initiated everything was far more relaxed. It's much tougher now. Back in the 1960's everything was going our way. We had influential people in governments, in the media, in the music industry and in big business. Then it all changed in the 1970's. An important member of our organisation suddenly found God and became a born-again Christian. He betrayed a large number of our members to our opponents. The result was that some were sacked, others were frozen out of decision- making positions and a few were murdered. It couldn't have happened at a worse time."

"Between the 1930's and the 1970's Western governments were competing with Communism for the hearts and minds of the people. The ruling elite in the West was frightened that if it didn't give people what they wanted, they'd become Communists. So they relaxed their stranglehold a bit. The gap between rich and poor shrank, human rights groups sprang up and there was a lifting of sexual repression. The Women's Liberation movement burst onto the scene. In those days we were working behind the scenes, giving help and feeding ideas to activists. But it all went wrong.

"In the 1970's it became clear that Communism was at the point of collapse. The expenditure of the Cold War was putting too much strain on the economies of both the Soviet Union and China and they wanted peace. When they realised that Communism was no longer a threat, the Western ruling elite changed everything in a flash. Keynesian economics, which is the economics of full employment, was replaced by Monetarism, which creates high levels of unemployment."

"You've mentioned Keynesian economics before," I interrupted, struggling to remember the context.

"Do you know much about it?" he asked.

"A bit," I said. "I looked it up on the Internet but I didn't get a clear explanation of how it works."

"It's quite easy to understand," James explained "It was used to take Western countries out of the Depression of the 1930's. What you do is find or make work for everyone, creating full employment, however artificial. This results in everyone having surplus money. People spend their money in shops, which creates a demand for factories to produce more goods. That way the economy is kick-started to full production again."

"Sounds like a win-win situation," I said.

"It is for the poor, but in the long term it means losses for the rich and wealthy. Unfortunately they are the ones with power. As soon as Communism stopped being a threat, they went for Keynsianism's throat and killed it stone dead."

"I never read anything like this at University."

"You might have done in the 60's and 70's," he said feelingly, "but not any more. Censorship rules."

"I thought we were supposed to have free speech and a free press in the West."

"Of course we don't," he said scathingly. "Even you ought to know that most media outlets are owned by a handful of people who filter information ruthlessly, often at the behest of governments and special interests. Control of information has always been the best tool of oppression next to violence. The important point to note in the West is that the censorship is cleverly disguised. We have the illusion of freedom but not its reality."

"I didn't realise," I said lamely. "I suppose there's so much mention of freedom that I believed we had some."

"Back to economics," James continued. "The 'powers that be' claim Monetarism holds down inflation. What they don't tell you is that it does this by keeping unemployment high. That reduces the power of the ordinary workers. They put up with poor pay and conditions because they're afraid of losing their jobs. In a Keynsian economy of full employment, they might leave for something better if they're dissatisfied. Anyway, what we have now is a widening gap between rich and poor. Not only that, we make sure Third World countries can't compete with the West by engineering huge debts. They stay poor, we stay rich. It's been a depressing time, the last thirty years."

"But you've recovered?" I asked hopefully.

"Slowly, very slowly," he said. "We've had to reorganise ourselves to survive. The initiations are a lot tougher too, to try and eliminate spies and traitors. That's why you've been given a hard time. Also, I have to say that some young women today are nothing like the women of my generation. They're aware of what's been done to them by the patriarchy and many of them want blood!."

"You don't have to tell me," I said, trying to find a way to sit comfortably. I was still shifting restlessly in my seat when another thought popped into my head.

"If you've been betrayed by traitors, then your opponents have the same knowledge of the past as you have."

"True," James agreed. "The difference is they're not interested. All they want to do is preserve their power, which means removing any agents of change today. Yesterday is irrelevant. We see our ancient knowledge as a means to enlighten humankind, they see it as dangerous to their position. I really wish our opponents were stirred by what falls into their hands; they might learn something."

"Do you keep your secret stuff in underground libraries or something?" I asked him.

He laughed.

"You don't expect me to tell you, surely? All you need to know is that it's completely safe, in a place where our opponents can never find or destroy it."

"That sounds a bit mysterious," I said, grinning inside my hood, "I'll have to treat it as a riddle. It sounds like one."

I had no more questions to distract me from my pain. It was a relief to reach James' house, where I could stand again and down a stiff drink to ease the ache. James seemed sympathetic.

"Did she hit you hard?"

"As hard as she possibly could," I told him, wincing at the memory.

"I'm afraid that some of the young women today are completely ruthless," he commiserated with me.

"Does it happen to them?"

"Of course not," he said with an abrupt laugh. "They're taught to be dominant."

"So a dominant man or a submissive woman wouldn't be able to join your organisation."

"Not usually," he agreed, "though it's complicated by the fact that most people are neither one nor the other. Most of us are a mixture; we have both dominant and submissive traits in us, triggered in different situations. You can have a man, for instance, who regularly goes to a Dominatrix to be beaten and humiliated yet is married to a very submissive woman. Or you can have a woman who runs her own company but wants to play the submissive role when she has sex. We've had apparently dominant men amongst the spies who've infiltrated our opponents' organisations. In the workplace they behaved like a macho man, yet they were excited by Goddess worship and often risked their careers and sometimes their lives to help us."

"So are there men who pass the sternest test - being beaten and humiliated by women - who can still betray you?"

"I'm afraid so," he said gravely, "and it's happened more than once. Sometimes it's easier to be a traitor than admit what you are."

"I know we've been over this before," I said hesitantly, " but I still don't understand how you've survived all these years of persecution, betrayal and infiltration. You should have been eliminated long ago."

"You're right, Arthur. I can't go into detail, but take it from me that we'd have disappeared if we hadn't received assistance from a special source that's kept us alive even at the worst times. You'll find out more after your final initiation and test, but for now let's just say that we've led a charmed life."

"You're being mysterious again," I said, slightly peeved by this second riddle. I hated not knowing.

"It's not such a big mystery," James reassured me, "as long as you're willing to consider the possibility that we are not alone. If you believe that human consciousness is as good as it gets, think again."

"What do you mean? Are you talking about spiritual help or aliens or what? And why doesn't whatever it is intervene and give us direct help and guidance?"

He smiled sadly. I could tell I was disappointing him.

"It doesn't work that way. We've chosen to be individuals, to see ourselves as completely separate from each other, especially if we're male. We've even acquired a body that symbolises this; it says 'inside this skin is me, outside this skin is not me'. We are a long, long way from an awareness of the One, the unity that really describes who and what we are. It might be exciting being a separate individual, making our own decisions and living with the consequences, but when things go wrong, it's difficult to connect with our Source to get help. We've forgotten how to do it and where it is. Because we were the ones to leave home, as it were, the Great Mother has to wait for our call before she can help us. She can't rush in without our permission."

James leaned forward to emphasise the importance of his next words.

"What is difficult for almost everyone to understand is that the help and succour that's given benefits everyone. You can't be helped to hurt others, because The One doesn't see you that way. So you're given information and insight that might seem incomprehensible because you still think in terms of 'what's in it for me', and you reject it. All over the world people are insisting that god is on their side, or at least he ought to be, and failing to listen to what will save them, because they think they already know what the answer should be. They're missing the point entirely."

I wasn't sure I understood anything of what he'd just said and my butt was still throbbing, so I moved back to my original complaint.

"I can't see how beating me up helps me!"

James sighed patiently. I seemed to have this effect on him a lot of the time.

"Now I have to admit I don't really approve of this, it was a decision by a teenage girl and I don't believed it was sanctioned by the Sisterhood. Not if it was done against your will, but I could be wrong. I am not privy to the decision of the Sisterhood."

"So will you report her," I asked.

"I will mention what happened," said James, "that is all I can do."

"So what if they don't take any notice and allows my teacher to continue to cane me?"

"I can't say," admitted James, "all I can say is that I really doubt they will let your teacher continue to do this, if you haven't given your consent."

I shook my head.

"I really don't want to be caned again." I said.

"You seem to be very unfortunate in being given a sadistic teacher," commented James, "If you don't want to face a situation like this again I personally would suggest using science of mind."

"Are you suggesting it is my fault," I said angry, "because I haven't used your affirmation."

"Certainly not in the short term," James admitted, "but in the long term if you want to stop getting into situations like this, then I would strongly suggest you use positive affirmations."

"So this is how you see it," I said continuing with my anger, "you think this I all my fault because I have created this reality. Well I can tell you straight, it is something I really didn't want."

"Off course you didn't create this reality consciously, but that is not the issue. It doesn't matter who is to blame, the point is that you are in a reality that you don't like, and the surest way to change this, is to use science of mind to change your reality. I can help you to do this if you are willing."

I just shrugged my shoulders, in defiance.

"All right, perhaps you are not ready yet," commented James quietly

He got to his feet and I followed suit

"Don't think about it now. You need some rest, before you can see straight. Go home,"

"Just one more thing," I pleaded. "What's the name of the organisation I'm being initiated into."

"Very well," he said, "I can't see the harm in telling you. It's called the Sisterhood of Naked Isis."

"Why Naked Isis?"

"Because the Goddess has been censored for thousands of years, so the Sisterhood is of the true Isis, who hasn't been dressed in patriarchal clothing, like the Virgin Mary has. Also, nudity is a symbol of seeing another person as they really are, without cultural adornment or bias, so it's about the true self."

James had opened the door by this time, but I ploughed on.

"Is that why Witches traditionally worshipped in the nude?"

"One of the reasons," he admitted, pushing me gently into the drive. " I have to say that Naked Isis is a fairly modern invention. In the past we've called ourselves after ancient names of the Great Mother. Each name was then turned into that of an evil male god by our opponents, seeking to undermine us. So today we use the word Isis; it hasn't been denigrated or given a bad press yet, so it will do for the present."

He saw me to my car, waving cheerfully at me as I drove off and I settled down uncomfortably in my seat for the journey home. I tried not to think about my teacher, but with no success. She seemed as contrary and complex as me. On the one hand, she'd been genuinely happy and supportive about Mary, yet it hadn't stopped her wanting the sadistic pleasure of caning me. Then there was my own internal conflict. One part of me was resentful and angry at the abuse meted out to me, but another part longed to worship her. I wondered how it would be possible to resolve all these contradictions within me.

# CHAPTER FOURTEEN

I visited Janet as usual the following Saturday. By now it was routine for me to strip off before I did her housework. As I removed the last of my clothing, Janet was watching me and noticed the cane marks striping my rear.

"What are these?" she asked, rubbing her hand over the welts.

"I had an accident," I mumbled, immediately moving away to get my cleaning equipment. It was the only excuse I could come up with at short notice. Janet didn't buy it.

"An accident! What sort of accident!" she exclaimed. "This looks more like cane marks to me. Who did it!"

"I went to a Dominatrix," I lied, digging a very large hole for myself. I couldn't tell her the truth but it was a stupid evasion to try on someone with Janet's proclivities.

"Why spend money going to a person like that?" she asked resentfully. "I would have done it for nothing. I didn't realise you enjoyed heavy punishment."

"I don't," I explained. "I just did it as an experiment. After one stroke I knew it wasn't for me, no way. I never want to be caned like that, ever again."

"Well there's definitely more than one stroke on your ass," she said excitedly. "You sure you didn't like it? You seem to have taken a long time to tell her to stop."

"We agreed on six strokes, beforehand." I said lamely, wishing I was a better liar. Janet snorted in disbelief.

"Oh come on! That's a crock of shit. Tell me the truth."

"Honestly, I hated being caned," I insisted. "It was a total misunderstanding. I didn't think it would hurt so much and I'm never going to repeat the experience. Never."

She looked at me thoughtfully. I could see she didn't believe me, but she just shrugged and left the room. It was a relief to see her go, but short-lived. Half an hour later, as I bent to pick something off the floor, I felt a hard blow across my bottom that brought tears to my eyes. I turned round to see Janet grinning at me, a thick strap in her hand.

"Gotcha!" she said maliciously.

"Please," I begged her. "That really hurt. The scars haven't properly healed yet."

"I've got you worked out," she said, ignoring my plea. "You like to pretend that you don't like being caned, but deep down it's what you really want."

"No!" I protested. "Honestly! I'm not playing that sort of game."

"Off course you're not," she laughed. "Now tell me what safe word you used with this Dom."

"I didn't use any safe word. It was only an agreement beforehand."

"Did she tie you up?"

"No, of course she didn't." It was the truth, but it only made the situation worse.

"So you bent over for six strokes, voluntarily, " she said, her eyes glistening with excitement, "and then you tell me you didn't want it. Yeah, right!"

Before I could react, she danced to one side of me, swung her strap and fetched me another hard slap on my ass. I clutched myself for protection and backed away from her.

"Listen. Please believe me," I pleaded. "I honestly don't want to be hit."

Unfortunately, I'd backed myself into the coffee table. As I lost my balance, Janet pushed me and I fell across the table on my side. She was quick to seize her chance. Within seconds she'd delivered two more stinging whacks with her strap. The pain moved me all the way from frightened to angry in one jump. Gripped by an uncontrollable rage, I grabbed both her hands.

"Listen!" I yelled into her face. "You fucking, stupid woman! That really hurt! I do not want to be spanked! How many fucking times do I have to tell you!"

She was completely shocked by my reaction. Tears briefly welled in her eyes before her own anger rose.

"How dare you speak to me like that!" she screamed.

"It's the only way I can get you to fucking listen!" I bawled back.

I was still gripping her wrists. She began to twist her arms to extricate them, all the while hurling abuse at me. Realising I was still restraining her, I let go, but my timing was out. I released her at the same moment that she violently pulled away from me and she went sprawling on the floor. I bent forward to try to help her up but she rolled away from me, screaming.

"Get out! Get out of my house!"

"Look, I'm sorry," I said, calmer now that I was safe from attack. "This is just a mistake. I didn't mean to yell at you."

"I don't care!" she shrieked. "Just get out and don't ever come back!"

It seemed prudent to leave. There was clearly no way to reason with her while she was upset, so I quickly put my clothes on and left. It was only when I was driving away that the implications of what had happened hit me. Was this another test? If so, did I fail it? I wondered if she would rat on me to James.

I didn't have long to wait. Shortly after I reached home, the phone rang. My heart sank as I heard James' voice.

"I've had a hysterical phone call from Janet," he said in his usual calm tones. "I think you'd better come round and explain it all to me."

I drove to his house with a sinking feeling in my stomach, which intensified when I saw the video camera set up in his living room.

"This interview is being filmed," he said formally. "Please sit over there." He indicated a straight-backed chair opposite the camera and I thought wistfully of his soft leather couches as I took my seat.

"Janet phoned me about an hour ago," he said, after placing himself at some distance from me. "She was greatly distressed. She claims you yelled at her and hit her."

"I may have shouted at her," I responded as calmly as I could, "but I certainly didn't hit her."

"Tell me exactly what happened."

"Janet likes me to do her housework in the nude," I began, then recounted the whole sorry tale to him as best I could. It sounded childish and tawdry to me, but I was still convinced I'd had no alternative. Surely James would see that.

"So you admit you lost your temper with her."

"Well, yes, I did. But she was totally convinced I was playing some sort of 'no means yes' game - and it became impossible to convince her otherwise. The only way I could get through to her was to shout."

"And you grabbed her."

"It was the only way I could stop her hitting me."

"She also claims you held her so tightly that you bruised her wrists."

"She was struggling with me!" I protested. "I was only trying to restrain her! I certainly didn't want to hurt her in any way."

"Yet you struggled with her so fiercely that you pushed her to the floor." His voice had a relentless quality I'd never heard before. It scared the hell out of me.

"She only lost her balance!" I whined. I could feel anger rising up in me again. James was my friend; why couldn't he see what had happened and back me up?

"You also swore at her and called her stupid."

"It wasn't that bad! All right, I did use a few swear words, but like I said, it was the only way I could get through to her."

"Very well," he said, quietly. "Is there anything else you want to say."

"It was just a complete misunderstanding from start to finish. Janet got hold of the wrong end of the stick and she wouldn't listen. I lost my temper out of complete frustration. She was hurting me, for God's sake!"

"That's it?" he asked calmly.

"I think so," I sighed. "I certainly never intended to harm her or be rude to her and I certainly didn't hit her. I am willing to go around and apologise if that will help."

"I wouldn't advise you to do that," he said darkly.

He got up and turned off the camera.

"I'm sorry I had to act as prosecutor, but it's the role I'm expected to play."

"How does it look?" I asked nervously. "Will they accept that it was only a misunderstanding?"

He shook his head sadly.

"I can't say. It's in the hands of the Sisterhood."

"I wish there'd been a witness there. They'd support me. So when will I know the verdict?"

"I don't know that either," he said. "All I can say is that you should hear within a week. They won't drag it out."

I drove home feeling sick, realising just how much the organisation meant to me. I had been given a chance to read uncensored knowledge about the true history of the human race. Now, because of one silly mix-up this opportunity might be taken away. I fretted endlessly over the next three days until a call came from James. He wouldn't tell me what the verdict was. When I got to his house, he looked very sombre and I feared the worst.

"Sit down," he said gravely, pouring me a drink.

"They don't want me, do they?"

James sighed deeply.

"They are split about whether to keep you."

I leapt to my feet.

"But it was only a misunderstanding," I protested. "Surely they see that."

"Maybe it was to you, but the Sisterhood saw it as an opportunity to witness your true nature. Had you run away from her they would have understood, but instead you became aggressive."

"I couldn't have run out of her house in the nude!"

"It might have been better if you had. I know it was a difficult situation, but the bottom line is that aggression from men is never tolerated by the Sisterhood. You had a choice; run or attack, and you attacked."

"Can't I appeal?" I said desperately. "Is there any way I can redeem myself? I'm willing to be tied up and whipped as long as they like, if that's what it takes."

He shook his head.

"I'm afraid it's not about your ability to endure pain; it never has been. The experiences you've had were designed to bring you to the point where pretence couldn't work and what was hidden was revealed. You showed that you capable of being very aggressive with a women, which doesn't go down well with the Sisterhood. But on the other hand your teacher spoke up on your behalf; she said she probably pushed you too hard too quickly."

"So there is a chance they will overlook me losing my temper." I said hopefully.

"There is that chance," admitted James, "Anyway they will want to speak to you in person."

He picked up a hood from the table and I was soon on my crazy journey in his car. When we reached our destination I went through the usual routine of removing my clothes.

"When you go in, do not try to speak before you are allowed to," James warned me.

Then there was a knock at the door and with sweaty palms and a racing heart I crawled into the room. I was surprised to find there was now five veiled women looking down at me. Some were bare breasted others wore a dresses where the neckline was cut at an angle exposing one breast while the women in the centre had both breasts covered up.

"You know why you are here," said the women in the middle of this group. She had a unfamiliar voice and so I hadn't met her before. She seems older than the others.

"Er, yes," I said nervously.

"Then tell us in you own words exactly what happened," She said, "starting with your relationship with your teacher."

As calmly as I could I told the whole story. I had rehearsed countless of times in my mind, over the last few days, what I was going to say in my defence, so I found it easy give a clear description of what happened.

When I had finished the women looked at each other and some nodded to each other and I didn't know if that was a good or bad.

The woman in the centre turned to me again.

"You description of events are very similar to what your teacher told us, who incidentally has spoken up strongly in your defence. It is very different to the story Janet told James, but we also realise she is a drama queen and will normally greatly exaggerated anything that happens to her."

"First of all we all want to apologise for you, to have to endure violence inflicted onto you without your consent. We don't condone it and it should never have happened. Will you accept our deepest and most humble apology?"

That shocked me I didn't expect them to do that!

"Um, yes off course," I stuttered.

"Thank you," She said with a slight bow. "Now the other problem is that you were very aggressive with a woman, which we also don't condone. We understand you were defending yourself and we know Janet has a history of violence against men. The only problem we have is that you didn't handle the situation very well and did lose your temper and was no longer in control of yourself. We sent you to Janet to test how you would behave with a difficult women and you have clearly failed that test. But in your defence, the test was made far more difficult than we intended. Though I have to say, we women have had put up with thousands of years of violence from men. So what you had to endure from your teacher and Janet is very mild compared with what women even today have to accept from men in many third world countries and even in western countries. So you will be given a second chance, you will be tested again but if you do ever lose your temper with a woman again and lose control, you will be out. Is that clear."

"Yes, very clear," I said in relief.

"You may go."

"Oh thank you, thank you," I said as I backed away.

I was surprise at the emotion in my voice and realise just how important this group had become to me. On my way home in James' car I felt very confused. I now knew I wanted to stay in this group and yet I was also spying on it. I now began to question if I really wanted continue to do this, but how could I stop? I certainly didn't know how this shadowy government organisation would react if I tried to resign. I now wanted to tell James what I was doing but I didn't think it was the right time to tell him. I had just had a narrow escape from being expelled from the group, if I told James I was a spy, they more than likely would throw me out. Then I thought about my teacher who had it seems spoken up for me.

"Will my teacher be punished or told off because she beat me against my will?" I asked James.

"Very unlikely," he replied.

"Oh," I said in surprised.

"We try to get people to be as honest about themselves as possible. Which means that if we punishing or censoring people's behaviour, then this is the sure way to make people secretive. The Sisterhood would see it as a good thing that your relationship with your teacher brought out into the open her sadistic desires. This means they can find ways to deal with this by finding ways for her to some understanding why she has these feelings."

"How will they do that?"

"By getting her to talk about her feelings but not in a way that does not condemn her or make her feel ashamed of herself."

"So you are saying it is perfectly all right for her to be a sadist."

"No, it is not something that the Sisterhood encourages in their membership. Yet at the same time they know that to condemn it will not overcome this desire because all it will do is drive it underground into the unconscious mind. So the only way to bring such behaviour into the conscious mind, where it can be dealt with, is to treat people with love and understanding."

"Well what about me," I complained, "I was on the receiving end of this sadistic behaviour."

"What happened to you was unfortunate, but again it brought out into the open a behaviour pattern that the Sisterhood doesn't encourage. It seems that you can be provoked into violence against a woman, even if it was very mild. It does suggest you need more training and testing."

I didn't know how to respond to this and kept quiet. Our journey soon came to an end and when we had sat down he had poured me a large drink, and looked at me sympathetically.

"Arthur," he said gently, "Would you accept you might have a very negative programme within your unconscious, in your relationship with women?"

I looked at him in surprised.

"I don't understand," I said.

"I know many men, whom, if they had the same experiences as you. Would claim women treat them very badly. Do you think that is true?"

"Well, yes, I do seem to be unlucky. What is your point."

"Your girlfriend Mary has given you what many people believe is a hard time, and has left you in limbo for many years. Now you suddenly have had very bad experience with both your teacher and Janet. Do you think that is just bad luck or do you see a pattern in all this."

"I suppose you are now going to say I created this." I said sourly.

"Only on the unconscious level," he said smoothly, "but don't you think your reality in your relationships with women, might be self-destructive."

I very much resented this suggestion, but it also frightened me. I began to think about Mary.

"It wasn't my idea to get involved with my teacher or Janet. It was suggested by you and the Sisterhood."

"I agree, but you have had difficult relationship with women before you joined our group and this pattern of behaviour is still continuing, and seems to be getting worse. I want to help you to change this."

"Your not suggesting that it is impossible for me to have a relationship with my girlfriend Mary, because I have this self-destructive programme?"

"I can't say, but it is a possibility I would like to discuss with you. You just had a experience where your teacher broke the rules and caned you without your consent. Then Janet done the same and nearly had you thrown out of the organization. Don't you find it strange that you had a very difficult time with two women is such a short space of time?

"Like you said, I just put it down to just bad luck," I admitted.

"You must be aware by now, that I don't believe in luck."

"All right, if what you say is true, what can I do about it?"

"Can you imagine yourself having a loving and caring relationship with a women where everything works out for best for both of you?"

"Well yes, I suppose so."

"That is all you have to do, but do it every day."

"That sounds too easy."

"It may not be as easy as it sounds. If you do have a self-destructive program in your unconscious mind, then doing this will provoke it into flooding your conscious mind with negative memories and thoughts about relationships. This is where you then have to be strong and do not give in to these negative memories and thoughts. See it as a opportunity of self-awareness, of finding out what is going on in your unconscious mind. Then feed yourself with positive thoughts about the relationships you want to have with women. If you find this too difficult, then use positive affirmations like; 'I always have loving and caring relationships with women'. That is only a suggestion, it is better to find your own affirmations that suit you. Remember your conscious mind is the boss, the programmer of the unconscious mind. For many people who are not aware of the science of mind, their unconscious mind is in charge, and this is not how it should be. The unconscious mind is a very willing and faithful servant but can be a tyrannical master if it takes control."

"Oh, I see," I said, the thought of trying to battle with my unconscious mind frightened me. James picked this up.

"You look apprehensive," he said.

"I don't know why, I find it scary."

James frowned in thought.

"There is another way to look at this," he said, "do you think that unconsciously you want to be punished by women?"

"Why should I want to do that?"

"This is becoming increasingly commonplace nowadays. Many men will paid a lot of money to go a dominatrix to be tortured and humiliated. While others are greatly attracted to sadistic women and will allow these women to physically and verbally abuse them. Even though they are bigger and stronger than the woman."

"Well, I'm not like that!" I said forcefully.

"Perhaps not now, but it does seem to be the direction you are heading."

This upset me, not only had I been abused by both my teacher and Janet. James was now suggesting I was, 'asking for it'.

"Why should I want to be punished by women," I demanded.

James lowered his head in thought. Then he raised his head slowly.

"We men," he said gently, "have been abusing women for thousands of years. And it still goes on today in many third world countries. To understand the nature of this abuse I would recommend you read the book, 'The Colour Purple" by Alice Walker. It is about a girl whom is raped regularly from the age of 14 by her step-father. She conceives two children from this rape and the step-father sells the children for money. The only way the girl can cope with this extreme abuse, is to not allow herself to feel anything. Now this is just the story of one woman, but similar abuse has happened to millions of women all over the world."

"Yes, but I have never abused any woman in my life." I pointed out. "So why should I want women to hurt me?"

"We men, have been abusing women for thousands of years, and we all have a collective responsibility for this. From the pattern of your behaviour, you are also like this, which is a good thing, but you are also resisting it as well. Now men like you and me have two possible paths. They can try to make up for this collective abuse by learning how to love and care for others. Or we can go down the path of wanting women to take their revenge on us. You, it seems are using both paths. You are slowly learning how to love, care and serve women. But because of some resistance in this, you are also to some degree, wanting to be abuse by them as well."

I didn't know how to take this. I was very uncomfortable with the idea that I owed a debt to all women, for just being a man. Yet somehow it also rang true, I realised that as he said it, I did feel this way.

"Were you like this?" I asked, "have you been abused by women."

James paused before he answered.

"As a young man I did go to prostitutes that specialised in making men do housework. I know this is not a issue today, but back in the 1950s this was a big-deal, because it was considered 'unmanly' for men to do housework then. Then when I got married I discovered that my wife was a sadist. Because I was incapable of resisting her she became increasingly abusive towards me. She also took lovers and enjoyed telling me about them but forbade me to do the same. Fortunately at about this time I joined the Sisterhood and they taught me why she was behaving like this and how to serve her. I then discovered that the better I was in serving her, the less she became abusive towards me. To the degree she overcome her sadism and was invited to join the Sisterhood."

This was news to me, I never realised he had a wife.

"So are you saying," I said, "if I learn to serve women better, I won't be abuse by them."

James gave a small sigh.

"There is no strict rules about this. I know this worked for me, but I can't claim it will work for everyone. Because we men have been abusing women for thousands of year, we assume that if women took control of our world, they will want their revenge. The trouble is that hatred and revenge are very negative emotions and many women will not want to feel them. They far prefer the emotions of love and nurturing. So men will find themselves in the position of being only able to pay back a karma debt to women through service. Which will be far more preferable to many women."

"Oh", I said in surprise, "So are you saying that the Sisterhood doesn't agree with women taking revenge on men. If that is the case why did you send me to a woman like Janet?"

James gave a shake of his head.

"No, it is not about disapproving of revenge and hatred. The Sisterhood finds it perfectly understandable that many women hate men and want revenge. As well as understanding why some men want to be abused by women, to pay back a karma debt. It is just about a personal preference. The aim of the Sisterhood is to create a feminine world of love, compassion and nurture. Hatred and revenge do not have a place is such a world. But it is not a rule or command. It is just the realisation that hated is a negative emotion that doesn't bring joy or happiness to the person feeling this emotion. It is love and caring that brings us happiness. Women understand this, better than men. We men try to look for happiness through ego gratification of winning or power or possession of material goods. But it is love that brings about true happiness and this is why men need to be encouraged to learn how to love."

"Oh," I said again, "how do I do this?"

"You are doing this already, by following your feelings of wanting to serve and worship women. Also you can use the affirmation; 'I live in a compassionate, loving and caring world' will also be a help."

"How can that be a help?" I asked in a puzzled voice.

James gave a slight shrug.

"The more you attempt to consciously fill your mind with thoughts of love. The more you will attract loving feelings and experiences to you."

"I'm not opposed to it, it is a wonderful idea, it just sounds so impractical. I really can't believe we all can live in a caring and compassionate world by repeating a affirmation like this."

"You say it is a wonderful but impractical idea. Can you think of a reason why living in a compassionate and caring world would be scary?"

"No?" I said in surprise.

"Think about it, you are unconsciously opposed to this, why?"

"I just don't think a compassionate and caring world is possible, I suppose." I said without much conviction.

James sat back and frowned, thinking about what he was going to say next.

"You've heard me use the phase, 'Know thyself,'" he finally said. 'The complete saying is 'Man, know thyself, and thou shalt know the universe and god'. Many people search for the truth in books, or religious doctrine. They go to far-flung places like India and Tibet, or join a secret society. Yet the complete truth is never outside you, it is within you. You already know it."

"But how do we access it?"

He smiled approvingly.

"A good question;" he said. "In order to answer you, I've got to take you back to the notion of the collective unconscious. It contains the wisdom and insight of the whole of human kind. Most people don't access this vast reservoir of accumulated knowledge because they believe they are alone, separated from communication with others and the One. It never occurs to us that it exists and can be contacted, yet we don't while the illusion of separation has such a strong hold on us."

"So how can I access the One," I said, "If I believe I'm separate from it?"

"The very fact that you are aware it might exist, is a good start. Like I said, the concept of separation is an illusion; it's not real. If we keep on questioning our belief that we are all alone, then it begins to collapse. Information and insight starts to reach us and eventually we trust it enough to let go of our conviction that our minds are locked away from others forever, behind a barrier of blood and bone."

"So all I have to do is deny my belief that I'm separate from the One and all the knowledge of the universe will be at my disposal."

He laughed.

"Not quite," he said. "It's a first step, though. Then you will have to learn how to tune in to what will best help you. It's like going on the World Wide Web for the first time. There may be a vast amount of knowledge on the Internet but you have to learn how to find it. This is also true of the collective unconscious."

"I see," I said. "Is this what you were hinting at when you said the knowledge you have cannot be destroyed by your enemies, because it's safe in the collective unconscious."

"Partly. Truth can never be destroyed, but the ability to access it can be lost or forgotten. Once intuition and spiritual insight are derided as impossible in a society, we lose our channels of information, or they become unreliable. It becomes difficult to distinguish between what is imagination or ego stuff and what is genuine insight. We have to be very cautious about accepting someone else's word on what is truth. It can be dangerous."

"Are you saying I need to become a medium or something, to contact the One?"

"No. Certainly not," he said, shaking his head vigorously. "All creative people tap into the collective unconscious, whether they know it or not. We all do. The only thing that stops us doing it full-time is fear. Somehow we've got hold of the idea that if we recognise our connection to others and the One, our freedom to choose for our selves will disappear; we will no longer be able to act as lone individuals, totally independent of others. They will have to be considered in our decisions. To safeguard this supposed freedom, we're willing to deny ourselves the love and wisdom of the universe!"

"I can understand that fear," I said. "When you talk about the One it sometimes sounds like you're describing the Borg collective."

"The Borg?" he said, startled. "I don't know what you mean."

"In Star Trek, the TV program."

"Oh I see," he said. "Yes, I've seen a few episodes. I remember now. The collective mind of the Borg as portrayed in Star Trek, however, would be more masculine than feminine."

"Isn't every collective mind feminine then? I thought you said it's the masculine mind-set, that leads to individuality?"

"I did, and the Borg are no exception. Their unity exists as a mechanism for efficiency. The main drive of the Borg is not union but violent conquest of others, the ultimate rape. The One, the feminine whole, has nothing outside itself to conquer; nothing at all exists except the One."

He paused for a moment to order his thoughts.

"It's more than likely that the Borg represents the masculine fear of the One, which runs away from the Great Mother because it's terrified it will lose its individuality. It's no accident that it's portrayed as a hive mind with a ruling Queen. The patriarchal assumption is that the One will engulf him without pity, blot out his will, not realising that the One is completely loving. No coercion, no force is ever used, nor can it be. We must return to the Great Mother of our own free will, because we realise how impoverished we are without

Her, how much we miss Her love and comfort."

"I see," I said, "well at least I think I do."

"Another way to contact the One," he continued enthusiastically, "is through unconditional love for humanity. This is what the Goddesses try to kick-start in all the male initiates. The more you love others, the more you receive love from the One. Your intuition develops, as it does in most women and you begin to know instead of relying on your intellect for guidance."

"So everything I've learned from the Sisterhood will help me to become more intuitive."

"That's right. Love and intuition go together, the more we love others the more we are in contact with the One and the collective unconscious and so the more we are intuitive. Now, there's one secret I wish to tell you. The Great Mother loves us all unconditionally. She is always ready and willing to help or guide us in whatever we do. Unlike the male gods, she does not blame us for the mistakes we've made or punish us for our supposed 'sins'. It's we who reject Her help because we are still learning to be individuals. We shut out Her voice and pretend it doesn't exist. If we do believe in a Creator, we choose a judgmental male one who is so unloving he threatens us with eternal damnation if we don't follow his rules. It's no wonder we're scared of him! Yet we prefer this to the truth – that we are all connected through love to each other and the Great Mother. Forever. All the help we need to get us out of the miserable existence we've created is ready and waiting. We just have to ask and it will be gladly given us."

"That sounds too easy and too good to be true. If it is that easy, why haven't we all done it thousands of years ago."

"Because as I have said before, most of us fear the One because we are frighten of losing our individuality."

"So what you are saying; that is the reason I am resisting affirming that we all live in a compassionate and caring world."

"Do you think that is true?"

"I'll have to think about that."

"I would strongly recommend that you do. It is the fear of the ONE that causes us to continue to live in a world of conflict and suffering. Perhaps you should try another affirmation first; 'I am loved unconditionally by the Great Mother'.

"Do you use this affirmation?"

"I still do occasionally, I was taught to use it and other affirmations like it, when I was still a student of science of mind. But I have also learnt self-awareness and I am now consciously aware of most of my thoughts. So I now do not have to use affirmations to bring new thoughts into my unconscious mind. It is now natural for me to be aware that I am part of the ONE most of the time. I can assure you I have never lost my individuality by learning how to be in tune with the One."

I suddenly felt very tired, and held up my hands in mock surrender.

"I've had enough, you always end up blowing my mind."

"I'm sorry, I hope I am not pushing you too quickly," his voice conveyed deep concern.

"No, I'm all right, but I now feel I have had enough."

"Are you interested in studying science of mind?"

"Well, yes, I think so."

"You don't sound too sure."

"I haven't liked the many of the positive thinking books I have read so far."

"Very well."

He got to his feet and was quickly going through his bookshelves. Then he came back with a half a dozen books.

"These are called New Thought books they were written in the 19th century and early 20th century. It was from New Thought that we get the present positive thinking books."

"I see," I said doubtfully.

James frowned at my lack of enthusiasm.

"Unfortunately the positive thinking books of today tend to be mostly about making money. The original New Thought revolution of the 19th century was more about healing. Something that is mostly forgotten about in modern, science of mind books."

"Do you want me to be trained as a healer?" I asked in a puzzled voice.

"If you want to, but it is important you know the principle of how true healing works."

"I see," I said but not for the first time, I didn't see at all.

"Try reading this first," he said picking up a book, "It gives a history of "New Thought, how it got started and a brief idea description of what it is."

He then showed me to the door and I went home trying to assimilate everything that happened to me that day.

## CHAPTER FIFTEEN

My time of my next session with Carol came up two days later. This time I had managed to book two hours with her in spite of the cost. The session started in exactly the same way before.

"All right," she said, after I kissed her feet, "What do you want to do?"

"Er, body worship," I said, "would it be possible to kiss you vagina as well?"

"No," she said firmly, "I only allow my husband to do that, you can either kiss by bottom or my feet."

I wondered what sort of relationship she had with her husband.

"Um, I want to kiss your bottom,"

She got me to do the same routine as before. As she ordered me to worship her PVC behind and tell her how beautiful it was. She then took off her PVC cat suit and I found myself again lying on back on the floor kissing and licking her arse-hole.

"You really like licking my arse," she commented, "I can feel it."

"Er, yes," I said, stopping my administrations briefly to say this.

"You don't sound very enthusiastic," she said in a mocking voice, "the tone in your voice doesn't match the enthusism you are trying to push your tongue into my arse-hole. Are you ashamed to admit you like licking my ass."

I didn't know what to say.

"No." I protested.

"You will have to show far more enthusiasm than that, if you want to continue to kiss my arse. I want to be able to really hear the devotion and appreciation in your voice, as you thank me for the great honour of allowing you to kiss me."

"Thank you for the great honour and privilege in kissing your arse." I said with as much feeling I could put into it.

## NAKED ISIS

She stood up and looked down on me, between her legs.

"Is that the best you can do," she said angry, "are you too proud to admit you want to kiss and lick my arse-hole?."

"No," I pleaded, "I do really want to worship you."

"That's better," she said, "that sounded like genuine emotion. Now if you want to continue to lick my arse you have to convince me you really want to do it."

I did try my best to tell her how much I want to do it.

"You find it hard," she said, with some sympathy in her voice, "I didn't find you at all convincing."

She stepped away from me.

"I really do want to lick your arse," I pleaded.

"The only time I heard any genuine emotion in your voice, is when I threaten to stop." She said. "Very well, you sound if you are really want it."

She stepped back and lowered herself onto my face again, and I was soon kissing and licking her once again. Then after a few minutes she reached out and took a mobile phone from a small table next to her and was soon taking to a friend of hers. I felt slightly outraged about her doing this and it dampened my ardour. Soon my tongue was getting a bit tired through trying to push it hard into her and I became contented in running it gently around her ring and kissing.

Then suddenly she finished her phone call, and slightly raised herself.

"All right," she said, "What's the matter? You are not licking away as enthusiastically as before."

"My tongue is a bit tired," I said.

"You only had been licking for ten minutes, last time you licked away for nearly an hour. So that is a poor excuse. Are you getting bored with it?"

"Oh, no," I assured her.

"So you want to continue?"

"Oh, yes please," I said, I now felt a lot better about it, when I realise that she was still very aware of me licking her arse-hole, even though she was on the phone.

"All right," she said, "But any slacking or lack of appreciation of the great honour I am giving you and your out the door. Understood?"

"Yes, Mistress", I found myself saying.

She lowered herself on my face once more and picked up her phone.

"Sorry about that," to the person she was speaking to, "there was a just a little problem I had to sort out..." she then continued with her phone call.

So I continued to lick her with as much enthusiasm as I could. Her phone call went on a long time but finally she finished and she stood up.

"You have nearly an hour left," she announced standing over me, "What do you want to do?"

My tongue was now far too tired to do anymore body worship.

"I think I'll like to try out one of your strap-on," I said nervously.

"All right, get to your feet and bend over that table over their." She said indicating to a table in the corner of the room. I done as I was told and she grabbed me by the hips and started pumping her genitalia against my bottom.

"This is what female rhesus macaques monkeys do to males to establish their dominance over them." She explained, then she gave a laugh. "Off course only a male would see this as a sign of submission, females don't see it that way at all."

She continued to do this and then after awhile she began to rub her herself up and down my buttocks telling me to arch my back downwards and clench them to make them harder.

"You have a really small sexy bum," she commented.

She kept on rubbing herself on my buttocks until finally her body gave a shudder and I wondered if she had a orgasm. I tried to sneak a look but was told sharply to keep my eyes to the front. She kept on rubbing against me, but more slowly now and then she stopped and stepped away to give my bottom two very hard slaps.

"Now I suppose you want a strap-on dildo up you."

She move away from me and I could hear her busying herself strapping it onto herself. I then sneaked another look.

"Isn't that a bit large," I said in horror.

She laughed.

"Off course not," she said picking up another strap-on from a table and showing it to me, "This is a large one."

I looked at it in dismay it must have been about a foot long.

"I'm not used to big dildos," I pathetically, "even the one you have on is too large for me."

"Your been getting away with it too easy," she said laughing again, "it is about time you felt what it is like to have proper size prick inside you."

She then proceeded in smothering her strap-on with oil. I suppose I could of stood up and refuse to go through with this, but somehow I felt unable to disobey her. She then grabbed my hips again and slowly pushed the dildo into my anus. It didn't hurt but it felt very uncomfortable and my whole body shook in reaction to it. She then began slowly pull out and push in again. That felt even worse.

"Please," I said, "I can't stand much more of this, could you please stop."

"Are you trying to tell me what to do?" she said sharply, and still continued her pumping motion.

"Er, no," I said, "I'm just saying this is very uncomfortable and I don't know how much I can stand."

"Who is in charge here?" she demanded.

"Er, you are," I admitted.

"Which means we finish when I am good and ready, not you."

Then she pushed hard inside me and then reach forward and grabbed my penis, it was hard.

"See how hard it is." She exclaimed, "and you think, you don't like this."

I didn't know what to say.

"It might help if you masturbate yourself," she suggested.

I cautiously done as she suggested and then realised I was turned-on in spite of my discomfort. Then within a short time I ejaculated.

"Look at the mess you have made on my floor!" She said in mock anger. "go and lick it up."

She then pulled out of me and I stood up unsure if she was only joking.

"Didn't you hear what I said?" she said more forcefully.

I bent down to floor it was tiled and looked clean, so I began to lick it up. I certainly didn't like the taste but she stood over me and made me lick it all up. She then unstrapped herself and handed it to me.

"Go to the bathroom next door and clean it, and do a good job because I will test its cleanliness by getting you to lick it afterwards."

I quickly done as I was told and cleaned it with both soap and detergent she had in her bathroom. I then brought it back and handed it to her and she processed to strap it back on herself.

"Kneel," she commanded.

I done as I was told and she pushed to dildo towards my mouth.

"Lick," she ordered.

I licked it and was relieved to find it only tasted soapy.

"Open you mouth," she said giving another order.

I done as I was told and she grabbed the sides of my head and pushed into my mouth. She then began to mouth fuck me which again felt very uncomfortable. Then suddenly she pushed it hard into my mouth and I gagged. Fortunately she only left it there for a second and pulled it completely out. She then unstrapped herself again.

"Right," she said, "go back to the bathroom and rinse off your saliva, dry it completely and bring it back."

I done as I was told and then she ordered me to dress and I was quickly hustled out of the house, fifteen minutes before my hour was up. But somehow I was incapable of objecting.

A week later on a Saturday, I need to go shopping and decided to look around at a newly opened out-of-town shopping centre. I was walking down a busy arcade thinking about what I was going to buy, when my eyes automatically fixed on the bottom of a girl walking in front of me. She had a pair of white slacks and the material was so thin for me to be aware she only wore a thong underneath them. Her back looked very familiar to me and I realised it looked exactly like the bottom of my ex-teacher. She was walking arm in arm with a older woman who also looked familiar to me. That increased my interest and I began to speed up my walk to overtake them, to see if I knew her. I have found in my experience that with some women, if you stare at their bottoms for too long they became aware you are doing this and look back at you. The younger women did this and looked back and saw me. A surprised and shocked expression appeared on her face. I also was shocked because I looked at her eyes and knew they were the eyes of my ex-teacher. The older woman seeing how the younger woman was reacting also looked back and I got another shock, she was my contact Angel Lyons.

"What are you doing here," she demanded, recovering from her surprise quicker than me.

"I was just doing some shopping and ran into you," I explained.

"We shouldn't be seen in public together," she said and grabbed the hand of the younger woman and hurried off into a shop.

I stood there trying to understand what had just happened. What was my ex-teacher a potential member of the Sisterhood, doing walking arm in arm with a women who was a member of a secret government organization, with the intention of infiltrating the Sisterhood. But something else also disturbed me, the two women looked very much alike, could be mother and daughter?

I walked on a bit further trying to make sense of all this, and different possibilities went through my mind. Was my teacher a spy like me? Yet if they were mother and daughter, would a mother use her daughter as a spy? Or was Angel Lyons a double agent working for both sides? This would mean that James and the Sisterhood would be fully aware I was a spy. I now felt very vulnerable. Angel was the only contact I had with the government agency I worked for. This would mean I had no-one to turn to, I could trust.

I now felt a strong desire to have it out with Angel to find out what was really going on. I retraced my steps hoping to find them again, but among the large crowd I soon realised the task was hopeless.

That evening I tried to contact Angel in a pay-phone using the number she had given me to memorise, she answered the phone.

"I really need to see you," I said, "I don't understand what is going on now."

"Right," she said, "meet me at our pre-arraigned destination, at 2'clock tomorrow."

The next morning I called my work explaining I was sick. Then in the afternoon I had a long drive to the common we had previously agreed to meet. After a long walk through the common I found the agreed destination. I was then relieved to find the seat where we arraigned to meet was empty. I sat down and look at my watch I was nearly five minutes early.

I had another twenty minutes wait before she finally turned up.

"All right what is your problem?" she asked, sitting down. I never seen her aggressive as this before.

"That young women you were with, was my teacher in the group," I said

"How can you be sure, you said you never saw her face."

"I am very sure, her body, eyes and hair were all exactly the same." She gave a sigh.

"It is very unfortunate that you saw us. You must realise you are not the only spy we are using to penetrate this organization."

"Yes, but, she also looks very much like you, and could be your daughter."

"I don't have to answer to you," she said with some anger in her voice. "You now know far too much. I will be recommending that you should be pulled out of this job, because you could inadvertently betray another spy better placed than you."

"Oh, I see," I said and felt completely deflated at this unexpected news.

"The next time James contacts you," she went on, "you will to tell him you no longer want to be part of his group. You then will be paid for your time as a agent and you must never tell anyone what you have been doing, or you will be prosecuted, under the government secrets act, is that clear!"

"Yes," I answered

"Good," she said, and got to her feet and looked down at me

"You were doing well," she said in a softer voice, "and I thought that perhaps you stood a good chance of being initiated, it is a shame that you accidentally saw something you were not meant to see."

She then bend down and briefly kissed me on the cheek, and then quickly walked away.

I continued to sit there in a daze. I certainly didn't want to tell James I no longer want to be part of the Naked Isis. It was then at that moment, I realised that my sympathies were now more with the Sisterhood, than with the shadowy government agency I had been working for.

I had decided that I didn't want to leave the Sisterhood but didn't know how the government agency would react to that. So I continued as normal and when James phoned me a ten days later. I had decided to tell James the whole story that I was a government spy but at the last minute I bottled out completely, when we met at his place.

"So how did you like my Science of Mind books?" he asked.

"I found them a bit hard to accept," I said, "They are claiming that all illness is caused by the mind."

"Off course," said James, "if we are to believe in a compassionate and caring Goddess created our world. Then in no way can She have created illness and pain. It can only be created by us."

"So you are saying that if a person dies of say cancer or any other illness. Then it is their own mind that has created this illness, even to the point of killing them."

"That is correct."

"I find that hard to believe."

"That is understandable. If you have been taught since a child that illness is caused by germs, virus and other explanations. Then you would find it hard to accept any other explanation. It is easy for me because I have been using science of mind for nearly thirty years now, I have also seen amazing cures of illness brought about through the healing power of the Great Mother."

"Is it possible to see proof of this healing?"

"Not until you are initiated."

My heart sank, it was now very unlikely that would happen. Then I had a sudden thought.

"You say we unconsciously create our own illness, but what about children who are born with a mental or physical defects?"

James smiled.

"We all have an existence before we were born. On this earth we live in a sort of frozen reality. That is to say, what we think doesn't effect our reality straight away. Which does protect us, to some degree, from many of the many negative thoughts we may have. When we die we move into a reality, where, what we choose to think immediately changes our reality. Now this can produce an instant heaven or hell. If we have positive thoughts then we find ourselves instantly living in a heaven. Unfortunately for people who do not have any control over their minds and habitually have very negative thoughts, they will create a instant hell. It is these people who need to be born back into our frozen reality, to protect themselves from their own minds. Unfortunately their negativity can be so strong that they bring on to themselves incurable illnesses, even before they are born."

"Oh," I said I didn't know what to make from that. There was no-way I could find out if that was true or not, so I changed the subject.

"Another thing that surprised me," I said, "Was that there was a lot about Christian Science in your books."

James shrugged

"Christian Science, is just a Christianised version of science of mind," he said.

"So do you practice healing like the Christian Scientists?"

James frowned and thought about what he was going to say next.

"It is similar, except we use the healing power of the Great Mother rather than a father and mother god, what the Christian Scientists use. We also are a bit more flexible in the way we use healing, but the basic principles are very similar."

"So I could learn how your organization heals, from Christian Science?"

"You could. Though I would like you to study other science of mind groups as well. Read about Franz Anton Mesmer, Phineas Parkhurst Quimby, Emma Curtis Hopkins, The Brook Sisters, Myrtle and Charles Fillmore and Ernest Homes. All these people are mentioned in the books I lent you. Some of the Christian Science ideas are a bit inflexible. For instance Mary Baker Eddy claim that; 'matter has no reality'. Whereas we would say; reality is whatever we have made it into. So a illness like cancer has a reality because that is what we have created. What we would say, is that if we take responsibility for creating it, then we have the power to un create it again. In other words; if we accept we have the power to create illness, then we have the power to heal the illness we have created."

"I see," I said slowly thinking about what he had just said. "So what part did your organization play in the New Thought movement."

"You may of noticed that there were many women who were New Thought teachers we greatly encouraged that. Though also, many New Thought teachers and helpers were also Freemasons."

"Is science of mind a essential part of the teachings of the Sisterhood?" I asked.

"Yes it is."

That was the answer I didn't want to hear, as I had real problem with science of mind.

"Well what about going to professional dominas, is that essential,"

"Not at all, we only send some men whom we believe might benefit from this."

"So why me?"

"Because you had a difficulty with becoming a carer."

"All right," I said accepting that, "well why is science of mind so essential to the Sisterhood."

"Because it would be impossible for us to survive without it. Some time ago you did asked how it is possible of a secret organization like us to survive for thousands of years. A example of this is what happened when I first joined. At that time the Sisterhood was allowing people in who had doubts about the importance of science of mind. This made us weak and allowed us to be betrayed to those who hated us. Since then we realise our mistake and reinforce our science of mind, teachings."

"So how does science of mind protect you," I said puzzled.

"A secret organization can only be betrayed and destroyed if it allows that to be part of it's reality. If it is not part of the reality of its members, then there is nothing that can be done to harm it. A case in point would be the Knight's Templar. They grew very rich and powerful using science of mind. Unfortunately as they grew rich, they began to rely more on their great wealth and material power, for protection, rather than the thing that brought them wealth and power in the first place. This then made them very vulnerable to their enemies, who took full advantage."

"So you are saying that it is impossible to destroy your organization, because you practice mind power."

"There we always be individuals in the organization who are lax in practising science of mind. So those people will always be vulnerable, but the main organization is stronger than ever before."

This made me feel better and gave me the incentive to confess.

"James," I said quietly, "what would you say, if you knew I was a spy."

"Tell me all about it," he said smiling.

I started of telling him how I was originally recruited and finished telling him of my last meeting with Angel.

"I'm very glad you told me," said James calmly.

I looked at him suspiciously.

"You don't seem surprised at what I told you," I said, "did you already know?"

"I think at present, the less you know the better," he replied.

"Why," I asked.

"Because the government agency that recruited you, would not be happy if they knew you had betrayed them. I am sure they will never find out, but if they did, it would be a big advantage to be ignorant of the facts."

I took a minute to digest this.

"All right," I said, "but there is something I really want to know. I have always been puzzled why a spiritual group like you sent me to professional dominas and to sadistic women like Janet and my teenage teacher. You also tried to get me to care for homeless people. Is that what you normally do? Or did you make it tough for me because you already knew I was a spy?"

James gave a short laugh and then shook his head.

"I can't even tell you that," he said, "like I said before, you are better off at present being ignorant of the facts."

"So what happens now?" I said.

"It is best to do what your boss Angel told you to do."

"So that means I won't be coming back here."

"That's correct."

"Oh." I said and began to feel really upset.

"Arthur," said James quietly, "there would have been a time during your initiation where we would of stopped and gave you a rest, to see how you would cope on your own, with all knowledge and teachings we have given you. A good time to stop would be now."

"So are you suggesting we can continue at a later date?"

"We might. What you really need to study is science of mind to make this happen. You do have a real barrier because if you do come back with us at a later date and one of the government secret services found out, they may call you in for questioning because you once worked for them. So it is up to you to create a reality where you would be protected from this."

"I wouldn't even know how to start."

"I have given you a way you can start by simply affirming; 'I live in a compassionate and caring world'. You can use other affirmations like; 'I am loved unconditionally by the Great Mother'. 'I am one infinite wisdom and healing power of the Great Mother'. Or, 'I am guided and protected by the Great Mother in everything I do'."

"Um, can I write all these down?" I said frantically search for a pen.

"Don't worry, I have a page of affirmations I can give you."

He went to his desk and after a brief search came back with sheet of A4 paper.

"All the affirmations I mentioned are on this page, plus some more we use."

"Thank you," I said gratefully.

"But do not get too hooked up with only affirmations. You can use visualizations as well, also practice self-awareness, so you become aware of negative thoughts within you that hold you back"

"I don't know how you would use visualizations."

"I would suggest that when you use a affirmation like; 'I live in a compassionate and caring world', you attempt to visualise it as well. So just imagine people helping and caring for each other. Or, 'I am love unconditionally by the Great Mother' imagine a cosmic mother who is loving all the people on this earth."

"I see," said thoughtfully, "So would just using these affirmations protect me from being targeted by the government secret services?"

"They would if practised every day, and don't expect instant results from this. The affirmations have to overcome the negative reality you already have created. What is need most of all in making mind power work, is persistence. The longer you persist and practice it, the better it works."

"So are you saying that everyone in your organization has to practice science of mind."

"Yes. Remember you once asked how it was possible for secret organizations to survive for thousands of years. The key to this is mind power. It is about the members creating a reality where they cannot be betrayed or destroyed."

"So if you are so powerful, why can't you change the world for the better?"

"We have. The ruling elite over the last few thousand years have tended to support religions or philosophies that empathise fatalism. So everything is seen in terms of; 'It is the will of Allah', or 'the will of God'. Even atheism is a fatalistic creed where everything the creation of the universe and life happened through blind chance. Now such beliefs leave people completely powerless, which makes them far easier to rule. We had to directly intervene, and gave out secret teachings the general population that we are not powerless and have the power to make our world a better place. This is why over the last few hundred years the European and North American civilizations have become the most dynamic and powerful in the world."

"How did you give out these secret teachings?" I asked in a puzzled voice.

"Freemasonry. We watered down many of our secret teachings to make them more acceptable to he general population and created a popular secret society in Freemasonry. Then to those who were opened minded we taught to them, how to use the power of the mind. We even tried to go beyond Freemasonry with the New Thought movement. We managed to get this going in the USA and positive thinking has permeated right through this society and this is why the USA is now the most powerful and dynamic country in the world."

I stared at him with surprise and disbelief.

"So why the USA and not other countries?" I asked.

"It is just the way it worked out. Many of the first Europeans that settled in USA were from secret societies, who saw the opportunity to strongly influence a new country from the beginning. Also the new settlers were not so bound by traditions of older countries and were more open to new ideas. We also had a powerful effect on Britain and other European countries but we weren't as effective as in the USA in the teaching of mind power."

"Well if mind power is so powerful, why aren't you ruling the world?"

"The downside of teaching mind power to the masses is that some people use mind power solely for purpose of gaining wealth and power. Which in itself is not a problem, but having gained power and wealth, many of these people become competitive and don't want to share it with others. It is these people who become our enemies. Because although they have benefited from our teachings, they don't want the rest of the world to know about it, because they don't want more competition from others."

"So why don't you use mind power to gain wealth and power. Then take over the world and rule it as you want to?"

"We do to a degree, we even have had some of our members leaders of countries, but as we have found with experience a leader is still limited in what he or she can achieve. We need to dominate the whole ruling elite to make a difference and unfortunately this is what we have completely failed to do. Yes, at times in history we have welded great power in certain countries. But when we have given out the secrets of mind power, we have found many of our pupils use mind power for different purposes than we intended."

"So why didn't you keep the secrets of mind power to yourselves?"

"Because it is so important that the whole human race finds out about this power. We all have the power to create a far better world than we have at present. The problem is, that the common people are unaware they have this power."

"Yes, but surely your first priority is to concentrate in gaining political power and then use that power to educate the people."

"The power does not reside with the ruling elite it always has been with the people.."

"I can't believe that!" I said interrupting him.

"The ruling elite have only gained power over the people by convincing them that they are powerless, the rulers, are all powerful. In other words the power of the ruling elite is simply the power of propaganda, deception and keeping the people ignorant."

"So why can't you enlighten the people?"

"We have tried in many different ways. The problem is that if you teach the common people the secrets of mind power you are in effect giving away the power you have gained. So it has been tried to create a benevolent ruling elite. Then when in power, these people have been very reluctant to teach mind power to the masses, because they knew they would be giving their power away. It is not in the nature of people who want political power, to give power to the people. It is a catch 22. I'm afraid some of our most powerful enemies have come from our own ranks, because they have been corrupted by power."

"So what are you doing, about this?"

"We have unfortunately discovered you cannot rush these things. We found this out in the Witch hunts at the end of the medieval age. We were then secretly teaching women all over Europe the secrets of mind power, who where using it for healing. We imagined that this would kick start a new matriarchal age. Because of the way we used mind power the Church and the state were powerless to stop us but then we encountered a even great power. Unfortunately we were moving too quickly and the people began to fear these women, who had a power they didn't understand. It was the power of this fear that was greater than our mind power. The Church took advantage of this and played on the fears of ordinary people to launch the infamous Witch hunt. In which millions of women were tortured and murdered, most of whom were not Witches at all. I'm afraid it was a very bad mistake on our part. We since learnt you need to be patient and only go as fast as people will allow you. Because if you push too hard, you frighten people. So it means we have to drip feed the knowledge of mind power to the people, who will only accept it when they are ready."

He paused but I didn't know what to say as I was trying to digest all of this. So he continued.

"We started to do the same again in the 18$^{th}$ century though this time we went far more slowly. Anton Mesmer in Austria learnt the secrets of mind power as a Freemason and believed strongly that this power should be used by doctors to cure their patients. He had the courage to go out and do this and even though he proved conclusively that mind power does work, he knew that he couldn't say so in public. So he tried to invent a scientific theory, which he called Animal Magnetism to explain it and make it more acceptable to doctors but the theory was easily disproved.."

"Wait a minute," I said interrupting again, "I know a bit about this. Wasn't one of the people who disproved Mesmer theories, Benjamin Franklin and he was a prominent Freemason."

"Like I have said before, we and all not united in our aims. Many Freemasons greatly disapproved of what Mesmer was trying to do. They feared that if he was too successful he could frighten too many people and create a new Witch-Hunt. The only reason he was allowed to continue was that he received great support from the French lodges, though even they finally became frighten and stopped their support of him. Fortunately his work did continue after he was forced to retire, in the form of Mesmerism which later became acceptable to doctors in the form of Hypnotism when the healing aspects of Mesmerism was removed..."

I realised the irony of this and gave a brief laugh. Then he continued.

"Fortunately some Mesmerists began to realise that it worked through mind power. One of these men was Parkhurst Quimby, who fortunately did receive some support from local Freemasons. Then he healed Mary Baker Eddy whom later Christianised his methods and single-mindedly created a new Christian Sect called Christian Science, based on healing. She was also supported by Freemasons and the Sisterhood. Unfortunately her single-minded attitude also made her difficult person to deal with. One of her best pupils Emma Curtis Hopkins, was forced to leave Christian Science through Mrs Eddy's uncompromising attitude. Fortunately Hopkins was more open-mind and continued to teach science of mind which resulted in the New Thought movement. Which again was supported by the Freemasons and the Sisterhood. Today it continues as Positive Thinking which is Science of Mind with, again, the healing aspect removed."

I didn't laugh this time, as I realised this wasn't a joke. We both lapse into silence as I tried to make sense of what he was saying.

"You seem to be suggesting that people are frightened of healing," I said finally.

"Only because healing can be the most dramatic demonstration of mind power. A successful healer creates a real problem. In the minds of many people he or she has either got to be a Jesus Christ figure or a Witch or Wizard. Or if the healer is honest and says directly they heal through the mind. It suggests we can all do this, and people are forced to question the reality they believe they live in."

"Are you saying that if a person has the power to heal, they also have the power to harm and this is why people fear healers?"

"That would be one reason. Another reason would be that people fear their own minds. If a healer was to say to a sick person; 'it was your own fears that gave you cancer'. That person would be very upset to know their illness was self-inflicted. They would also be even more frighten because they don't know how to quell their fears. If you are told that it is the fear of illness that creates the illness, then you are going to be even more frighten of your fears. Because how to you stop being afraid? Some people may be able to suppress their fears but all they will do is drive it into the unconscious mind, where these fears will continue to do harm to the body without the awareness of the conscious mind."

"So what would a person do in this situation?"

"To learn how to overcome fear, using mind power. There are many ways like; learning meditation, learning that our Creatrix is all powerful and loves us all unconditionally or by affirming 'we live in a compassionate and caring world.' As I have pointed out before, the invention of angry and judgemental gods has done great harm to the human collective unconscious."

"If what you say is true why can't it be taught to all of us?"

"Because the human race still has the mentality of children who are not willing to take responsibility for the world they have created. We are all are creating the world we live in, both individually and collectively, and if we don't consciously create our world, then we do it unconsciously. It then become like someone driving a powerful sports car with no understanding that how the car is controlled. So it is no wonder we drive off the road and have accidents. This means, by chance, people find themselves living in poverty, or becoming depressed or insane or the victims of bullying and crime or life threatening illness, not realising that it is their own unconscious mind that is creating all these problems..."

"Wait a minute," I interrupted, "I thought you were blamed the problems of the world on the ruling elite. Now you seem to be blaming the people themselves."

"It is not a question of blame," said James patiently, "the ruling elite do what they do because they are only interested in power. While people who live lives of suffering, do so because they have no knowledge of mind power. We have to acknowledge there is great resistance among people to the concept of mind power. The main one is the fear of responsibility. If we accept that we create our own reality, then we become responsible for everything that happens to us. And if we all accept mind power, on the collective level, then we all become responsible for the world we live in. This means we are no longer children with no responsibilities, we have to become adults and take responsibility for ourselves and the world."

I stared at him, not knowing what to say, as usual he was overloading my mind with too many new concepts.

He stood up and faced me for the last time.

"That's all you need to know," he said. "It's time to say goodbye."

He escorted me to the door. In a daze of disbelief, I thanked him for all his help. Gravely, we shook hands and went our separate ways. Two weeks later I flew to America to visit Mary and to start a new life